CO-AZH-750

3 4028 08952 7338
HARRIS COUNTY PUBLIC LIBRARY

Gilmor
Gilmore, Kylie
Restless harmony

$14.99
ocn958935268
First edition.

REST

KYLIE GILMORE

This book is a work of fiction. Names, characters, places, brands, media, and incidents are the product of the author's imagination or are used fictitiously. The author acknowledges the trademarked status and trademark owners of various products referenced in this work of fiction, which have been used without permission. The publication/use of these trademarks are not authorized, associated with, or sponsored by the trademark owners. Any resemblance to actual events, locales, or persons, living or dead, is purely coincidental.

Copyright

Restless Harmony © 2015 by Kylie Gilmore

Excerpt from *Not My Romeo* © 2015 by Kylie Gilmore

All rights reserved. No part of this publication may be reproduced, distributed, or transmitted in any form or by any means, including photocopying, recording, or other electronic or mechanical methods, without the prior written permission of the writer, except in the case of brief quotations embodied in critical reviews and certain other noncommercial uses permitted by copyright law.

First Edition: April 2015

Cover design by The Killion Group

Published by: Extra Fancy Books

ISBN-10: 194223807X

ISBN-13: 978-1-942238-07-2

To Zeke and unconditional love…

CHAPTER ONE

"If I happened to publish an e-rot-ic story, or three, can they legally kick me out of church?"

Gabe Reynolds shifted uncomfortably as Maggie O'Hare smiled sweetly across the desk from him. He was the only lawyer in Clover Park, Connecticut, and had cornered the market on ridiculous and absurd cases.

Maggie's grandson and Gabe's longtime friend Shane sat at his grandmother's side, cheeks as red as his hair. Shane rolled his eyes. "Gran insisted I drive her over here for an *important* legal question. I thought it was her will."

"I ain't dead yet!" Maggie exclaimed. "Now let the man talk."

Gabe rubbed the back of his neck. "Are you telling me that you, Grandma O'Hare, wrote an e—" He choked on the word. It just didn't go with the white-haired woman with spiky hair, who'd taken him in like family way back in seventh grade when he'd desperately needed a haven from his own home. She was sweet and motherly, even if slightly inappropriate for a woman her age. For example, today she wore a black and white polka-dotted dress with an extremely high slit to show off one pasty-white seventy-something leg. And that was one of her more modest outfits. Then, of course, there was her "legal" question. He cleared his throat, unsure where to start in this incredibly awkward conversation.

"Erotic," she supplied helpfully.

"Erotic story," he choked out. "Or three, you said?"

She glanced at Shane and said primly, "I can neither confirm nor deny that claim."

"You're not under oath," Gabe said.

"Just answer the question, Counselor," she snapped. Someone had been watching a lot of *Law & Order*.

Gabe took a deep breath. "I would have to say no. Legally, they can't kick you out of church."

Maggie giggled. "I have a pen name, but you never know what those dirty church-going ladies are reading. It's an e-book, so you can read it with a nice plain cover on your e-reader and no one's the wiser." She winked. "Isn't that genius? I'm Madam M, if you're curious."

Gabe's stomach rolled. "I'm not."

For the first time in four years, he thought longingly of his old job at Reynolds & Taft, LLC, where he'd been working his ass off to gain partnership, until his father, the Reynolds in Reynolds & Taft, died of a heart attack at the age of fifty-seven. The shock of his father collapsing at the office mid-tirade right in front of Gabe's eyes made him reevaluate what he was doing with his own life. He'd been racing along in his father's footsteps, and for what? To end up stressed and rich and dead? He'd inherited his dad's money and city apartment, not because he was an only child, he had two younger brothers, but because he was the only child that lived up to his father's expectations by becoming a lawyer. Gabe had returned home to Clover Park and bought the house he'd grown up in from his mom and stepdad, who'd wanted to downsize. He'd figured small-town life would help him get back to the basics.

Now he had to wonder which was worse—death by stress or death by the ridiculous. Truthfully, death had stalked him his whole life. He was up to three people close to him that had died, including a fiancée, which was why he'd made no effort whatsoever in the last four years to find a girlfriend. People close to him were doomed.

"I'm joking, dear! Ha-ha-ha!" Maggie exclaimed.

"Though it's been a lot of fun. I mean"—she straightened and tried for a serious expression—"it seems like it would be a lot of fun. If you were into that kind of thing." She nodded once and looked between the two frowning men. "Anyhoo, Shane, would you like to ask Gabe your question?"

"Thank you, Gran," Shane said between his teeth. He turned to Gabe. "I just wanted to see if you were busy on Valentine's Day."

"Why? You want to be my valentine?"

Shane barked out a laugh. "Yeah. Get in line. I've got three girls on my arm already." He smiled, probably thinking of his two young daughters and wife. "So you're not busy?"

Maggie raised her brows, eagerly waiting for Gabe's response.

"Nope," Gabe said. "No valentine for me."

"Ohh, I could help you with that, honey," Maggie said.

"No need," Gabe quickly replied. Maggie was an interfering, notorious matchmaker. In the nicest possible way. It was funny when it was happening to someone else.

Shane shook his head with a smile. "Could you help with the catering at the Valentine's Day dance?" He was a chef and, along with his wife, owned three businesses in town—Book It, Shane's Scoops, and

Something's Brewing Cafe. The cafe often catered local events.

Shane went on. "My usual ladies have dates, and I don't want to ruin their Valentine's Day. Rachel's five months along, and I don't want her on her feet the whole time."

"Sure, no problem."

"Great. Thanks a lot." Shane stood. "We'll see you at the dance."

Gabe walked around the desk to see them out. "Yup."

Maggie looked Gabe up and down. "Good, very good."

Gabe suddenly felt uneasy. "This isn't a setup, is it?"

"Nah," Shane said. "I do need your help."

"You need my help, Gabe," Maggie said. "A thirty-five-year-old man should be married with a babe in his arms. Like my Shane."

"I'll just hold one of Shane's kids," Gabe said. "I don't need any help meeting someone. Thanks, anyway."

She just smiled, making him even more nervous.

He whispered in her ear on the way out. "Your pen name might not be so secret if you try to set me up."

Maggie merely smiled. "Don't mess with the woman who knows you inside-out."

He gulped. She did know him well enough to do some serious matchmaking damage. In the nicest possible way.

"Bye," Shane said. "Thanks again."

"You got it." He waved them off and heard Shane giving his grandmother a stern lecture on putting things out on the Internet that could be seen by some as inappropriate, all while holding her arm and guiding her carefully down the icy sidewalk to his minivan. She countered with freedom of artistic expression, which was as much as Gabe heard before they drove off.

A bright pink stroller caught his eye followed quickly by the beautiful woman pushing it right toward him. It was Zoe Davis, the waitress from Garner's Sports Bar & Grill. He was shockingly disappointed to see that stroller. She must already be married with a baby, though he'd never noticed a ring. Not that he wanted a girlfriend, and for a damn good reason, but his attraction to her had grown stronger every time he saw her. It was getting to the point where he thought he might have to do something about it.

Something temporary. But satisfying.

Then she got closer, waving and smiling at him, with her bright brown eyes and cute purple hat on dark brown hair, and he found himself smiling back.

She stopped in front of him. "I need a lawyer. The landlord wants to evict me and Fred."

He peered through the black mesh covering the front of the stroller and just about choked on his own laughter. "Is this Fred?"

"Yes." She frowned. "It's not funny."

Why should he ever have a case that wasn't completely absurd?

"Hi, Fred," he said.

Arf! Arf! Arf! Fred was ready to plead his case.

Gabe opened the door to his office with a smile. "Come on in."

~ ~ ~

Zoe parked the stroller in the foyer and lifted the hood. Fred leaped out and started running in circles around the small space. She grabbed his squeaky bone toy, hoping to keep him occupied while she filled Gabe in on the problem, but then Gabe snagged the toy right out of her hands and tossed it back toward his office. Fred took off after it, and Gabe gestured for her to follow.

"Have a seat," he said, indicating the leather cushioned chair in front of his desk.

She sat, unzipped her long down parka, and pulled the lease out of her purse, handing it to Gabe. "It says right here that I can have a small dog." Gabe glanced uneasily over at Fred, who was attempting to hump his rubber toy. "Fred might've put on a few pounds now that he's one year old, but he's still a small dog." Fred was a keeshond with thick gray and black fur. "Fred, come!" The dog bounded to her side. "Sit." Fred sat, and she pushed down the huge mane of fur around his head to show Gabe. "See? Look how small his head is. He's just fluffy."

"Uh-huh," Gabe said.

Fred leaped up and put his front paws on her leg, trying to climb into her lap like he did when he was a puppy. She hauled him up and peered around Fred's shoulder. "So can you help us? I've got two months left on my lease. And there's no way I'm getting rid of Fred. My landlord knew very well I had a dog. I've had him for eight months already."

Gabe studied the lease for a few minutes and finally looked up. "How much does he weigh?"

"I don't know. I haven't weighed him lately." She stroked Fred's thick mane. "He's just fluffy," she said defensively.

"The lease says you can have a dog under twenty-five pounds."

"He was under twenty-five pounds when I got him."

His sharp blue eyes studied her. "Did you piss off the landlord?"

"Me?" she huffed. "Why do you think it's me? Maybe John is the one with the problem."

Gabe reached across the desk and pulled a folder from Fred's ever-chewing mouth. "You say you've had Fred for eight months with no problem."

"That is correct."

"This isn't a courtroom," Gabe said.

"Can you rephrase the question?" she asked with a grin.

One corner of his mouth lifted in a small smile that revealed a dimple in his stubbled cheek. Her mind wandered to what that stubble would feel like scraping against her as his mouth—Fred licked her cheek, distracting her. She ruffled his fur.

Truth be told, she'd had a little crush on Gabe for weeks and always waited his table whether or not he was sitting in her section. She'd held back on the flirting, though, on account of his reputation as a "ruthless, money-grubbing, slick city lawyer just like his dad" and, what really gave her pause, some dark whispers about his ex-fiancée's death she'd heard at Garner's, aka gossip central. Still, she'd been drawn to him and found it hard to reconcile the reputation that preceded him with the man who always left a generous tip and seemed to help so many people in town with legal problems. In any case, if he was as aggressive and ruthless a lawyer as reported to be, she wanted him on her side.

Gabe spoke up. "If I'm going to be your lawyer, I need the whole story. To be honest, with this lease you signed, you don't have much of a case. Unless we can prove the eviction is malicious."

Zoe's lips formed a flat line. Gabe waited patiently. Did she want to tell him all the embarrassing details? She didn't know him all that well. He'd been five years ahead of her in school. She'd only been his waitress for about a month, ever since she'd come back to town from her six-week gig singing on a cruise ship. She knew his brothers better. Luke, who was in her class (a clean-cut cutie); his younger brother Jared (a rough, grubby boy) a grade behind; and his stepbrother Nico, a grade ahead, that every girl in the whole school crushed on. His other two stepbrothers, Vince and Angel, she didn't know well and hadn't seen in years.

Fred started choking, and Zoe rescued Gabe's stapler from his devouring mouth. Honestly, Fred would eat anything. She'd caught him with cat poop in his mouth last time they'd visited her sister, Jasmine's house. The kitty litter all over his nose was a dead giveaway.

She let out a breath. "It's possible this is a revenge eviction. I might have had a teeny, little—" she lowered her voice and brought her pointer finger and thumb together to show him just how tiny "—fling with the landlord, but that's over." She raised her chin. "And P.S. he's a sleazy asshole."

Gabe raised a brow. "P.S.? Were we corresponding?"

"Corra-what?"

"You have a strange way of speaking," Gabe said.

Zoe narrowed her eyes. "Can you help us or not?"

Fred leaped off her lap and ran to the front door, barking his head off. Probably another plane overhead. He went nuts for planes and helicopters.

Gabe shoved a hand through his already disheveled light brown hair. "I could talk to the landlord."

"You would? That would be great." She beamed at him. He looked back at her, all lawyerly and professional, his dark blue eyes giving nothing away. He'd be excellent at poker. "Can you speak lawyer to him? Really put the fear of jail into him."

He folded long fingers together in front of him, and her mind wandered to what those long fingers could do to a woman. Her cheeks heated. She was just getting out of an impulsive, ill-advised fling. The last thing she needed was to jump into another one. Especially with her lawyer in his preppy lawyer-guy white button-down shirt and khakis. She mentally unbuttoned the top two buttons of his shirt, imagining golden skin and just a smattering of chest hair, maybe some nice pecs—

"I'll speak to him as your lawyer," he said. "I doubt I'll put the fear of jail into him."

Gabe was all business. Clearly his mind wasn't wandering in the same slutty direction as hers. She brought her mind back to the task at hand—making her case for Fred. "John deserves it the way he preys on innocent fluffy dogs."

Gabe wrote the phone number from the lease on a Post-it and handed the lease back to her. "I'll be in touch."

She stuffed the lease back in her purse. "That's it?"

He raised his brows. "Were you expecting something else?"

"Well, are you going to bill me or put me on retainer?"

He shook his head with a smile. It made him look younger, that smile, and less like an intimidating lawyer. "You would put me on retainer, not the other way round."

"Oh. So how much?"

"Zoe," he said gently, "can you really afford a lawyer on a waitress's salary?"

"Not really," she admitted. A waitress with singing gigs (that she had to split four ways with her band) didn't have much, or anything, saved in the bank for a rainy, I-need-a-lawyer day.

"It's pro bono." He stood, snagged Fred's toy from

the floor, and walked around the desk to her side. "On the house for being such a good waitress and always keeping my coffee cup full."

"Thank you. If there's ever anything I can do for you. Extra fries or something."

He laughed, a deep, rumbling sound, like he hadn't laughed in a while.

"Your bone," he said, handing her the toy. Now why did that sound dirty? She took the toy, and his long fingers brushed hers, leaving a warm tingle. Okay, she was prone to tingling with good-looking guys, but she was only human, right? Of course, that path had never ended well for her. She should really look for a nice clean-shaven, boy-next-door type like her brother-in-law, Will. He treated her sister, Jasmine, like a goddess.

"I heard you were a singer." He gazed down at her, and she found she couldn't look away from those dark blue eyes that seemed warmer now. His voice turned husky. "Let me know if you ever perform locally."

She breathed in his clean, masculine scent. They'd never stood face to face before. Usually he was seated at a table, and she was standing. He wasn't overly large, maybe five foot nine to her five foot four, but he somehow radiated strength and something in her responded with a secret thrill. She felt suddenly shy and awkward, not at all like herself. "Waitressing just pays the bills."

"I figured. I'd love to hear you sing."

"I've got a gig on Valentine's Day!" she chirped. She tried to cover up her embarrassing nervous voice by grabbing Fred and tucking him into his stroller. "At the dance at the Jorge Chavez Dance Studio," she said over her shoulder, "if you want to give a listen."

One corner of his mouth lifted in a small smile. "Actually I was already planning on going. I'm helping Shane with the catering."

She handed Fred his toy and straightened. "Great! I'll see you then." She headed for the door.

"Can I ask you a question?"

She turned, her heart pounding. Was he going to ask her out? She was torn between hormones and common sense and had no idea what answer would come out of her mouth.

"Sure!" she chirped. She tried to zip up her long parka and ended up fumbling it, zipping and unzipping over and over as the zipper caught on the fabric. She smiled tightly and dropped the zipper. She was overheated already. A cool, winter breeze would feel good about now.

"Why do you put your dog in a stroller?" he asked.

She stiffened. "He likes it." Fred gazed out, a happy panting smile on his face.

"I can see that," he replied. "But don't dogs like to

walk?"

"I can take him into stores and offices, like yours, in a stroller with no complaints. Can't do that if he's just walking on in."

He inclined his head. "Fair enough."

Her lips formed a pout. "You think I'm weird."

"I think you're very interesting," he said with a hint of mischief in his eyes. Oh, he thought she was weird for sure, but then he gave her a warm smile, and she found she didn't mind being weird so much.

His cell phone rang, and he glanced down toward his pocket, seeming surprised to hear it.

"I'll let you get back to work," she said. "Thanks again, Gabe."

"My pleasure," he returned, and the way he said "pleasure" had her halting in her tracks as heat rushed through her.

She met his eyes, took in his heated gaze, and knew he meant it exactly as she'd felt it. Fred barked to move things along, and she sailed out the door, wondering what the heck was Gabe's story. And P.S. if she was throbbing from just one word, she was in trouble.

CHAPTER TWO

Zoe had played all sorts of clubs in New York City with her jazz band, Sizzling Coda, but nothing compared to playing for the hometown crowd. She could feel the love in the room at the Clover Park Valentine's Day dance as she sang "Soul Riff." Jordan Banks on trumpet mouthed, "All you," with a wink before backing her up on a fun improv part of the song where she liked to run up and down harmonic chords in her *ba-daw-daw-baw* riff. Wade Peterson on piano and Alex Higgins on drums kept up with her.

The improv section ended, and she segued back to the lyrics, moving forward to sing near the enthusiastic little girls right up front, Alice and May, the two-year-old twins of Liz and Ryan O'Hare. The girls were alternating bouncing and spinning each other in their pink party dresses while their parents and other couples danced nearby. The Valentine's Day dance had become more popular with each passing year. This was her third time at the gig. Not only did it attract singles looking for a special someone on Valentine's Day, but a lot of couples went to enjoy the live music, dancing, and catering by Shane O'Hare, master chef extraordinaire.

The song ended, and she took a quick swig from her water bottle while she scanned the room for Gabe. She found him helping Shane set up the hot food station in the back of the room. Shane's wife, Rachel, stood nearby, pregnant and holding one little girl on her hip while her other daughter hung onto her leg. Gabe looked up suddenly, seeming to sense her stare, and she wiggled her fingers at him. He smiled, raised a hand, and went back to work. He'd been having trouble getting a hold of her landlord, John, no surprise there, but she hoped something would come through soon. She'd run into John this morning, and he'd snarled, "Get your lawyer off my ass." Since he still wanted to evict her by the end of the month, she wasn't being so helpful in that regard.

Her bandmate Jordan appeared in front of her, totally in her personal space. She was used to it. He always said it was the best way to get her attention when her mind tended to wander. "Let's do some swing, Zoe-bean," he said, giving her hair a playful tug. "I think this crowd can handle it."

"Can you?" she shot back with a grin.

"Keep up, sassy girl," Jordan said with that slow smile that brought women to him in droves. She'd been one of them once, many years ago, but they'd agreed they were better off as friends, which was fine, given that Jordan liked to spread the love to as many women as possible.

Jordan turned to the band, shouted the song, and counted off a silent one, two, three on his fingers for the start. The crowd went wild for Jordan's bright and peppy trumpet sound. All of the older couples got on the dance floor to swing, even Maggie O'Hare, in her seventies and still going strong, got out there with her much younger husband, the owner of the place. She couldn't help but smile while she sang. Some of their songs were covers of other more famous jazz bands, but this song, "Swing Me Up, Baby," and a lot of others in their repertoire, she'd written herself.

After the first set, she chatted with the band in their usual postmortem about how it went and where they might improve. Jordan wanted a harder backbeat from Alex on one song, but otherwise things were rolling smoothly. They took a break and went their separate ways to mingle, eat, or in Alex's case, head outside for a smoke.

She headed over to the hot-food station for a quick snack and a chance to talk to Gabe. He wore a red apron embroidered with white letters that read

Something's Brewing Cafe. Shane and Rachel stood nearby in identical aprons, serving up the food.

"Hi, guys!" Zoe said. "Where are the little ones?"

"Wearing themselves out on the dance floor," Rachel said, pointing to where Hannah and Abby were running in gleeful circles around their Uncle Trav, who pretended to be looking for them just as they ran out of sight. "We're hoping for an early bedtime."

"Gabe's got this, and the girls are occupied," Shane said to Rachel. "Why don't you get off your feet?"

"I'm fine," Rachel said, scooping up the next helping of ziti.

Shane narrowed his eyes. "Have a seat, sweetheart, before I show you what's what."

Rachel's head shot up. "How do you think I ended up like this?" She pointed to her baby bump. Gabe chuckled.

"That's right," Shane said all cocky-like before he wrapped his arms around her from behind and pressed his lips to the side of her neck.

Rachel closed her eyes for a moment. "Okay, fine." She stepped away, and her apron was already loose and untied, probably Shane's doing. "You're sneaky," she said, handing him the apron. "Call me if you need me."

"I won't," Shane muttered as he set the apron on a nearby chair.

"I mean it," Rachel called.

Gabe appeared at Zoe's side. "Your landlord is avoiding my calls. I'll stop by in person tomorrow."

"Tomorrow's Saturday," she said. "You work weekends too?"

He shrugged. "I just want to put your mind at ease."

"Thank you," she said, touched that he cared enough to keep pursuing her problem when she wasn't even paying him.

She pointed to some chicken in lemon sauce and asked Shane for some. "John's usually home Saturday mornings because he parties late Friday nights."

"Perfect," Gabe said.

"You want to join me?" Zoe asked, pointing to the chairs where she planned to eat.

"Can't," Gabe said. "I promised to help out here."

She tried to hide her disappointment with a quick nod. What had she expected, really? They were both working tonight. And she was getting all hot and bothered over nothing. She was his client. Sort of. Whatever.

"All right," she said breezily. "See you." She turned and headed to the chairs.

"You sound great!" Gabe called. "I'm impressed."

She turned with a smile. "Thank you!" She walked to the chairs with a little spring in her step and sat for a quick meal.

Zoe ate and watched some of her friends dance. Someone had put on a slow jazz playlist while the band took a break. She knew nearly everyone at the dance because she grew up in Clover Park. A lot of people stayed in town or came back to raise their families. It was nice that way, and New York City was only a train ride away if you needed more excitement than Main Street with its cute shops had to offer. She did love this town, even as she longed to break away and make a name for herself in the music world.

She finished her chicken, tossed the paper plate, and was about to head over to talk to her friend Daisy O'Hare when Gabe appeared at her side. The apron was gone. He wore a maroon button-down shirt with the top two buttons undone, giving her a glimpse of golden skin just like she'd imagined. Every cell in her body stood up and said, *Yes, please*.

"Would you like to dance?" he asked.

She smiled up at him, intending to say I'd love to, but what came out was, "I thought you had to work."

"Shane gave me a fifteen-minute break. It's in the labor regulations." His lips twitched.

"Did you threaten a lawsuit to dance with me?"

"Would you say yes if I did?"

"No!"

He took her hand, his grip warm and secure. "I

didn't. Come on."

She followed him onto the dance floor, her smaller hand tucked in his, as both excitement and something else, an odd feeling, ran through her. She stopped in front of him. He gazed down at her, wrapped an arm around her waist, and took the lead in a waltz. And, in that first step, she knew. Safe. She felt safe. A feeling she'd never felt with any man besides family. The rumors about him couldn't possibly be true if she instinctively felt safe, right? Unless her instincts were dulled by overwhelming lust. It wouldn't be the first time lust short-circuited her brain.

She met his dark blue eyes. He gazed back with a heated expression that made her throat go dry. She'd never felt so strange, sort of light-headed, giddy, and yet grounded. Like she was standing out in a lightning storm with a protective shield around her. She was getting squirrely. What was this, a sci-fi movie?

"You look beautiful in that dress," he said. "I mean, you always look beautiful, but that dress is really nice." It was one of her regular singing-gig outfits, a simple form-fitting A-line dress with a flirty, twirly skirt, red for Valentine's day, with red pumps.

"Thank you," she said, feeling herself come down from that strange electric place. Gabe was just saying all the regular lines that guys always said when they wanted to hook up. "You look nice too," she added.

He smiled. "I'm glad we've established that we both look good. What are you doing after this?"

"Can I cut in?" Jordan asked. His eyes were on Zoe.

"No, you can't," Gabe said, maneuvering Zoe away from Jordan.

"Is he bothering you?" Jordan called.

Zoe's cheeks heated. She shook her head. "I'm fine."

Gabe spun her around and away, even further from Jordan, until they were dancing just the two of them in a quiet corner. "Ex-lover?" he asked.

She didn't answer right away. Things with Jordan were complicated. They always had been.

~ ~ ~

"Zoe?" Gabe prompted. He wanted to know the answer, but he could barely focus on the words because now that she was in his arms, lust hit him like a blow to the head, dizzying in its intensity. His pulse thrummed through him, his pants were uncomfortably tight, and he could barely focus on conversation. He'd been in a deep freeze these last several years since his fiancée, Alyssa, died and he felt like he'd just dropped into the hot, carnal deep end.

"I grew up with Jordan," she finally said. "He looks out for me."

He noticed she deftly dodged the real question. Clearly Jordan had some unfinished business with Zoe, but Gabe was the one dancing with her, and he wasn't going to waste his fifteen minutes worrying about an ex. He subtly pulled her closer, felt the heat of her through the dress, breathed in the scent of strawberry. A primal urge surged through him to take. He spread his fingers wide on her back to touch more of her.

"Gabe?" She was staring at him, brows raised, waiting for some response.

"What?" he asked, forcing himself to focus.

"I said you can really dance," she said. "You waltz beautifully."

"Thank you."

"Did you take lessons?"

"Yup. Me and all my brothers."

"You're telling me a bunch of guys took ballroom dance lessons?"

He twirled her around and brought her back. Her smile was infectious, bright and beaming. "Yup," he said with a grin.

"Tell me how that happened. You, Luke, and Jared just asked for ballroom dance lessons?"

"And my three stepbrothers."

"Six boys taking ballroom dance!" she exclaimed.

"Yup. We were like *The Brady Bunch* hepped up

on testosterone."

Her brows shot up. "The who?"

"How old are you?"

"How old are you?" she returned with a grin.

Probably too old for her. She looked so young and fresh. "Older than you," he said, feeling ancient. "You seriously don't know *The Brady Bunch*? They're on reruns all the time."

"My parents didn't let us watch much TV. So tell me about six boys dancing."

A smile tugged at his lips. "My mom insisted my stepfather, Vinny, take lessons before their wedding. Then she sent all of us boys too, so we'd bond."

Zoe laughed. "That's how she wanted you to bond? I can just imagine it. Especially Jared."

He chuckled. Jared had run around the room more than he'd danced. "It was bad. But Vinny was so in love with her, he went along with it. Of course, I didn't understand that at the time. I just thought he was whipped."

"How old were you?"

"Fourteen." He was damn grateful for the six weeks of forced lessons now because women loved a man who wasn't afraid to get out on the dance floor.

He spun her again and pulled her closer when she returned to his arms. She didn't pull back. Her soft curves pressing against him felt incredible. And she smelled good enough to eat. Or lick.

She looked up at him with wide eyes. "Fourteen and you didn't give them any attitude about ballroom dance lessons?"

He forced his mind back to the conversation. "Well, I'm the oldest, and Vinny offered to pay me ten bucks a lesson to set an example for my brothers."

"Ten bucks is pretty good."

"I negotiated to twenty." He grinned. "I cleaned up good."

"You sure did."

"I like dancing with you." His gaze caught on her cherry red lips, full and sweet. He desperately wanted to kiss her just then, screw the dancing.

"Me—ah!" She bumped into his chest as a little girl wrapped herself around her leg.

"Zoe! Zoe! Save me from the monster!"

Zoe pulled away with a laugh. Gabe glanced down, and his throat got tight. It was one of Ry's twins. Gabe had once been a twin, though he tried not to think about it. Ry approached and neatly scooped up the little girl, tucking her under his arm like a football, and left without a word.

Gabe pulled Zoe back into his arms, only this time he didn't bother with the waltz position and merely wrapped his arms around her waist and pulled her close. "This way you won't fall over from another twin attack," he said by way of explanation.

Zoe laughed and wrapped her arms around his neck. "I think we're safe. And P.S. I'm the big three-oh."

He smiled. "I'm the bigger three-five. You look much younger, by the way."

"Awww, thank you. I bet you say that to all the girls. You lawyer types are so smooth."

He shook his head with a smile. And then the words were out before he had time to second-guess himself. "I've been meaning to ask you..." He trailed off as Zoe turned away to talk to the guy who'd just tapped her shoulder.

"We're up," the guy said. He thought it was the drummer.

"Be right there," Zoe said. She turned back and gave Gabe an apologetic smile. "I gotta go. Sorry. What were you going to ask me?"

"Zoe!" Jordan hollered.

"It can wait," Gabe said.

"Sure?" She turned and raised a finger to her bandmates, and then turned back to him. "Okay, thanks for the dance."

He let her go. "My pleasure."

She studied him for a moment, her expression at once curious and, yes, definitely interested.

"What?" he asked in a show of innocence.

She blushed. "Nothing."

He knew what. He wanted to do dirty, dirty things to her, and he was testing the waters, throwing pleasure into the conversation.

"You owe me a dance," he said, "since we were interrupted. Come find me after your gig."

"But there's no music after," she said as she backed away.

"I don't need music."

She cocked her head to the side, opened her mouth and shut it again. "I gotta go."

"I'll wait," he said.

She nodded once and headed back to the other end of the room where the band was set up. He watched as Jordan scowled at her. Zoe smiled in return, her hand on his arm, and said something that pulled a reluctant smile from him. What was their deal?

Gabe returned to helping Shane while still keeping an eye on Zoe and Jordan. The man frequently ogled her ass when Zoe moved forward, center stage, and joked with her between songs. In fact, his eyes rarely left her at all. Still, Zoe had seemed interested, or at least curious about Gabe while they danced. Fuck it. He was going to ask her out as soon as they were done playing, death curse or no. He wouldn't get too close to her. He just wanted to spend a little time with her.

Naked.

He listened and watched Zoe for the next hour. There was something about her when she was singing that was different, almost divine, though that sounded so sappy. Sometimes when her voice rose in a building chorus, he actually got chills. It was electrifying, that voice. Her talent was wasted here in small-town USA. She belonged in the spotlight on the world stage, or at least with her own album. Why didn't she have a recording contract? He'd never heard of her singing career until he moved back to town four years ago. He hadn't seen much of her, as she flitted in and out of town for various jobs, but this past month she'd been putting in a lot of hours waitressing at Garner's, and he'd finally gotten the chance to talk to her when she brought his lunch.

The dance ended, and he helped Shane pack up and load the chafing dishes back in the van, trying to keep an eye out as the band packed up, hoping he wouldn't miss his chance to see Zoe. Shane asked him to help with the folding tables and chairs, which required several trips to a back storage shed. He'd just returned for the last of the chairs when he saw Zoe leaving with Jordan, his arm slung over her shoulders. Gabe continued on to the shed in the back of the parking lot. He was about to call out her name when Jordan stopped at an obnoxious yellow Corvette, opened the passenger-side door, and guided her in, one hand on her shoulder. The man couldn't keep his hands off her, and Zoe wasn't pulling away. The car peeled out of the lot.

She'd forgotten all about him. He slammed the shed door closed.

CHAPTER THREE

Gabe pulled up to Zoe's apartment Saturday morning intent on straightening things out with her landlord. Whether or not Zoe was interested in him, she'd come to him with a serious problem, and he intended to help her to the best of his abilities. That was what being a lawyer in Clover Park meant, it was in the job description—fixing problems. The place wasn't much to look at—a run-down Victorian house that had been converted into apartments with a gravel lot in what would've been the backyard for tenants' parking. He headed for the front door and buzzed the landlord's apartment multiple times.

Several long moments later, the door opened to a guy in his thirties, standing in Homer Simpson boxers that read Beer Pressure, looking horribly hungover. The guy ran a hand through his shaggy blond hair. "What the hell do you want? No solicitors, man."

Gabe would bet good money the guy had inherited

the house. He didn't look like much of a real estate investor.

"John, I'm Zoe Davis's lawyer," Gabe said, handing him his card. "She would like to finish the last two months on her lease before she looks for another place. She says you didn't have a problem with the dog until recently."

John smirked. "You stop sleeping with the landlord, you stop sleeping with your dog."

Gabe shoved his hands in his pockets so he wouldn't throttle the guy. "She's not giving up her dog because you say so. It's been eight months, and you had no problem with the dog. You'll need a court order to evict her, or we can take you to court and then you get to pay my lawyer fees." This was not exactly true, as Zoe was still in violation of the lease by having an over-twenty-five-pound dog, but this guy seemed about as bright as the character on his boxers.

"Whatever." He shut the door, but Gabe shot his foot out to stop it from closing.

"At least let her out of the lease so she's not out two months' rent."

"Fuck that. She signed it. I get the last two months whether or not she's here." He smirked. "And that lease says no dogs over twenty-five pounds."

Gabe stared him down. John stared back insolently. He couldn't believe Zoe slept with this jerk.

Women were blinded by muscles and tattoos.

"What makes you think the dog is over twenty-five pounds?" Gabe asked.

"I fucking weighed him."

"When did you weigh him?"

"When Zoe was in the shower."

Gabe ground his teeth, hating the idea of this asshole with Zoe at all, let alone pulling shit like this. "You have no proof."

John snorted. "I've got a picture on my cell."

"Show me."

John rolled his eyes, went into his apartment, and returned a few minutes later, shoving his cell phone picture in Gabe's face. There was Fred sitting on the scale. The picture was from over the dog's shoulder, but it looked like Fred with his distinctive gray and black fur. The large digital display clearly read forty. Dammit.

Gabe switched gears. "How much is two months' rent?"

John crossed his arms. "Two grand."

Gabe thought the guy might try to fleece him, but two grand was the exact amount for two months' rent. More than fair. "I'll write you a check. But you can't come after her for more. This is it, and she gets her security deposit back. Deal?"

"Who are you?" John sneered. "Her sugar daddy?"

He raised a finger. "You get the check only if you don't say a word about it. I'll take care of the rest."

John shrugged. "Whatever."

"The check will be delivered on Monday. She'll be out by the end of the month."

"One week." John turned and walked back to his apartment.

Gabe barely resisted slapping him upside the head. This asshole was turning Zoe's life upside-down, and he sounded as concerned as ordering a pizza. He left before his temper got the better of him. Problem solved. Zoe wouldn't be out any money. She just needed a place to stay on a temporary basis, until she could find a new place. He had an idea where she could stay, if she was agreeable. He'd ask her later today at Garner's, where he usually ate lunch on Saturdays. At least he had since he'd noticed Zoe worked the Saturday shift.

A few hours later, he sat at a table for two, studying the menu, debating ordering something different, and finally deciding to stick with his favorite. Once he liked something, he always liked it. Chocolate ice cream for the rest of his life? Yes, please. You can keep the other thirty flavors.

Zoe approached and lust pounded through him, making him feel alive and hyperaware of her. She was so beautiful, even in the required waitress uniform of white button-down shirt and black pants. The shirt open enough to expose her collarbones and luscious skin. The pants that clung to her curves. He always subtly checked out the rear view as she moved about the restaurant. Each time he saw her at Garner's, he fell deeper in lust. And now that he'd had her in his arms and had this chance to bring her closer, he was knocked off his feet. No other word for it. It was shocking after so much time avoiding entanglements. *Play it cool.*

She set down his usual club soda. "Howdy, stranger. BLT?"

"That's right. Hey, let me know when you get a break. I want to talk to you about your landlord."

"Did you finally get a hold of him?" she asked eagerly.

"Sure did. Long story, though." He needed time to put his idea to her in the best possible persuasive light.

"I've got a fifteen-minute break coming up in half an hour."

"I'll be here."

"Great!" She rushed off to help the next person. He watched her—the way she cocked her head, her beaming smile, the way she joked around with the customers. It was like the world had never touched her, never worn her down. A beautiful thing. Doubt swamped him. Should he still make the offer? Would it really be in her best interest? Lust messed with his head, making it hard for him to think logically. He couldn't take his eyes off her, so lust won that round.

A half hour later, she slipped into the chair across from him. "So, what's the news? Good, I hope?"

"Good news," he confirmed. "I got you out of the lease, so you won't owe him anything."

"What a relief! Now I can start looking for a new place."

"That's the other thing I wanted to talk to you about." He hesitated as inconvenient morals prodded at him. Was this in her best interest or his?

"Gabe? What?" she asked.

The hell with it. He could go a round or two in lust without harm, right? It had been so long, and he felt alive when he was near her in a way he hadn't felt in years. "I have a studio apartment over the garage that's available. If you'd like it, it's yours."

"How much?"

"No charge."

"Gabe."

"What?"

She shook her head. "You can't do that. Of course I'll pay rent. Really, how much?"

He shrugged. "I don't need the money. The house is paid off."

She stared at him. "I'll pay you what I paid in rent

for the other place."

"Why don't you just check out the place?" he asked in his best impression of a man with no sex drive whatsoever. He didn't want to scare her off. "It's a temporary solution. There's a fenced-in yard for Fred."

"There is?" Her face lit up. "Fred's never had a yard before."

Thank you, Dad, for being a miserable, antisocial man, who'd put up a six-foot privacy fence around the backyard so the neighbors couldn't look in.

"You and Fred could stop by," he suggested. "Check it out."

"Okay, we'll do that." She stood. "Tomorrow ten a.m. okay?"

"Sounds good. Just a minute." He pulled out his business card, wrote the address and his cell number, and handed it to her.

She took the card and chewed on her bottom lip, which sent a jolt to his groin, before she backed away. "Okay, see you soon." She flashed a smile that seemed a little forced.

"See you soon," he replied, unsure if he'd done the right thing. The fact was, he had a large four-bedroom house and a separate studio apartment all to himself, and he was damn lonely at home. He tried to be there as little as possible. He left some bills on the table and quickly left.

What was he doing bringing her closer? Just because he selfishly wanted her. He couldn't offer her anything more than a casual fling. Not with a clear conscience. Not with his track record of death.

No, no, it was fine. He was helping her out. She'd probably be flitting off to the next gig soon. He'd ask her about her schedule tomorrow.

If she just needed a temporary place to crash, no one would get hurt. This could still work.

~ ~ ~

Zoe pulled into Gabe's driveway the next day. "Wow," she muttered under her breath. She'd ridden her bike down this dead-end street as a kid and thought the homes were like castles back then, so big and majestic on large wooded properties, but even as an adult, the three Victorians on Lover's Lane were magnificent. The street sign had famously been stolen numerous times over the years by couples that wanted to hang it in their own home, but it was always replaced.

His house was painted a cheery yellow with dark green shutters, and had a wraparound porch and a large yard with a tall privacy fence. The two-car detached garage, set a little further back from the house, would be her new place if she moved in.

She unbuckled Fred from his doggie seatbelt and hooked his leash on him. "Ready to play?"

Fred gave her his happy panting face and leaped onto the sidewalk. His tail moved a teeny bit back and forth, which would've been an enthusiastic tail wag on any other dog, but his tail was curled and so fluffy, it was hard to tell when it moved.

She rang the bell and waited. The door swung open to Gabe in another button-down shirt, but this time with faded jeans that looked downright tasty on him.

"Hey, Zoe." He turned to her fur baby. "Hey, Fred." He ruffled Fred's fur and he presented his back side for a hip rub. Gabe obliged, and Zoe's heart melted a little. "We'll put him in the yard while I show you the apartment. I'll meet you out back by the gate."

"Okay." She led Fred back to the gate just off the driveway, slid open the latch, and stepped through. Wow. It was a huge yard, definitely an acre, maybe more, all covered in pure, untouched snow. She unhooked Fred's leash. He took off, jumping, running, and frolicking joyfully in the snow. Fred was made for this weather with his thick double coat.

"Looks like Fred likes it here," Gabe called from the back deck. He crossed to her. "Ready to check out the apartment?"

"Sure."

He led the way, ushering her through the gate and quickly shutting it behind them so Fred wouldn't make a run for it.

"It's empty," he told her, "but I've had the cleaning lady keep it clean. I put the heat on yesterday, so it should be comfortable."

"Great!"

She followed him up the outside stairs. He unlocked the door and stepped inside, his hands on his hips. "Well, what do you think? Good place to crash?"

She walked around, taking it all in. The unfurnished studio apartment with a private bathroom and a small kitchen area was smaller than her last place, so she'd have to ask her dad to keep some of her extra furniture. Still, it could work. It had nice light from two large windows in the front and back of the space. She glanced over at Gabe still standing by the door. It was private with its own entrance, she told herself; it wasn't like Gabe was going to be in her apartment all the time.

"You can move in as soon as you're ready," Gabe said.

He said it nicely enough, but she felt a tension in the air. She chewed her bottom lip. It seemed like a no-brainer, but something about Gabe, or maybe just what she'd heard about him, made her cautious. She should find out more about him before committing to anything. Because somehow moving in felt like it would be inviting him into her life. There was no denying an attraction between them. She'd felt that big time when they'd slow danced together, and if she was honest with herself, before that too.

"If I did move in, it might only be for a month or so," she said. "I might be going out to L.A. for a four-month gig." She'd received an offer to be a contestant on *Next American Voice*. The prize was a boiler-plate contract with a record company. Not that great, and she'd have to go on as a solo artist; they only wanted her, not the band. All of which made her hesitate, but the *exposure*. That she needed. She'd been so restless since she got back from the cruise ship, living in the town she couldn't seem to shake, still waiting for her big break.

"Whatever works for you," he said with a smile. "Let's see how Fred's doing." He opened the door.

The tension left her in a whoosh. "Yes! I bet he's having a blast."

She followed him to the backyard, where Fred met her with joyful jumps and yips. "Hey, Freddie!"

He took off, a furry streak running the perimeter of the yard. She'd never realized how much he must've needed regular runs. He looked so happy. She looked at the center of the yard with its untouched snow and couldn't resist. She walked over, flopped back in the snow, and made a snow angel just for fun. Fred came by, licked her cheek, and stole the fleece hat right off her head. "Fred! Get back here! I need that!"

He raced in circles around the yard, his prize in his mouth, as she tried unsuccessfully to catch him. He was just too darned fast. "Fred, drop it!"

Fred took off again.

Gabe whistled. "C'mere, Fred!"

Fred ran over and dropped the hat at Gabe's feet, looking up at him expectantly. Gabe snatched the hat and headed for Zoe. He set the hat on her head. "Hope you don't mind a little dog drool in your hair."

"I'm used to it. I can't believe the way he listens to you."

"Just call me the dog whisperer," he said, rubbing Fred behind the ears as he wiggled enthusiastically, bumping against Gabe's leg.

She laughed. "I'm surprised you don't have one of your own."

"I'm not home all that much."

"You travel a lot?"

"No, I just, you know, busy with work and stuff." He looked away. He sounded kinda lonely.

She scooped up some snow and tossed it lightly, hitting him right in the chest.

His jaw dropped comically. She giggled. He recovered fast, bending and scooping up a wad of snow and packing it in his big hands. She took off, and the snowball sailed past her shoulder. She turned. "Ha-ha, missed!" And that was when another one hit her right on the shoulder. "Hey! You tricked me!"

"All's fair in snowball fights." He was already forming another snowball. She quickly made a few snowballs and took off at a sideways run, pelting him as she went, until she ran out of ammunition. He tossed another one that hit her arm at the same time as Fred leaped in the air to catch it, knocking her to the ground. Oof.

Gabe knelt beside her. "You okay?"

She sat up, a little sore on her rear end, but she wasn't going to mention that. "Yeah, the snow's soft."

Gabe threw a snowball in the other direction, and Fred took off after it. She grabbed some snow and smashed it in his face for revenge.

"Hey!"

He grabbed some snow and put it in her face, and they wrestled for the next snowball, which ended with him straddling her, flat on her back, her wrists pinned above her head. "Never wrestle with a man who grew up with five brothers."

"Look out!" she shouted. "Behind you!"

He got off her quickly to face the threat. She grabbed some snow and threw it at him just as he turned back. "Ha!" she shouted, perhaps unwisely.

"You'll pay for that," he growled.

She squeaked and took off. Gabe chased her, and

Fred chased them both. Gabe caught her around the waist. "Got you now." His voice, low and husky, sent a delicious shiver through her.

She looked over her shoulder at him. "What are you going to do with me? Throw me over your shoulder and take me to your secret igloo lair?"

He loosened his hold on her. "Sorry. Didn't mean to be grabby."

"I was kidding."

He stepped back.

She turned. "Relax, Gabe. No big deal."

"Your boyfriend probably wouldn't like that."

"I don't have a boyfriend."

"What about that trumpet player—"

"Jordan and no."

A smile dawned slow and sure across his face, revealing that dimple again, almost hidden in his stubbled cheek. He looked entirely too appealing—hot and slightly dangerous. If what they said about him was true, if he really did dump his fiancée when she needed him most, well then she needed *that kind* of guy like a hole in the head. If it wasn't true, if he was the man that, from her perspective, seemed like a nice guy, well, he probably shouldn't get involved with her. Every relationship she'd had ended when she was away on a gig. Except for Eddie Thomson, the very famous A-list actor she'd gone out with before her landlord.

He'd picked her up in a jazz club and dumped her a month later in a very public rejection at his star-studded, cocaine-riddled party when she refused to join him in a threesome. She'd left for the cruise-ship gig shortly after that, desperately needing to be alone on the ocean. Except, of course, for the other three thousand passengers that she didn't socialize with.

When things settled down for her, once she proved to herself and her family that she could make it in the music industry, then she'd find some boy-next-door type that was good for her. Like vegetables.

A lima-bean boyfriend. Yum.

His dark blue eyes gazed warmly at her.

She absolutely, positively needed boy next door. Later. In the distant future.

But wouldn't that be exactly what he was if she took the apartment? Literally, boy, no, she corrected herself, nothing about Gabe said boy. He was *the man* next door. She swallowed hard. Gabe was definitely not her lima bean and this was definitely not the right time. She repeated the mantra to herself so she wouldn't be tempted. *Not my lima bean, not my lima bean—*

"Zoe?"

"Huh? What?"

"I said do you want to come in for a cup of coffee?"

She forced a smile. "A friendly cup of coffee?"

"Is there any other kind?"

"Good point." Fred barked. "Can I bring Fred?"

Gabe eyed her fur baby. "Uh, sure."

Zoe followed Gabe up the back steps and stomped her boots on the mat. "You should probably get a towel for Fred," she said when they got inside.

Fred took that opportunity to shake all the snow off him and onto the hardwood floor.

"Two towels," Gabe said.

She grabbed Fred's collar to keep him in place while they waited. Gabe's kitchen was gorgeous— white cabinets, dark gray soapstone counters, stainless steel appliances, double oven, six-burner Viking range. It was also spotless.

Gabe returned and handed her a towel. She dried off Fred while Gabe dried off the hardwood floor. Fred shook one more time, just enough to get Gabe wet. "Thanks," he muttered. He stood and held out his hand. "I'll take your coat."

She stuffed the hat in the sleeve, handed it to him, and left her boots on the mat. He left, and she sat at the kitchen island to wait.

"So, coffee?" he asked when he returned.

He'd changed into a Henley that emphasized a broad-shouldered, definitely muscular chest. Her heart thumped a little harder. *Fight impulsive nature. Be strong, girl!*

"You changed your shirt," she croaked.

He looked at her strangely. "Fred got it wet."

"Oh." She rubbed her icy cold hands together. "Coffee sounds perfect."

He went about making coffee in some fancy machine with way too many buttons and switches.

"You're really into your coffee, huh?" she asked.

"I got spoiled with Shane's coffee, so he set me up at home."

"Your kitchen's beautiful. Do you cook?"

He looked around and smiled sheepishly. "Never. I hired a decorator. I should learn, huh?"

"If you like cooking, this place could be a lot of fun."

"Not much point in cooking for one. All that leftover food."

"Yeah, I know what you mean." She glanced around. "Wait, where's Fred?" It was never good when Fred sneaked off somewhere. "Fred! C'mere, boy."

Fred trotted out with her boot in his mouth. "No," she told him sternly. "Leave it."

Fred took off. She chased him into a living room with lots of leather furniture, wood tables, and industrial metal lamps. Some black-and-white pictures of the moon in different phases hung on the wall. Fred leaped on the leather loveseat. "Off!" she hollered.

He leaped off. She chased him around the coffee table, and he leaped on the sofa. Keeshonds were jumpers. "Fred!"

Gabe appeared. "Leave it," he commanded in a tone that had her straightening up. Fred dropped the boot and looked to Gabe for the next command. Clearly, Fred thought Gabe was the alpha here.

She called Fred, and he trotted over to her side. "You've got the voice of authority," she said, rubbing Fred behind the ear. "Even I was ready to obey."

Gabe lifted a brow. "Oh, yeah?"

She flushed. "Must be an older brother thing. I'm the youngest, so I'm used to being bossed around."

He gave her a slow smile. "And I'm used to doing the bossing."

The gleam in his eye had her backing up a step. She bumped into Fred, who had circled around behind her when she wasn't looking. "Ah!" She stumbled and was about to fall backward when Gabe reached out, grabbing her arm, and she fell forward instead, bumping into his chest.

"Easy," he said.

"I am easy," she chirped.

He chuckled. That hadn't come out right.

"I mean, I'm relaxed." She straightened. He still held her, his hands on her upper arms, warm and firm. "You can, um, let go now."

"Let's get you warmed up," he said, snagging her boot in one hand and placing his other hand on the small of her back as he guided her back toward the kitchen. Holy cow. One hand, and she was burning up. Imagine what two hands could do.

Fred trotted ahead of them and pressed himself against the cold glass of the back patio door. He loved the cold.

Gabe set her boot back on the mat and returned to the kitchen, pouring them both a cup of coffee. He leaned against the island across from her, holding his mug and studying her.

She self-consciously smoothed her hair. She probably had hat head. "What?"

"How have I never spent any time with you?" he asked. "You grew up here, right?"

"Yes. I know your brother Luke, but you were too far ahead of me in school to bother with." She took a sip of coffee. Wow, that was good. She sipped some more. She loved Shane's coffee.

He sipped his coffee too. "Did you move back home after college?"

"Never made it to college. I was learning so much from my vocal instructor and, well, playing in Greenwich Village was an education all on its own." Greenwich Village was her favorite part of New York City. "It's like a Mecca for jazz musicians. People from all over the world play at the clubs there. But the city was too expensive, so I moved back home and became a commuter." She laughed ruefully. "Like most everyone else."

"I used to live in the city too, but I never hung out in the Village."

"More of an uptown guy, huh?" She grinned. "I got you pegged with your preppy outfits and your fancy schmancy job."

He chuckled. "What do you know about my fancy schmancy job?"

"Not much. Tell me about it."

She sipped her coffee while Gabe told her about wealthy clients, high-profile cases, and the need to always win. The hard focus on the bottom line, the insane hours, and the burnout that eventually got them all.

"Wow," she said when he'd wound down. "I guess you don't miss it, then?" *And do you miss your fiancée? Did you really bail because she had a brain tumor?* She was having trouble believing it from the guy who so generously offered her an apartment rent-free. She shouldn't listen to gossip. She wouldn't bring up such a painful memory as his fiancée's death. It was none of her business. Not unless something happened between them, which it definitely wouldn't.

"Don't miss it at all." He sipped his coffee. "I want

to hear more about your career. You sing beautifully."

"Thank you."

"I can't believe you don't have a recording contract," he went on, which thrilled her, until he continued. "You're much too talented to be stuck playing small-town dances."

She lifted her chin. "I like small-town dances, especially when it's my small town." The familiar burn of ambition returned, making her restless. She had to make something happen soon. For so long she'd been chasing that dream, and it wasn't any closer now than it was twelve years ago. Unlike her family, who'd all had their big break young. Her mom had been an actress in several popular movies in her twenties, her dad was a jazz pianist and singer in The Davis Trio and booked *The Pete Macauley Show* at twenty-five, and her sister, Jasmine, scored her first Broadway show as a dancer at nineteen. It was way past time for her.

"Surely you want more," Gabe said, somehow sensing her true feelings.

She warmed her hands on the mug, suddenly depressed. "Maybe some things just aren't meant to be," she said quietly.

"Maybe. But what about your L.A. gig? Maybe that will lead to something."

She met his eyes. "It's to be a contestant on *Next American Voice*. If I won, the contract isn't great.

Everyone in the industry knows that. It's kind of limiting, especially for someone like me that also writes my own songs."

"Still, it's something," he said. "At least people would know who you are. They should know you. You're amazing."

She met his dark blue eyes that looked back at her with such sincerity that she found herself confiding in him. Something she hadn't had the nerve to say out loud yet to anyone.

"This doesn't leave this room," she started.

"Lawyer-client confidentiality," he said with a straight face, his eyes sparkling in amusement. "Got it."

"I've been thinking about renting studio time and doing my own album. You know, just go indie."

His palm slapped the counter. "You should. That's a great way to get noticed. Hell, even a YouTube video could lead to something."

She frowned. YouTube was for amateurs. Her dad always said that. She came from a family of professionals.

"Everyone in my family has been a success in the arts," she told him. "Everyone but me, that is. I don't know if going indie would count, you know?"

"It only matters if it counts for you."

She stared at the counter. "I guess."

"So your sister danced on Broadway and your dad's band was on *The Pete Macauley Show*." Everyone in town knew about her family.

"And my mom was in the movies, the *Eye on Top* trilogy." It was a lot to live up to. Not that her family ever acted like she was a failure, but the fact was she was still just a waitress scrambling for gigs, and they all knew it.

"You have good show-business genes," Gabe said, "but that doesn't mean you can't forge your own path."

"Is that what you did?"

He didn't answer for a moment. Finally he said, "No. I followed in my father's footsteps, climbing that corporate track to partner as fast as I could, until he died of a heart attack at fifty-seven. That was a wake-up call. I quit. I've been practicing law here ever since." He shook his head. "I'm not sure why I'm still here. I'm just killing time, I guess. I can't believe four years passed so quickly while I solved the case of the smashed mailbox."

She laughed. "The what?"

"Mr. Jacobs's case of the anonymous mailbox basher—never mind." He grinned.

"Say no more." She raised a hand. "Mr. Jacobs says it all. What are you passionate about?"

"Passionate?" he drawled.

She felt herself flush. "I mean—" She cleared her throat. "You have to find what you're passionate about and follow your bliss."

"Like you?"

"Yeah." She frowned. "And here we are in the same place." Guess her grand plan of following her bliss hadn't worked out any better than Gabe's lack of a plan, and wasn't that depressing?

He reached out and squeezed her hand. "Hey, that's not necessarily a bad thing."

"Uh…" The tingling was back. *Not my lima bean, not my lima bean.* Fred ran by with something shiny in his mouth. "Fred!" Gabe released her hand, and she headed for Fred, prying Gabe's cell phone from Fred's mouth.

She scolded Fred, who looked back at her with his happy panting face. She handed Gabe the phone. "Sorry."

"That was brand new," he muttered. They both looked at the screen that was cracked in several places. It was one of those big expensive phone tablet thingies. The edges were chewed off too.

"I'm so sorry," she said. "I'll buy you a new one just as soon as I get the money. We'd better go." She grabbed Fred and headed for her coat in a hurry.

Gabe appeared where she was busy yanking her coat on while she tried desperately to hang onto a pulling Fred, who wanted to explore more of Gabe's house.

Gabe took Fred's leash. "So are you going to take the apartment?"

She avoided his eyes, instead focusing on Fred, who looked lovingly up at Gabe. Geez, even her dog was falling for him. "Let me think it over," she said. "I'll call you."

"Okay." He handed her Fred's leash and walked them to the front door. "Bye."

"Bye," she called over her shoulder, already out the door. "Thanks for the coffee!"

She hurried to her car, buckled Fred in, and headed home, feeling like she'd dodged a big gorgeous snowball.

Only to get one in the face when she arrived home. A bright yellow eviction notice was taped to her front door.

Chapter Four

Zoe pounded on John's door, eviction notice in hand.

The door swung open, and John looked her up and down. "Yeah?"

She shook the notice in his face. "What is this?"

He shrugged.

"By the end of the week?" she shouted. "What the hell? How am I supposed to be packed, moved, and find a new place in one week? You could at least have given me to the end of the month! Would two weeks have killed you? I already paid this month's rent."

John turned away and flopped on his sofa, picking up his video game controller. She followed him in, grabbed the remote, and turned off the TV.

"Hey!" He snatched the remote out of her hand and got in her face. He smelled like beer and nacho cheese. "Law's on my side. You broke the rules with your dumb dog."

She was so mad she wanted to spit in his face. She

headed for the door. "I'm calling my lawyer!"

"Go for it," John said.

She left, slamming the door behind her. Great. Now she had no choice but to take up Gabe on his offer. She couldn't stay with her parents because her mom was allergic to dogs. Couldn't stay with her sister because she already had a cat and a baby. She didn't want to add to the chaos over there. She marched back to her apartment, hating the position this put her in. She still wasn't so sure about Gabe. She'd ask Daisy about him. If anyone knew the scoop on Gabe, it was Daisy. Gabe was close with the O'Hare family, and Daze was one of them ever since she married Trav.

When she got home, she let Fred out of his crate and spent a long time petting him and getting some love. Fred always seemed to sense when she needed comfort and leaned against her in his form of a doggy hug. After she'd calmed down, she called Daisy, who told her to come over after lunch because talking on the phone was impossible when her boys were running around.

A short while later, Zoe rang the bell at Daisy's house. It was a brand-new addition with a separate entrance from the original house that her husband, Trav, still used for his landscaping company. Daisy answered the door with four-year-old Bryce and two-year-old Cole at her side. The boys wore knitted monster hats over their blond hair. Bryce had Daze's blue eyes while Cole had hazel eyes like his daddy. Bryce was the mischievous instigator while the more mellow, easygoing Cole did his best to keep up.

"Daisy and her little flowers!" Zoe exclaimed.

"We're not fwowers!" an indignant Bryce said.

"Yeah!" Cole chimed in, bobbing his head, making the ear flaps wiggle.

"You must be monsters, then," Zoe said. "Grrrr!"

"Roar!" Trav said from behind them. Both boys shrieked and took off. Trav grinned, hazel eyes sparkling with glee. Clearly, Bryce got his mischievous streak from his daddy. "Hey, Zoe, gotta run." He took off after the boys, his arms straight out in front of him, his hands grabbing the air.

"Hey, Z!" Daze was gorgeous as ever—long, wavy blond hair, bright blue eyes, and a sunny smile. She still had her figure and showed it off in a form-fitting white V-neck long-sleeve tee, jeans, and ankle boots. Daze gave her a big hug. "Come in. What's up?"

"I'm moving!" Zoe exclaimed.

Daze frowned. "Oh, no. Did he really go through with the eviction?" Zoe nodded, and Daze gestured to follow her to the kitchen. "Wait. Let me get the chips and drinks, and then you can tell me the whole story."

Zoe relaxed a little. Daze always had the potato chips she loved from the health food store. They were organic, so they both felt better about finishing the bag. She sat at the breakfast nook with its wraparound bench. Daze joined her a few minutes later with the bag of chips and two glasses of water.

Daze pulled out a handful of chips. "Okay, talk. Where are you moving?"

"Gabe Reynolds offered his place. So…" She lifted a shoulder up and down.

"His house?"

"He has a studio apartment over the garage with a fenced-in yard for Fred." She paused, knowing Daze would morph into big-sister mode at this next part. Her friend was seven years older, so they hadn't known each other in school, but when Daze heard a young girl from Clover Park was booking gigs in the city, she'd invited eighteen-year-old Zoe to stay over at her apartment whenever she had a late-night gig. They were close, even more so when Daze moved back to Clover Park, which was great, except Zoe was no longer a naive eighteen-year-old, and she already had a big sister on her back.

Zoe continued. "He says I can stay there for free, but of course I'll pay something for rent. I'll probably say yes. I should just do it, right?"

Daze's eyes widened. "Rent free? Are you two—"

"I know what it sounds like, but…" She took a sip of water, thinking about Gabe, and what exactly were his intentions with the offer of a rent-free place? "He's just being a friend," she finished lamely.

At Daze's concerned expression, Zoe flashed a big smile to put her at ease.

"Sweetie, you seem worried," Daze said. "You know you can always stay with us. We have a guest room and the kids love Fred."

"Aaahhh! Roar! Roar!" came from the other room. *Crash! Wa-aa-ah!* Then a moment later, "I'm otay."

Daze held up a finger and headed out to the living room. "All monsters must report to nap duty."

"Awww…" the boys said in unison.

"Daddy will read you a story," Daze said. "Not a scary one, Trav."

"Those are the best kinds, right, guys?" Trav asked.

A few moments and more squeals later, the noise level dropped.

"That's okay," Zoe said when Daze returned to her seat. "You guys are pretty busy without me and Fred being in your hair."

"We don't mind," Daze said. "It's already chaos. You and Fred would blend right in."

Zoe laughed. "I think I'll go with Gabe's place. Unless…" She paused. "Any dire warnings? Things I should know? I've heard some rumors, but I know I shouldn't jump to conclusions."

Daze cocked her head. "What did you hear?"

"I shouldn't repeat it. Just tell me what you know about him."

"Trav always said Gabe was a good guy. He's been friends with Shane for years."

"That's good enough for me."

Daze held up a finger. "But—"

"What?" Zoe sighed.

"Sweetie, just listen. Trav also said he used to be a shark in the courtroom. He won nearly all of his cases for corporate clients, and let's just say those corporations weren't always innocent."

Zoe shrugged. "So he's good at his job. No big."

"The point is he can be very persuasive. Be sure it's what you want."

Zoe waved that away. "It's just a temporary place to crash." She munched on a chip, then finally asked her real concern, "Is it true about his ex-fiancée?"

Daze cringed. "Gabe won't say much about it. Shane said she was hit by a truck, but no one's sure if it was an accident or suicide. And after the collision, the truck driver swerved off the road and smashed into a building. He didn't live to tell what happened."

"You think it was suicide because Gabe dumped her?" Zoe whispered.

"We'll never know."

So far everything she'd heard about Gabe was true, and she was almost afraid to ask this next part, but she had to know. Had to find out what kind of man Gabe really was. "Did he break up with her because he couldn't handle her being sick after his dad died? Because of her brain tumor?"

Daze shook her head. "I don't know. He told Shane very little, and Shane didn't push because it was such a sensitive subject. But, honey, people do strange things when they're grieving. His dad had died only a few days before they broke up. She died the very next day."

For some reason, she was disappointed. She wanted Daze to say Gabe would never do that. That he really was the nice guy he seemed to be, helping others, leaving generous tips, petting her dog.

Daze lowered her voice. "Are you into him?"

"No! Not as long as he's my landlord." Maybe she was worrying for nothing. If no other gig panned out, she'd probably be heading to L.A. in a month and none of this would matter anyway.

Daze frowned. "I just worry about you, after this eviction and Eddie."

"Have I told you I'm on a boy-next-door diet?" Zoe asked. "Only sweet boys next door with side parts in their hair." She nodded once. "It's the right thing to do."

Daze snorted. "Gabe is next door!"

"It'll be fine." Zoe ate more chips. "Right? Daze, I

need it to be fine."

"I'm sure you'll be fine," Daze said reassuringly. "Just, you know, be careful." She looked into Zoe's eyes. "Call me if you get persuaded."

"Yeah." She blew out a breath. "Yeah, I will. It's fine, it's fine, it's fine."

"It's good to have a mantra," Daze said with a grin.

"I've also got 'not my lima bean.'"

Daze sputtered. "What does that mean?"

"My next boyfriend will be good for me like lima beans."

Daze burst out laughing. "That sounds awful."

Zoe lost it. "I know!"

When they both calmed down, Daze said, "Call him right now and tell him."

Zoe grabbed her cell from her purse, pulled out the business card with his number, and dialed.

"Hi, Zoe," Gabe answered. His voice resonated on a deep, rumbling level through the phone, sending a thrill through her.

"Hi, I'll take the place. I have to make a few more calls, but I hope to move in this Saturday, if that's okay."

"Perfect. I'll get a copy of the key made."

"Okay, thanks." Daze was gesturing like crazy for the phone. "Daze wants to say hi. I'm at her place."

"O-kay," he said slowly.

"I've got my eye on you, shark boy," Daze said.

She couldn't hear Gabe's reply, but Daze laughed and hung up.

"What'd he say?" Zoe asked.

"He said *da-dun, da-dun, da-dun*." Daze cracked up.

Zoe gulped. "Is it wine-o-clock yet?"

~ ~ ~

Gabe was having difficulty focusing on his client Tuesday morning, knowing Zoe would be stopping by soon to pick up her key. The fact that she might only be at his place for a month left the door wide open for him to make a move. He'd satisfy this aching, throbbing lust he had for her, she'd leave, and no one would get hurt. No one would die.

He pinched the bridge of his nose and looked across the desk at the elderly woman who'd been his first grade teacher. "Mrs. Peters, I'm sorry, but there is nothing illegal about your neighbor having a bird feeder in his yard."

Mrs. Peters narrowed her eyes behind her pink cat's-eye glasses. "It's all well and good to feed birds, but it also brings mice. And ever since my..." She sniffled and produced a lace hankie from her purse. "My sweet Princess died, I've had a mouse problem." She pursed her lips and leaned forward. "I hear them scurrying around my basement. They're probably building an entire mouse city down there." She threw the back of her hand over her forehead dramatically. "I couldn't possibly go down there now. They're organizing, just waiting for an unsuspecting human to arrive so they can swarm and devour." She eyed him, waiting for his response to this grisly situation.

"Could you possibly call an exterminator?" he asked.

"And kill all those innocent mice!" she exclaimed.

Gabe didn't know how much longer he could practice small-town law. He was considering hanging up his law practice and taking up juggling on the back of a bucking bronco. He smiled to himself. It made more sense in its way. Not that he'd ever rode a bronco, or juggled, for that matter.

He brought his attention back to Mrs. Peters. "Have you considered talking to your neighbor about the problem?"

"Pfft. Not like old man Harvey would listen to anything I had to say. The man gets his mail in his pajamas."

He had no idea what that had to do with anything. "How about another cat?"

"No one can replace my Princess," she said. "She was one in a million—loyal, affectionate, trainable. Did you know I trained her to use the toilet?"

Did she flush too? He kept that to himself.

"I'll order some humane traps," he said with a note of finality, hoping she'd take the hint that this case was now closed. "They'll trap the mice, but not kill them. And I'll talk to Mr. Finkle."

"Who's going to get rid of the traps?" She lowered her voice, though they were the only two in the office. "You know, once the mice are trapped in there."

He let out a breath of resignation. Mrs. Peters was a widow, and her only daughter lived thousands of miles away in Oregon. "I will."

She stood and shook his hand. "Thank you, Gabe. Nice doing business with you."

"You too." Not that he'd get more than a handshake out of it. This town had a strange definition of what a lawyer was for. Aside from a few wills and small-business paperwork, he spent most of his time acting as The Fixer.

He heard the door open and then Mrs. Peters exclaimed, "How are you, Zoe, dear?"

Gabe stood abruptly, then sat again, not wanting to appear too eager. The two women chatted, then Mrs. Peters left, and Zoe was in his office.

"Hey," he said. Brilliant opening line.

She beamed. God, he loved that sunny smile. "Hey there," she said. "Got the key?"

He fished it out of his pocket and handed it to her.

She stared down at it for a long moment and then tucked it into her tiny pink purse with a purple flower on it. He loved that she was so girly. He grew up in a house filled with testosterone.

"So, Gabe," she said hesitantly, "I thought maybe we should talk about the rent. I don't feel right not paying anything. Just tell me what you think is fair so I'm not caught by surprise. I mean, maybe we should sign a rental agreement." She warmed to her topic. "A legal contract that spells out exactly what's expected. I dunno, you're the lawyer. What do you think?"

"No need," he said. "It's still free, and you can stay as long as you need to. At least someone can get some use out of the space."

She narrowed her eyes. "Is this one of those deals where I think I'm getting it for free, but you really want—" she lowered her voice and leaned forward "—services rendered?"

He chuckled. "What kind of services?"

She straightened and raised her brows. "You know."

He folded his fingers together on top of the desk. She stared at his fingers. "What would your trumpet player say about that?"

She tore her gaze from his fingers and stared at him with wide eyes. "Jordan? He'd be mad as hell."

He leaned forward, really needing a straight answer

on this guy. "Why is that, Zoe?"

She shifted in her seat. "We go way back," she said, neatly avoiding the question again. "So you don't want…" She looked side to side in case anyone was listening in, which made him smile, given that it was his private office, and they were very much alone. "You know what."

He chuckled.

She flipped her hair over her shoulder. "Um, you have to actually answer the question."

"Do I, Counselor?" he asked in his best intimidating lawyer voice.

She shook her finger at him. "I've been warned about you and your lawyerly ways. You're like a shark."

His lips twitched. "Daisy told you that."

"Yeah."

He smiled. "That's mighty nice of her to say."

"Oh, so you don't deny it? Proud of our sharkiness, are we?"

"It helped me win cases, so yes. That was courtroom Gabe."

"And who are you now?"

"Just a guy helping out in the community." She just sat there, studying him across the table, so he added, "Who do you want me to be?"

"Never mind." She pushed up from the chair, and

he snagged her hand.

"Sit." When she just stood there, looking pissed off, he added, "Please."

She sat.

"I was just joking around," he said. "I want you to feel comfortable. I really and truly want to help. That's all." He raised a brow, curious if his innocent act worked. Because there was no question that while he did want to help her, he also wanted her. Badly.

She smiled uncertainly. "I guess the whole landlord-tenant thing makes me itchy. You know, after John. Things went south pretty fast."

"This is purely out of the goodness of my heart," he said. That might've been pushing the innocent act.

She looked at him suspiciously. He didn't want her nervous and tense around him. He wanted her open and friendly. Really friendly.

"I won't make a move on you, if that's what you're worried about," he said. "Honest."

She pursed her lips, clearly thinking that over.

"Unless you ask me to," he added, unwilling to completely close the door he really wanted open.

"Okay, let me ask you this." She hesitated, and he held his breath, knowing she was going to try to corner him into admitting that he secretly lusted for her. "Would you have asked me out if this whole apartment thing had never happened?"

He knew it. How to answer? He'd wanted to, but he'd hesitated because he knew he couldn't do the relationship thing. That was definitely not what she'd want to hear. It wasn't personal, he hadn't asked anyone out since Alyssa died, and he really didn't want to talk about that. But if he said he didn't want to ask her out, well, women were touchy about that kind of thing. This felt like one of those does-my-butt-look-fat-in-these-jeans questions. There was only one right answer.

"No." That was technically true because the apartment thing had happened, and so answering as if it hadn't happened wasn't a fair question. It was a loophole. He was trained to find loopholes.

"Oh." She frowned and looked at his desk.

Now he felt like an ass. "I would love to go out with you," he answered truthfully. *On a temporary basis.* "But only if you were comfortable with it." He crossed his arms, working on looking unattainable. "The only way anything would happen between us is if you made a move on me."

She stood and flashed a smile. "Then there's no problem," she said in a perky voice that made his heart sink. "I've got to get to work." She pulled on her coat and grabbed her purse. "I can't wait for Fred to have his own yard. See you soon, neighbor!"

"See ya," he managed.

The door swung closed behind her, and he quietly thunked his head on the desk. Brilliant strategic move, Counselor.

CHAPTER FIVE

Zoe sang with a heavy heart at her last gig at her favorite jazz bar in New York City on Friday night. The Blue Tizzy would be shutting down on Monday, as the rent had doubled, and they couldn't afford to stay in business. Things were rough all over for musicians and the smaller venues that supported them. They finished their last set and she hugged the owner, Judy, who'd given Zoe her very first gig. Judy, a sixty-something jazz fanatic, liked to dress like a flapper from the 1920s Jazz Age. She wore her dyed-blond hair in a cute bob with a rhinestone headband with a rhinestone feather. A shiny silver sequined dress and black Mary Jane pumps completed the outfit.

"I'll miss you," Zoe said.

"I'll miss you too," Judy said in her rough smoker's voice. She pulled back, her blue eyes soft. "But I'll be relaxing in the Florida sun, finally retiring, so it's not all bad. You make me proud, ya hear? I want to hear those pipes on the radio one day."

"I'm trying," she said, blinking back tears. She wanted so badly to make Judy proud. "You know I'm trying."

Judy cupped her cheek. "I know you are. I'm so proud of how far you've come. Remember how your voice shook your first time here?"

Zoe nodded.

"Now you own that stage. Hell, you own the whole damn room."

"Thanks, Judy." They chatted for a while, and then she joined her bandmates at the bar.

An older man on her left bought her a drink. "You're the most beautiful singer I've ever met," the man said.

"Thank you," she said.

Jordan interrupted, wedging his large body between them. "Excuse me, this is my wife."

The man held up a hand and shifted further down the bar. Jordan took his seat, his dark brown eyes gleaming with a fire that said *don't mess with me*.

She turned to him and whispered, "Jordan, I told you to stop doing that."

He tipped her chin up with one finger. "I'm just looking out for you, Zoe-bean."

"I know," she said with a sigh.

"Don't drink what he got you," Jordan said, taking

the drink from her. A harmless glass of white wine. "He probably slipped you something." She shook her head. Jordan always suspected people were at their worst. He signaled to the bartender, returned the drink, and ordered her usual dirty martini and a beer for himself.

When their drinks arrived, Jordan took a pull on his beer and gave her a sideways glance. "Your gears are turning. Whatcha thinking about?"

She'd been thinking about how badly she wanted her big break and how, performing tonight, she really wanted it to be with her band, who'd been with her the past five years. Jordan was the most recent addition to Sizzling Coda, two years ago, but he'd blended in seamlessly because of their history. He wanted to prove to his father he could make it to the top just as much as she did. With that much inner fire to succeed, why couldn't they do it their own way?

"I'm thinking maybe it's time we went indie," she said. "We're no closer to a recording contract now than we were five years ago. Clubs like this, our bread and butter, are going out of business. We should raise some money, rent a studio, hire a producer, and put out our own album."

He set his beer down. "No."

"That's it? No? Why not?" She sat up straighter, annoyed. If something didn't come through soon, she was going to end up on *Next American Voice*. There was just no other way to break out.

The corner of his mouth lifted. "My feisty one. Because I'm not giving up that easily—"

"It's not giving up! It's just a different path."

He leaned close and pushed her hair back to whisper directly in her ear. "I'm working on something."

She barely resisted rolling her eyes. Jordan was always working on something. "Whatever," she muttered. Maybe she could raise the money to do an indie solo album. It wasn't ideal, but it was something. If the band wasn't behind her on this, what could she do but strike out on her own? If she found a good producer to work with her in the studio—

"Zoe, I mean it. I'm working on something that could be our big break."

"I'm tired of waiting for our big break." She was getting nowhere fast and she just *had* to do something about it.

"Just hang tight. A little longer." He squeezed her hand. "Please."

Jordan hardly ever said please. "How long?"

He smiled because he knew he'd won. "Not long. I don't know exactly. One month, two, tops. There's a lot to work out before they get to us, but we're on their radar, thanks to me."

"Who? What?"

He pressed one finger against her lips, shushing her. "All in good time, my dear."

She nipped his finger, which only made him smile and pretend to snap at her like a crocodile with his gleaming white teeth. She turned to her other side where Wade and Alex sat, munching on mixed nuts and drinking whiskey. "You guys know what Jordan's up to?"

"He's always up to something," Alex said.

"Yup," Wade put in.

"They don't know," Jordan said in her ear. She shoved him away.

"Stop talking in my ear," she said. "It's very sensitive."

"I know," he cooed in her ear.

She huffed out a breath of frustration and gave him her back. "What do you guys think about putting out our own album?"

"Cool," Wade said.

"Hold that thought," Jordan said, leaning his arm against the bar next to her and somehow making it feel like his arm was around her at the same time. He spoke to the guys. "Our big break is just around the corner."

"Ain't it always?" Alex said before downing his whiskey.

She looked from Alex to Wade. They'd been with her the longest, seeming content to play whatever gigs she and Jordan scrounged up for them. Wade worked for his family's produce company driving the morning delivery route, sleeping days, playing gigs at night. Alex had a trust fund. His family pretended he was a percussionist in a symphony to their friends. She sighed. These two never hungered for success the way she did.

"You've got one month," she told Jordan. And then she'd do something on her own, *Next American Voice* or a solo indie album, she wasn't sure which, but something.

Jordan pulled her right off the stool and into his arms, rocking her from side to side. "I knew I could count on my girl."

She pulled away. "I'm not your girl."

"You know what I mean," he said, lifting his beer again. "We all call you our girl. Right, guys?"

"Yeah, yeah," Wade and Alex muttered, well used to this argument.

She moved back to her bar stool. "Give me a hint, Jor."

He leaned close and grinned, his eyes full of mischief. "Promise not to tell a soul?"

"Yes!" she said, thoroughly exasperated with him, but unable to help smiling.

"Ever hear of Hep Six?"

"Omigod!" Hep Six was an internationally acclaimed jazz band that did regular tours of Europe. Their music was amazing, and they even had several hits that got regular radio play.

"Shh!" He smiled, seeming pleased with her response. "So just think about that."

Wade and Alex leaned in. "What are we omigod about?" Wade asked.

"Hep Six might want us!" Zoe exclaimed.

Jordan shook his head. "Keep it down."

Wade and Alex looked at each other, brows raised. She bounced up and down in her seat. "As backup, or as an opener?" She smacked Jordan's arm. "What? Tell me!"

He chuckled. "They're considering us for an opener, but it's not a sure thing. They're considering a lot of bands. Keep it under your hat." He put his hand on top of her head to keep it there.

She just stared at him, slack jawed. She couldn't believe it. Even just singing backup for Hep Six would be such an honor. To open for them would be a dream come true. Maybe they'd get a chance to jam together, hang out, learn from them. She got goose bumps. This was huge. The big break she'd been waiting for, and she'd have it with her band.

Jordan put one finger under her chin and closed

her mouth for her. "That was exactly the right response," he told her.

"Cool," Wade said.

"Let us know when you know," Alex said. "Pool?"

"Nah, you go," Jordan said. "I need to talk to Zoe." Wade and Alex nodded and wandered off.

"How well do you know your new landlord?" Jordan asked.

She sipped her martini. "Well enough."

"You see him much?" Jordan asked. "He bothering you?" That last part came out quiet and menacing.

She sipped her drink. Did hot and bothered count? Now that they were adults, Jordan played the protective older brother role. As kids, he'd teased her relentlessly. And as teenagers, well, that was when all hell broke loose. At least for her. Jordan, two years older, had morphed overnight into a gorgeous six-foot hunk of man. He was her first kiss, her first time, her first love. She was none of those things to him, and he'd treated her as carelessly.

She'd run into him at twenty at a party in the Village when he'd returned home from college, sure that now that they were both grown up, they could be together. She practically threw herself at him, had secretly been in love with him since he'd obligingly kissed her at thirteen when she'd brazenly asked him that summer. Again, he took what she offered, and the next morning sent her on her way, saying he hoped they could still be friends. She saw him the next night kissing another woman at yet another party.

She'd made the mistake of confronting him. "Jordan, what are you doing? Who's she?"

"Cherise," he said with a smile, "this is Zoe, a family *friend*."

Cherise wrinkled her nose. "She's so cute. How old are you? Are you allowed to be here?"

Jordan laughed. "Old enough for some things. Right, Zoe?"

She sputtered, so furious she couldn't get a word out. And then she turned and walked out, her cheeks burning in humiliation.

She stopped going to Village parties for a while after that. She'd moved on. Years later, as their paths crossed at jazz clubs and the occasional family get-together, he'd apologized for how he'd treated her. He promised he was no longer a man slut and hoped they could move past that. And while she'd forgiven him, she'd turned down his offer of a date a month later. Years after that, as the hurt wore off, she accepted him into her band. Ever since, he'd been her number one protector, big brother, and friend all rolled into one.

"Zoe," Jordan prompted, "I said is he bothering you?"

"No. I think I'm bothering him."

"How so?" he asked, deceptively calm.

"Fred ate his cell phone."

He grinned, returning to his easygoing tone. "How did that happen?"

"We were having coffee—"

"Where?"

"Um, in his kitchen."

"So you were in his kitchen in his house?"

"Yeah, and we were talking—"

"What were you doing in his house?" he demanded.

"I told you, we were having coffee."

"Don't get involved with your landlord again," Jordan said. "My back can't take two moves."

"Ha-ha."

"I'm serious."

"I'm not getting involved. What do you think I am, an idiot?"

He took a lock of her hair and rubbed it between his fingers. "Of course not. You're Zoe-bean the great."

She laughed at the childhood nickname. "Jordy the Horn."

He kissed her cheek. "What would I do without you?"

"You'd be bored and wandering around in a daze."

He laughed. "You got that right. Come on, I'll

walk you to the train station. I don't want you getting back too late."

"All right, thanks." She finished her drink and left, knowing Jordan had her back. Just like always.

~ ~ ~

Saturday morning was the big moving day. Zoe had her dad, Jordan, and her brother-in-law, Will, coming by to help. With three men, she'd be moved in no time flat. Her cell rang while she waited for them. It was her sister, Jasmine. She hoped Will wouldn't be delayed.

"Hey, Jaz," she answered.

"You talk to Will and not me? Now I know something's up. How well do you know Gabe? What's the deal?"

"He's helping me out, he's a good tipper, and he eats at Garner's." He was also a shark lawyer apparently, but she didn't think the shark part would go over big with Jaz. And he may or may not have dumped his terminally ill fiancée who then died. Gabe's life was starting to sound like a tragedy. First his dad died and then a few days later, his fiancée. Even if it was true and he had dumped her after hearing she was ill, she still felt kind of sorry for him. The guilt must eat away at his soul.

Jaz's voice came through the phone loud and

mouthy as usual. "Oh, well, if he eats at the restaurant that everyone else in town eats at all the time, he must be okay."

Zoe sighed noisily. "Daze says he's good friends with Shane. You know he's okay, then, by association."

"Hmmm…have you heard the gossip about him?"

"I don't listen to gossip."

"Good. Just ask him yourself if you're worried. Are you worried?"

A little. "No, I'm not worried. I'm renting his apartment not marrying him."

"Do you think he's cute?"

"Jaz! Nothing's going on! He just happens to have an apartment, and I just happen to be getting evicted from my apartment on account of Fred."

"Your landlord is a sleaze."

"I know it." Of course she knew that now. At first John had been so uber-supportive of her singing career, cheering her on, going to all her gigs in the city. But it was all fake. He just wanted the free drinks and entertainment from being her invited guest (as he'd informed her when she'd caught him kissing another woman at the bar).

"Don't sleep with your new landlord," Jaz said. "You'll screw things up for Fred again."

"I'm not going to sleep with Gabe!" First Daze,

then Jordan, and now Jaz acted like she had no control whatsoever. Geez, it wasn't like she slept around. "I told you I just need a place. It's not even in his house! It's above the garage!"

"Okay, calm down. Is it nice?"

"Yes." Fred bumped his hip against her leg, asking for a hip rub. She obliged, and he wiggled happily. "It has a yard for Fred too."

"All right. Will's on his way." She heard a noise like they kissed.

"Were you holding Will hostage until you could butt into my life?" Zoe asked.

Jaz laughed heartily. "Good one. Just remember, don't get naked."

"Whatever!" Zoe exclaimed.

Jaz laughed again; then baby Ella let out a wail. "She's up. Gotta go! Love you!"

Zoe gritted her teeth. "Love you too. Bye."

A short while later, her stuff was loaded into the van the band used to move equipment and unloaded over at Gabe's place. She only had room for the bed, dresser, nightstand, small coffee table, and sofa. That was fine. It would be cozy. Besides, it was only for a month, maybe two if the gig with Hep Six worked out.

Gabe had come out to help too. After everything had been moved in, the men in her life felt it necessary to give Gabe the third degree.

"You single?" her dad boomed in his deep don't-mess-with-my-daughter voice. He'd scared off plenty of teenaged boys in high school that way.

"Yes, sir," Gabe replied in a voice that at once showed respect and an understated strength. She melted a little. She liked strength.

Her dad grunted.

"Zoe's off-limits," Jordan said. "Keep the landlord-tenant relationship professional." He gave Zoe a sideways look.

"I wouldn't say professional adequately describes Zoe living in my studio apartment," Gabe said. "It's more of a casual arrangement."

"What the hell is that supposed to mean?" Jordan said, getting all huffy and in Gabe's face. He was taller than Gabe and bulkier, but Gabe didn't back down.

Gabe spoke in an even, controlled voice. "It means exactly what I said."

She was about to tell Jordan to knock it off when Will cleared his throat. "Zoe is like a sister to me," he said in a voice that sounded almost rehearsed. Had Jaz coached him? "So, you know, er, hands off."

The three men stared at Gabe. He took them all in, his gaze lingering on her, before turning back to the men and saying in an authoritative lawyerly voice, "Your case has been heard. I am innocent until proven guilty."

Jordan made a growling noise and lurched toward Gabe. Her dad held him back with a solid hand slapping down on Jordan's shoulder.

"Calm down, son," her dad said. He always had seen Jordan as the son he never had.

Jordan huffed and continued glaring at Gabe.

"I'll go get Fred!" Zoe said brightly, leaving the men to their standoff at noon.

CHAPTER SIX

Later that afternoon when Zoe returned from grocery shopping, she found the kitchen sink still filled with water from when she'd washed out the few cabinets. She stared at it. The slow drain appeared to be stuck. She put the groceries away and contemplated what to do. Well, she had a landlord, right? She'd tell Gabe. She let Fred out into the backyard and headed around to the front door of his house.

Gabe answered the door, looking neat and preppy as always in a button-down shirt and jeans with loafers.

"Hey," he said warmly. "Come on in. No Fred?"

"He's romping around your backyard, eating snow. I just stopped by to let you know the kitchen sink is clogged. The water won't drain at all, so I don't know if we need a plumber or one of those plungers or maybe Drano? I didn't want to do the wrong thing, so I came to tell you."

"Let me take a look." He followed her back to her place, stopped in front of the sink, and stared. "Yup. It's clogged."

"Did you think I made that up to lure you to my place?" she asked.

"Wouldn't take much to get me here," he replied, sparing her a quick glance. She rocked back on her heels, the apartment suddenly feeling a lot smaller. He stuck his hand in the water and fiddled with the drain. Nothing happened. "I'll call a plumber."

"Wait! Plumbers are more expensive on the weekend."

"You can't live like this," Gabe said. "How are you supposed to cook or wash your dishes?"

"I'll be okay. Monday's fine."

He shook his head, washed his hands, and called anyway. He finished the call and turned to her. "Plumber will be here by five. You can have dinner at my place tonight. Okay?"

She swallowed. "You want me to pick up something or…"

"No problem." He gave her a slow, sexy smile. The shark was back. "I'll take care of everything."

"Okay, um, thanks."

Gabe nodded once and left. She sank on shaky legs to the sofa. This would just be a friendly dinner. Two neighbors getting together eating food. No big.

~ ~ ~

Gabe went a little nuts getting ready for dinner that night. This was his big chance. Zoe was coming over, just the two of them, and he was going to make it special. He put candles on the dining room table and ordered takeout because despite a top-of-the-line gourmet kitchen, he couldn't cook. Shane was always giving him grief about his untouched kitchen. His mom had left her china and crystal in the dining room cabinet, so he put that out too. Nerves shot through him. Was it too much? Was he putting on a show here he couldn't possibly live up to? Romantic dinner didn't scream fling. But she had to eat, right? He'd promised her dinner.

He put the crystal goblets back in the cabinet.

Took the goblets out again.

He heard a truck pull up and peered out the front window. The plumber was here.

He snagged his coat and walked with the plumber, Sal, over to Zoe's apartment, giving him a brief description of the problem.

Gabe knocked on her door. It swung open a moment later to a smiling Zoe. "Oh, good, you're here," she said.

Lust knocked him silly. "Plumber's here," he said, pointing out the obvious. *Get a grip.* Fred barked like crazy until the plumber gave him a pat; then he bumped against him happily. The plumber took off his coat and headed over to the sink. Zoe held Fred on a leash to hold him back.

"How's it going?" Gabe asked. "You getting settled in?" He glanced around. She still had a lot of boxes stacked up against the wall.

"Yeah. I'll unpack a little more tomorrow. I just wanted to get the necessities out."

Sal popped his head out from under the sink. "Just a clog. Be done in a jif."

Several minutes later, the plumber turned the water back on, and the sink drained perfectly. "There you go," Sal said. "Bill will be in the mail."

"Okay, thank you," Gabe said.

Sal grabbed his coat and left. Zoe released Fred, who started jumping all over Gabe. "Sit," Gabe commanded. Fred sat. He pet him lavishly as a reward.

"Do you still want me over for dinner?" Zoe asked. "I mean, I could cook here now."

Gabe squatted down to pet Fred, not wanting Zoe to see just how much he wanted her there. "Absolutely. Is Fred smiling?"

Zoe laughed. "Yeah, they call keeshonds the smiling Dutchmen. They're a Dutch dog, and they really do smile."

Gabe looked at Fred's big goofy smile and found himself smiling back. He stood. "Stop by in an hour."

"You want some help?" she asked. "I could stop by now."

"Nope. I got this."

"Okay." She wiggled her fingers. "See you in an hour."

He showered, shaved, and dressed extra nice in suit pants and shirt, the kind he used to wear when he was a stressed-out lawyer. He applied cologne and inspected himself in the mirror. That was as good as it got.

The delivery guy arrived with takeout from a really good Italian restaurant in Eastman. He emptied the containers and put them in various pots and pans to give the impression he'd actually cooked. Women went crazy for a man who cooked. He splattered some marinara sauce on the stovetop to further the illusion.

Finally, he put on some slow jazz. She was, after all, a jazz singer, and lit the candles. He dimmed the lights and inspected the scene. Definitely romantic like a nice restaurant. That didn't have to mean relationship, he reassured himself. That could just mean seduction. A few moments later, the doorbell rang, and his heart kicked up. It had been a long time since he'd been worked up over any woman. He felt like an awkward teenager on his first date.

He opened the door. "Hello."

"Hi." She stepped inside, and he helped her off

with her coat. She turned. "I, um, feel underdressed."
She wore the same clingy sweater with jeans and boots
she'd had on earlier. He loved it.

"Not at all," he said.

She slipped off her boots and left them by the
front door, losing a few inches in height. He placed a
hand on the small of her back and guided her into the
kitchen.

"Smells wonderful. Wait, I thought you didn't
cook."

"Only simple things," he said quickly.

She glanced into the dining room and stopped
short. "Gabe? This is all very nice. I mean, you look so
nice and the candles." She waved a hand in the air.
"The soft music. The food. But is this a date? I
thought it was just a friendly invitation?"

Gabe debated whether he needed to plow forward
or cover up a massive error in judgment. He'd thought
she'd seemed interested before, or maybe that was just
her way of being friendly, the way she was with
everyone. He turned to her, looking extremely
uncomfortable, and went with the cover-up.

"Definitely a friendly invitation," he said.

He crossed to the dining room and blew out the
candles. He shut off the music too. "I saw a dinner
party in a movie once with candles. But we don't need
them. Whatever. This could not be a more friendly

invitation." And if she believed that—

"Oh." She bit her lip, and he restrained himself mightily from doing the same. She had beautiful lips—full and pink.

He headed to the kitchen and gestured to all the pots and pans. "This is just takeout warming up on the stove. Very casual."

She cocked her head to the side, studying him. "You sure?"

"Yup." He shoved his hands in his pockets.

"I guess you're used to entertaining?" she ventured.

He never entertained. "All the time," he said. "Wine?"

"Sure."

"We'll eat in the living room on the coffee table. We don't need something so formal as the dining room."

"No, it's nice. We can eat in the dining room. You have the table set so nicely with…" She peered in there. "Is that crystal? And china and silver."

He shrugged.

She gave him a funny look. "We'll eat there, thanks."

He poured her a glass of merlot, poured himself a glass, and raised his glass to her. "To friendly dinners," he said.

She looked at him like he was crazy. He felt a little

crazy. Still, she toasted. "To friendly dinners," she said.

He took a long swallow of wine and turned to serve up dinner.

~ ~ ~

Zoe sipped her wine and stared at Gabe's broad back as he piled angel hair pasta, sauce, meatballs, broccoli rabe, and garlic bread onto two plates. She wasn't sure what she'd wanted tonight to be. On the one hand, he'd invited her to dinner at his home, which was very intimate and romantic. On the other hand, Daze's warning about Gabe's powers of persuasion made her leery. And the whole deal with his ex. She'd been on the fence over date or no date, so she went for casual. No makeup and no fussing over her clothes, just the same outfit he'd seen her in earlier today. Gabe had dressed up, and he smelled wonderful, some spicy cologne that made her want to breathe deep whenever he got close. She kinda wanted the music and candlelight back, it had looked so romantic, but she was afraid her uncertainty had squashed any romantic notions he'd had. Not many guys made that kind of effort, and it made her like him even more.

Gabe set dinner on the table and pulled out a cherry-wood chair for her to take a seat. He was such a gentleman. Maybe her worries were unfounded. "Thank you," she said as he scooted in the chair for her.

He took the seat at the head of the table, which was next to where she sat. They could hold hands if they wanted. Did she want that?

"The food is from Emilio's," he said. "Everything is made fresh from scratch. Homemade sauce, meatballs, even the bread."

"Sounds wonderful," she said, setting a cloth napkin in her lap. It almost felt like she was at a nice restaurant. "Gabe?" she ventured.

He set his fork down. "Yes?"

"I kinda liked the candlelight and music. I mean, if you don't mind, could we have that back?"

He gave her a slow, sexy smile revealing the dimple that she found so appealing. Now that he'd shaved, he looked more boy next door. "Sure."

He left for a moment, and the music returned. She relaxed a bit as the familiar voice of Billie Holiday filled the room. She looked up. There were speakers in the ceiling. Cool. He returned with a long lighter and lit the candles on the table.

"Dim the lights too," she said.

He did and returned to the table. "Does this mean you…"

She suddenly felt shy. "I don't know. I just liked it."

He raised his glass to her, and she clinked hers

against his. "To just liking it," he said in a husky voice.

Damn if she wasn't throbbing at the words. Unsure what to say in return, she took a long drink of wine. He took a sip, watching her over the rim of his glass. She felt herself flush. Thank goodness he couldn't see that in the dim candlelight.

She dug into the pasta. "This is wonderful," she told him after she chewed. "I love Italian."

"Yeah? Me too. What's your favorite Italian food?"

"Homemade ravioli. There's this place in the city I used to go to all the time just for the ravioli. I guess you need one of those pasta-maker machines if you want to do it yourself."

"My stepdad makes homemade pasta and sauce. Nothing like it."

"I can make a mean takeout," she joked.

"Me too."

They smiled at each other.

"So what made you move back into the house you grew up in?" she asked. "I mean, I thought you lived on this street."

"Yeah, this is it. I wanted to move back, and my mom and stepdad wanted to downsize. The timing just worked out."

She looked around. "So was it like this when you lived here?"

"Their furniture went with them or to charity. Just

the dining room set stayed. And I made some changes. Updated the kitchen. Redid the basement."

She grinned. "Did you make the basement into a man cave?"

"If by man cave, you mean a pool table, bar, and home theater—"

"That's a man cave, all right."

"Then yes, I did."

They ate in companionable silence for a few minutes. If this was a date, it was the most relaxed first date she'd ever had. Usually she'd be babbling a mile a minute just to make sure there weren't any awkward silences. And she hardly ever ate much of the food. She took another bite of garlic bread. Everything was so good.

"So what's the latest with your music?" Gabe asked.

She held up a finger and finished chewing. "Not much. Jordan says he's working on getting us something, but who knows if that'll pan out. He's always working on something."

"You should try the indie route. The world's much more connected now. Anyone can post their music online and get a following. That might even be better than that show. Although, if you do go on the show and win, as I'm sure you would, you do know a lawyer who could take that boiler-plate contract and negotiate a better one."

"It's pretty iron-clad."

"Nothing is iron-clad." His tone, so hard and confident, gave her a glimpse of the corporate lawyer he'd once been. He would be good to have on her side, that was for sure.

She took a sip of wine. "I've been thinking about my options. It's so hard, you know? I want to make it big with my band, but Jordan doesn't want to go indie. Besides, it's expensive if you do it right. You need to rent a recording studio and get someone who knows what they're doing to produce."

"I'd invest in you," he said.

"Gabe."

"What?"

"First you want to let me stay rent free, which I'm not doing; then you want to pay for my band's indie album?"

"Yes."

"You're much too generous with someone you just met."

"We haven't just met." He paused, his eyes trailing from her hair to her eyes and finally lingering on her lips. "I've had my eye on you for a month."

Her breathing hitched. "Oh."

"Forget I said that." He took a long swallow of wine.

A beat passed.

"Why didn't you ask me out?" she asked.

"I didn't want to strike out with my waitress and have you spit in my food."

She laughed. "I find that hard to believe."

"Why?"

"I think you go after what you want."

He studied her in that unnerving way of his. She had a feeling if he studied her long enough, all the answers he sought would be right there for him to see. All her lusty impulsive thoughts. Oh, this was not good. One day. She lasted one freaking day before temptation lured her in.

"Zoe, would you like—"

"I won't be persuaded to sleep with you!" she blurted.

He flashed a smile, looking darned pleased with himself. "I was going to ask you out," he said. "But if you want to jump ahead…"

Her face flamed. See what happened when big-sister types got in your head? Don't sleep with your landlord, don't sleep with your landlord, until all she could think about was sleeping with her landlord!

She finished her wine in one long swallow. "Maybe I'll go out with you," she replied, trying for cool.

"Maybe? How do you maybe go out?"

She put her glass down. "Can I be honest?"

"Please do."

"I have a long pathetic history of losers. My landlord, for one. Every guy that thought it was cool to pick up the singer after a gig, and not so cool to actually have a relationship with them." She blew out a breath. "And the truth is, maybe it's not just the guys I date, maybe I'm a bad bet. I want that music career so bad I can taste it. I fly off for every opportunity and things always seem to fall apart relationship-wise when I'm away."

His gaze was heated. "So you only want something temporary?"

A fling was not what she needed. That roller coaster was draining. She needed to focus on her career.

"Now's not a good time for me," she said. "For anything."

He studied her for a moment, and she worried he could see straight through to the walls around her battered heart. How she didn't want to risk another heartbreak, yet still deep down, beyond all reason, longed for a love that lasted. It was so Cinderella fantasy. If it hadn't happened for her by now, it just wasn't going to happen. She'd already been in love three times. The problem must be her. Something that made guys—

"What's the deal with Jordan?" he asked.

Her eyes widened. "What do you mean?"

"I mean he looks at you like he's in love with you."

"He does not!"

Gabe shrugged.

"He's a friend. We grew up together. His dad and my dad were in The Davis Trio. I thought I told you that."

"So you never…" He waited for her to fill in the blank. A flush crept up her neck. "Never mind," he said.

"We realized we were better off as friends," Zoe said.

He studied her again, making her feel positively jumpy. Like he could see right into her soul.

"Did you both realize that, or just you?" he asked.

"Both!"

He held up his palms. "Okay, okay."

He resumed eating, so she did the same. Gabe smoothly turned the conversation to favorite movies and TV shows, and she relaxed again. Gabe liked to watch classic car renovation shows (very guy of him), and she liked watching anything with vampires, especially if they fell in love.

When they finished eating, she thanked him for the meal and made an excuse that she had to get back to Fred. She wasn't sure what exactly was going on with this…chemistry between her and Gabe, but she knew she shouldn't act on it. The timing was bad, plain and simple. She was leaving soon for the next big thing.

Gabe walked her to the door and watched her put her boots on. "So we've established that you're single, and I'm single, so will you have dinner with me? I mean, out of the house, you know, like a date."

The shark lawyer didn't give up that easily, for sure.

She bit her lip. "This kinda felt like a date."

He inclined his head with a smile. "So how about another date? Next weekend?"

"I'm working Friday and Saturday nights."

"Sunday, then."

She should really nip this in the bud. Be strong, she told herself. She mentally rehearsed a nice rejection that a lawyer would understand. *Gabe, you are not my lima bean; therefore, this will remain a friendly relationship until such time as I'm no longer your tenant. With the additional provision that I have achieved some measure of success with my music and that you have some reasonable explanation for dumping the woman you were supposed to marry when you found out she was terminally ill. Quid pro quo latin, etc.*

"Okay," she said.

He helped her on with her coat, and then he lifted her hair from the back of the coat, his warm fingers brushing the back of her neck. He leaned down to her ear. "It's a date."

She turned. "Or just a friendly invitation?"

She jolted as his warm hand pushed a lock of hair back over her ear. "Zoe, I think we both know there's more here than friendliness."

She blew out a breath and started babbling. "I've got such baggage. This could get really messy with me living next door and—"

"I like messy."

She stopped. "You do?"

"I've got baggage too."

She stood very still. Was he going to give her the real story about his ex? "What kind of baggage?"

"My fiancée and I got in a fight when I said I was quitting my high-paying lawyer job. She wanted to keep up her shopping sprees on my credit card. I told her to go to hell, and she got hit by a truck the next day." He looked at the floor and said quietly, "How's that for baggage?"

She put her hand on his arm. "Did you lash out because of your grief over your dad?"

He was quiet for a long moment. Finally, he said, "I was in a bad place."

"I heard she was sick."

His expression was grim. "Yup."

"So…why exactly did you break up with her?"

His brows drew down. "She dumped me."

"Oh. So the breakup wasn't because of the brain tumor?"

He shoved both hands in his hair and blinked rapidly. "I didn't even know about the damn brain tumor until her mom mentioned it at the funeral."

Oh, oh, oh. Her instincts had been right. He was a good guy. He really was. And now he was upset. She'd brought up this horrible memory after he'd been so nice with the candlelit dinner.

"I'm so sorry, Gabe," she said before impulsively hugging him, trying to make up for her stupid completely unnecessary prodding at what was obviously a painful subject.

He pulled away. "It's okay. Now it feels like a pity date, so forget I said anything."

"I don't pity you. I'm relieved to hear the real story."

"Heard some nasty stuff, huh?" He shoved his hands in his pockets. "I know people like to talk around here."

Her heart squeezed. "We'll go out. Something casual and fun, okay?"

He studied her again for a long moment. "I'm not so sure. I think I need another hug."

She smiled. "Of course."

She hugged him again and this time he hugged her back. She pulled away, looking up at him to make sure he was okay. It was so sad about—

His mouth crashed down over hers. Her knees went weak, but she was in no danger of falling because he'd hauled her up against him, his arm banded around her waist, his other hand speared through her hair, cupping the back of her neck. Her mind shut down as his tongue invaded for a long, hot kiss that consumed her, causing a deep, throbbing ache. He finally let her up for air and gazed down at her with a hot look that told her he wanted more, a lot more.

He seemed to have forgiven her misstep.

"Gabe," she said shakily, "you said you wouldn't make a move unless I asked you to." She was still pressed against him, still clutching his shirt. She loosened her grip.

"Sue me."

"Aargh! You faked me out with that hug, you shark." She wiggled to get away, but that just made her rub against him because he still wasn't letting her go. "Gabe!"

He kissed her again, stealing the thunder right out of her outrage. She nearly stumbled when he suddenly pulled away. "See you Sunday."

She pursed her lips, torn between lust and aggravation. "I want to not like you right now."

He grinned, looking like an arrogant, sexy, shark lawyer who took what he wanted.

She pointed at him. "I don't want you."

"Zoe, Zoe, Zoe, do I need to show you what a liar you are?" His gaze ate her up, and she wondered how they'd moved so quickly from friendly neighbors to carnal friends. Just one short kiss away from lover land.

"I, you, gah!" She hightailed it out of there before she jumped in bed with the shark dressed in boy-next-door clothing.

She was halfway up the stairs to her apartment when she burst into song, so happy to know that Gabe was very much the good guy she'd wanted him to be. That didn't mean she was going to boink him. She giggled. But it was nice to know.

Really, really…nice.

CHAPTER SEVEN

Zoe woke with a start Wednesday night as Fred barked his intruder bark. She sat up in the dark and squinted at her radio alarm clock, three a.m. It was usually some noise he heard outside—a car nearby, a helicopter overhead. He quieted.

"Settle," she told him and tried to go back to sleep.

A few minutes later, Fred barked again and again, louder and more ferocious. She let him out of his crate and followed him to the back corner of the apartment, where he stopped and barked at the ceiling. She turned on the light, squinted, and saw a small access panel in the ceiling, probably leading to an attic. "Fred, shh." She wrapped a hand around his muzzle to quiet him for a moment and heard a flutter and banging around in the ceiling.

There was something there. Fred started lunging at the ceiling and barking ferociously. She got a chair, climbed up, and pulled on the small metal ring on the door. It creaked open and something black flew out. She turned as it swooped through the apartment, and Fred took off after it. She jumped down from the chair. It was a bat! She ducked down as the bat made multiple swooping trips through the small apartment.

She grabbed Fred's leash, clipped it to his collar, grabbed her boots, and rushed out the door. She hurriedly stuffed her feet into the boots and went straight next door to get Gabe. There was no way she could sleep with that thing swooping overhead. Didn't bats carry rabies? Fred was inoculated, but she wasn't. This was definitely a landlord problem.

She rang the doorbell frantically—it was freaking cold out—while Fred pulled to go back to the bat. Several long moments later, the door opened to Gabe wearing gray jogging pants and nothing else. She was momentarily distracted by his beautiful chest. His muscles were defined, and a smattering of light chest hair led to a happy trail that had her licking her lips.

"Zoe, what's wrong?" His voice was rough and gravelly from sleep.

She rushed inside. "There's a bat in my apartment! It's flying all over the place."

He rubbed a hand through his hair. "A bat? How did that get in there?"

"It was in the attic and when I pulled open the attic door, it flew out."

He turned and headed back inside. "I'll call someone."

"Who?"

"Critter Control."

That was a thing? He'd done this before?

He left briefly and returned a moment later, cell phone up to his ear. "Hey, Bert, it's Gabe Reynolds. We've got a bat loose, so could you stop by in the morning?"

He hung up and looked at her. "I left a message. He'll get back to us tomorrow."

"You mean he's not coming over right now?"

He checked his cell. "It's three in the morning."

"I know, but…there's a bat in my apartment. What if it sucks my blood when I'm sleeping?"

He chuckled. "You know bats don't turn into vampires, right?"

"Says you."

"You want the sofa?" He indicated the sofa in his living room. "I'd offer you a bed, but there's only mine." He raised a brow. "I don't mind sharing."

"I'll take the sofa," she said. There was no way in hell she was sleeping at her place with a bat. Or with Gabe, for that matter. Hell, she probably wouldn't sleep at all tonight.

"I'll get you a blanket and pillow."

"Thank you." She set her boots by the door and

headed for the sofa.

He returned a few moments later with a blanket and pillow that she clutched to her chest. She still felt weirded out by the middle-of-the-night bat encounter. Fred had already settled down on the floor to sleep, his legs in the air, his belly exposed. That dog could sleep anywhere.

"You all right?" he asked. "Need anything?"

"Can you stay with me for a little while?" she asked in a small voice.

"Sure. Nice pajamas."

She glanced down at her pink top and gray flannel pants with sheep all over them. She'd nearly forgotten she was wearing pajamas. "You too," she said, staring at his chest.

He sat on the sofa next to her and stretched his legs out to rest on the nearby coffee table. "C'mere."

She scooted closer to his warmth. He wrapped an arm around her, and she started to relax again as the adrenaline left her body. He reached for the lamp on the end table.

"Don't turn it off yet," she said.

"You really did get scared." He pulled her closer and kissed her hair. "That bat was more afraid of you than you were of him."

"I doubt that."

He tilted her face up, cupping her cheek. "You're

safe now," he said, brushing his lips over hers.

She leaned back. "You know you really are my landlord. I am going to pay you rent."

He sighed heavily. "This again? What are you trying to tell me, you just want to be friends? Fine. We're just friends." He made a big show of taking his arm off her.

"It's just that I tend to dive in with the physical and regret it later."

"Yeah, me too."

She turned, surprised. "Really?"

"No. Guys never regret diving in with the physical."

"Well, that's honest."

"It's three a.m. I'm too tired to put on a front."

She smiled to herself. "Tell me what's on your bucket list."

"You mean things I want to do before I die?"

"Yeah. What are your dreams?"

"I don't have any."

"Come on. Everyone has dreams."

"I don't."

She drew her legs up and wrapped her arms around them. "I've been following my dream of making it with a recording contract for so long, and it feels like it's further away than ever."

He grunted. "What else do you dream?"

She shook her head. "So much."

He grabbed a pillow and leaned back against the arm of the sofa.

She shifted to the other end with her pillow. "Here, you can stretch out." They sat on opposite ends of the sofa, legs stretched out and entwined. Her leg was between his.

"Be careful where you move that foot," Gabe said. "You're in a sensitive location."

"Don't worry, my legs aren't that long."

He looked more awake now. "Tell me what you dream. Maybe it'll give me some ideas for myself."

"I dream of my own album...ooh! To drive a Porsche and-and make homemade ravioli! And it would be so awesome to learn to surf and be a—" She stopped herself. "I'm a dreamer. I could go on and on. Enough about me."

He squeezed her foot briefly and then lifted it onto his lap, starting a slow foot massage. She would've pulled away, but it felt so good. She closed her eyes, relaxing even more.

"What was that last thing you were going to say," he said softly, peeling off her sock. "Be a what? Rock star?"

"It's silly."

"Anything you say here will never be held against you." His fingers pressed into the sole of her foot, warm and deep. She sighed.

She opened one eye. "Lawyer-client confidentiality?"

"Yes." He was massaging her foot again, stroking down to her toes.

"And no laughing?"

"Never." He chuckled. "Just getting that out of the way."

"It's sort of embarrassing."

He snagged her other foot, peeled off that sock, pulled both feet into his lap, and squeezed gently. "Now you have to tell me."

"Only if you confess something too."

His hand wrapped around her ankle while his other hand rubbed the top of her foot. "Okay. You first."

"I always wanted to be a princess in a castle, with a big, poufy dress." She covered her face with her hands. "I watched too many princess movies as a kid." Three to be exact, but she'd been very impressionable.

His hand slid up her pajama pants and squeezed her calf. "That's awesome, Princess Zoe. Here's mine."

She dropped her hands in her curiosity and watched him massaging her foot again. His gaze was entirely focused on her foot with its pink-painted toenails.

"I wish for once I could just relax and do

something spontaneous."

"Like massage my feet?"

He laughed. "That wasn't exactly spontaneous." He coughed out "seduction" and grinned. She pulled her foot out of his hand, but he just pulled it back and started massaging again. "No, I mean, like…just close my eyes, point to somewhere on the map and travel there. Like anywhere in the world."

Her eyes widened. "I love that!" She sat up in her excitement. "You know what would be even more spontaneous? Just show up at the airport and take the very next flight out."

He straightened up. "To anywhere?"

"Absolutely!"

"You want to go with me?"

"Oh. I-I don't know."

"Too soon."

She didn't know what to say. It was too soon, though she loved the idea of spontaneous travel. Just go wherever fate sent you. He turned off the light on the end table, and this time she was glad. She scooted back down onto her pillow and closed her eyes as he resumed massaging her feet.

"Tell me all about you," he said in the dark. "Start at your earliest memory."

"I was born in New York," she said.

"Keep going."

She talked and talked and talked, her life story coming out in fits and starts as different memories crowded in, taking her off on tangents. He was so attentive, so encouraging that she just kept going, telling him start to finish her love of music and all that she'd gone through to get where she was today. All of the hard work—the training, the auditions and rejections, the glory of performing.

"Tell me your story too," she urged.

"You don't want to hear about being a lawyer."

"Sure I do."

"Let me tell you about my family. They're more interesting." He slid to join her, rolling her out of the way to fit his larger body against the back of the sofa, nearly making her fall off.

"Hey!" she cried, but then he was pulling her back against him, tucking her legs against his, propping her head up on his arm.

"There."

She sighed. The perfect spoon. His bigger size somehow fit her perfectly. She tucked her feet between his legs to keep her toes warm. "Talk," she said.

They ended up talking all night, easier somehow in the dark, not looking at each other. Sleep finally claimed her just as the sun peeked through the front windows at dawn.

~ ~ ~

Gabe yawned at work the next day, trying to focus on the will in front of him. He'd never talked to a woman all night before. The more he knew about Zoe, the more he liked her. He couldn't sleep holding her in his arms; he wanted her too much for that. He'd stayed up all night, and then he'd slipped off the sofa, got in touch with Critter Control one more time, made sure the bat was gone, took Fred out, and gently woke her so she could feed Fred his breakfast.

She'd moved, zombie-like, stumbling around for a few minutes with Fred excitedly following her. Then she seemed to wake more fully, stopped, and looked at him. Her brows furrowed in confusion.

"Morning, sunshine," he said. "You slept on my sofa to avoid the evil bat."

She smiled and yawned. "Oh, yeah. Morning. How long did I sleep?"

"About three hours. The bat's gone if you want to go back to your place."

"Thank you!" She leaned up on tiptoe, kissed his cheek, grabbed her things, and headed home.

He wished he could've gone with her. Not just to hook up. When he was with Zoe, it was like being close to the sun. She pushed the dark reach of death further away from him. For as long as he could remember, death had haunted him. He'd shared the womb with his dead twin. His mom had always been honest about it. Had told him that he'd survived because he was the stronger one. For a long time, he'd felt guilty, like he'd taken what was rightfully his twin's chance at life. Later, when he'd finally confessed his guilt, his mom had explained that it was common for one twin not to make it in the early stages. Still, he'd spent his childhood looking out for his brothers, and later his stepbrothers, making sure they stayed alive. He even used to check that they were still breathing at night sometimes. Aside from a few broken bones, they'd all made it through alive.

Then there was his dad dying right in front of him. And a few days later, his fiancée Alyssa died. He'd let that slip when Zoe brought up baggage and immediately regretted it. Though it did score him a date, which he selfishly wanted even as he worried that getting close to Zoe would only doom her to the same horrible fate. He knew it wasn't logical, yet it felt so true he broke out in a cold sweat whenever he thought about it.

But he wanted Zoe's sunshine in his life.

She'd be fine, he reassured himself. She wouldn't be sticking around long. She had great things in her future, great opportunities.

He forced himself to focus and read the will a second time. "Miss Smith," he said patiently, "we've talked about this. You really shouldn't leave your house to your cat. I thought you were marking this up with changes."

"I left the library a larger donation," she pointed out. She'd worked for the library for fifty years and left the library exactly fifty dollars. She'd added a zero to the previous amount.

"Who's the next of kin?"

"It's the only home Oreo's ever known," she said. "How else will I make sure he's happy once I'm gone?" With that, she sniffled and quietly broke down crying.

He handed her a tissue. This was going to be a very long day.

~ ~ ~

Zoe hadn't seen Gabe since that night they talked all night. Their schedules were opposite. He worked days, and this week she'd worked long dinner and late evening shifts at Garner's to make up for taking Friday and Saturday night off for gigs. But she frequently replayed their conversation. The thing that came through for her the most was how much he loved his family, even when he spoke of his brothers' flaws and their battles growing up, the love just shined on through.

If she wasn't careful, he was going to steal her heart. Which was why when she absentmindedly asked, "What would you like to drink?" during her

Saturday lunch shift, she nearly jumped out of her skin to hear the masculine reply.

"Hey, sunshine."

"Oh, hi, Gabe." She giggled for no reason whatsoever. "How are you? Club soda, I know."

He took her hand and squeezed, reminding her of the foot massage he'd given her. Her heart thudded in her chest. "You promised me a date tomorrow."

"Yup," was all she could manage.

"Pack a swimsuit. I'll pick you up after lunch. One o'clock."

"It's too cold to swim. Is this one of those polar bear plunges?"

"Just trust me."

"Do I need to find someone to watch Fred?"

"Just a short day trip." At her silence, he grinned. "You'll like it, I promise."

"All right, shark boy next door."

He shook his head. "I have no idea if that's a good or bad thing."

"I'll let you know." She stuck her pen and order pad back in her apron pocket. "BLT coming up."

The next day she packed a bag—swimsuit, towel, flip-flops, toiletries—and puzzled over where they could possibly be swimming. Was Gabe taking her to the Y? What a strange place to take a date.

Gabe arrived at one o'clock on the dot. "Ready?"

Fred leaped all over him. "Sit," he told Fred, who immediately sat.

"Ready!" she chirped. She put Fred in his crate with some biscuits in a Kong toy to keep him busy. He still couldn't be trusted to have free rein. She followed Gabe outside and stopped short. A sleek cherry red Porsche waited in the driveway.

"Here's our ride," Gabe said. "My brother Nico will kill us if we get a scratch on it."

"Omigod!" Zoe rushed up to the car. "You remembered I always wanted to ride in a Porsche!"

"Not just a Porsche. A classic nineteen seventy-one nine-eleven E." He opened the passenger-side door and guided her in.

She sank into the black leather seats. The car was pristine—all black and silver with old-fashioned push buttons on the radio.

He slid into the driver's seat. "You can drive it back if you'd like."

"Yeah, I'd like!" She beamed. "Where are we going?"

"Ah-ah. No questions. You'll ruin the surprise."

He drove to the Big Bear Hotel and Resort an hour away. "Are we having a weekend getaway?"

"Come on, they have an indoor water park. You're going to learn to surf."

Zoe squealed and hurried in behind him.

Soon they were part of a small class of five people in a wave pool. Their instructor, a transplanted California surfer dude, kept telling them to "feel the wave" and also to "make themselves one with it," causing Gabe to roll his eyes. Which did nothing to take away from the gorgeous vision he presented in black swim trunks. He was all golden skin and trim muscle from broad shoulders to defined abs to muscular legs. Even his calves were swoonworthy. She'd done a double take when she'd first seen him as she stepped out of the locker room. He hadn't noticed, though, because he was too busy giving her a once-over in her modest pink tankini, which made her blush just enough to hurry into the pool to cool off.

Gabe put his hands on her waist and helped her up on the board. He'd been very handsy since they got in the water, which made it much more difficult to concentrate.

"Go-oo-od, pink lady," Surfer Dude said to her. "Now pop up." He popped up to his feet on his board.

She did, then a small wave came, her arms windmilled, and she hit the water with a splash. Gabe's hands went around her waist, lifting her right back on that board. He wasn't touching his board.

"Don't you want to learn?" she asked him as she straddled the board.

"This is your dream. I want you to have it."

Her stomach fluttered. He was so sweet. Also, his chest looked like an oiled-up centerfold when it was wet. She licked her lips and tore her gaze away.

"Pop up, pink lady," Surfer Dude hollered. "Feel the wave."

She popped up and stiffened as a huge wave rolled toward her. "Oh-hh," she said in a shaky voice. The board rocked, she tipped over, and the wave crashed into her, carrying her a few feet away. She came up sputtering.

"Bend your knees," Gabe said, handing her the board. She glared at him, acting like it was so easy when he hadn't even attempted it himself.

She kicked back to where the class was and climbed up on the board again. Hey, this wasn't that hard. She was much steadier on the board now. She glanced down to see Gabe was holding the board for her.

"Bend those knees," he said.

She did. He let go. The next wave came barreling down and her board went up and over. "Woo-hoo!" she hollered, splashing right into the next wave and toppling over.

An hour later, Zoe had managed to surf a series of three-foot waves. "I'm feeling the waves!"

Gabe threw back his head and laughed. She surfed for an hour, until the next class arrived.

"That was amazing!" she exclaimed as they got out of the pool.

Gabe smiled. "You looked like you were having a good time."

They grabbed a couple of towels to dry off. "I can't wait to surf in the ocean next!"

Gabe raised a skeptical brow. "We should start out in some small waves." He gave her a quick kiss. "Go get changed. You want to eat out or get takeout for dinner?"

"I should get back to Fred."

"Takeout it is."

A short while later, Zoe was behind the wheel of a Porsche for the first time in her life. Unfortunately, it was a stick shift, which was much harder than Gabe had let on. Even with Gabe coaching her, she stalled out several times and ground the gears before getting off to a fast start, only to stall at the first traffic light.

"Pull over," Gabe said between his teeth.

She started it again and pulled in a herky-jerky way to the shoulder. The car stalled again on the shoulder. "I'm sorry."

"No, no, it's okay," Gabe said in the voice of a saint. "I'll teach you to drive a stick another time. Just not on Nico's car. Believe me, he'll notice if the gears are ground down. Let's switch."

They did a quick run around the car, and Zoe

slipped into the passenger seat again. Gabe took off.

"At least I get to ride in it," Zoe said, enjoying the power and speed of the car.

When they got back home, Gabe turned to her. "Stop by whenever you're ready."

"I'm going to feed Fred and let him run in your yard a bit before I bring him back in."

"You can bring him with you."

She cocked her head to the side. "Gabe, last time he ate your cell phone."

"I'll get some baby gates for next time. That way we can confine him to a safe area."

She stared at him for a moment. He was being so accommodating of her fur baby, even after Fred had ruined his phone. Her heart melted.

"You're so sweet," she said.

"I'm really not."

She shook her head, kissed him on the cheek, and left to check on Fred.

~ ~ ~

When Zoe rang the bell at Gabe's place a short while later, Fred already back to napping at her place, she felt a very different vibe right away. Gabe let her in and stared at her for a long moment, taking her in from head to toe in her simple sweater and jeans—and it was far from boy next door. It was more like a rip-

your-clothes-off-and-have-my-way-with-you   look.
Something he'd kept hidden behind a friendly smile,
until now.

"What are we having?" she asked brightly.

He put his hand on the small of her back, burning
a hole right through her thin sweater as he guided her
into the kitchen. "You decide."

She sat at the kitchen island, and he handed her a
bunch of menus. They ordered Chinese, and then
Gabe took the seat next to her. He turned her swivel
seat and put his feet on the bottom rung of the chair
so his leg was between hers. His knee pressed lightly
on the inside of her knee, heating it.

"Zoe?"

She met his eyes and heated all over again because
she saw it clearly now. He was the lusty panther
closing in on its prey. And she was really not supposed
to be hooking up with her landlord again. Or shark
men. Oh-h-h, and the timing was bad. She could be
leaving as soon as two weeks if she went on *Next
American Voice. Not my lima bean, not my lima bean.*

"What?" she asked softly.

"You seem nervous," said the shark to the
minnow.

"Not at all!" she chirped.

His dark blue eyes burned into hers. "We had a
good time today. I mean, it seemed like you did. I

know I did."

"Me too."

"Then what's the problem?"

She sighed. "I really need a lima bean."

His brows shot up in confusion. "Lima bean?"

"I mean, you know, a good-for-you kind of guy wa-a-ay down the line." She nodded vigorously. "Keep calm and eat vegetables. That's my motto. All that good-for-you stuff."

His leg gently pressed against hers, spreading her legs wider. She felt herself flush.

"Zoe, can I be your lima bean?"

She giggled because he looked so darn sincere. "I don't know. Are you good for me?"

He leaned closer. "I could be very good…to you."

She wanted to turn from his unnerving gaze, but she couldn't untangle herself from his legs easily. "I'm sure you lure in a lot of women with your smooth talk."

"This is the first time I've tried the vegetable thing. Is it working?"

She thought for a suitable comeback to let Gabe know for sure that it was not working, no way, no how was she lusting for him, her landlord, no matter how good looking, how sexy, how…sweet he was. And she was leaving soon. Her next gig was just around the corner. Her big break. It would happen. She'd make it happen. Or, if she absolutely had to, she'd do that stupid show out in L.A., which she had to commit to in a week if she was going to do it.

She opened her mouth and nothing came out.

His long warm fingers stroked her cheek. "Let me be your lima bean."

Without waiting for her reply, he kissed her gently. He pulled back, gazed into her eyes, and she knew she'd lost the battle. The attraction was too strong, the temptation too great. She grabbed his head and kissed him breathless as her answer.

When she let him up for air, one corner of his mouth quirked up. "I'm sensing a yes."

"Yes," she said. "But I might be leaving soon."

He gave her a quick kiss and grinned. The dimple in that stubbled cheek appeared again, making her feel all swoony. "But you're here now. You play pool?"

She smiled. "I've been known to play."

He raised a brow. "You any good?"

"I'm terrible. Interested?"

He smiled wolfishly. "Very."

Hot tingles ran through her. "Care to make it even more interesting?"

"Strip pool?"

She sputtered. "I meant a wager."

"Loser strips?"

"Um…" She flushed and looked away.

He took her hand. "I'm teasing. You want to bet five dollars? I'll let you break."

"Make it a hundred. I need a new dress."

"I'll take you shopping."

Her jaw dropped. "A guy who shops? No way."

"I would love to if I got to see you model the dresses." His slow, wicked smile made her hot and nervous at the same time.

"You're doing that teasing thing again," she said.

His hands stroked the outside of her legs from her knees up to her hips, where they rested, holding her firmly. "Not really. Will you let me buy you a new dress?"

Her eyes widened. "You want to buy it? I thought you were just going to shop with me."

"I'll do both."

"You'll shop and...P.S. this sounds like a boyfriend thing."

"That's exactly what it is. Say yes."

She studied him—his dimple, those stubbled cheeks, sparkling blue eyes. "Yes."

"I love when you say yes." He kissed her again and then once more. "And I'm looking forward to our game of strip pool."

She leaned back, though she couldn't go far with his hands on her hips and his legs entwined with hers. "I never agreed to strip pool. Just regular pool. For money."

"Sure, sure." He smiled like he knew something she didn't.

"No stripping," she said. "Got it? I will not be stripping."

"Agreed," he said quickly.

Which had her wondering if Gabe would be stripping. Would that be so bad? She'd seen him without his shirt and that had been a very nice view. She glanced down to where his jeans were bulging and heard his soft chuckle. Face flaming, she jerked her eyes up to his.

"You're enjoying teasing me, aren't you?" she asked.

"Little bit."

"Hmph." She crossed her arms, but then he kissed her again, and she couldn't remember why any of this was a bad idea. Her arms stole around his neck of their own accord, feeling the silky hair at the nape of his neck. Long moments later, he pulled away, standing and walking clear across the kitchen.

"We'd better set the table," he said from a great distance. "The food should be here soon."

She tried not to pout. He was a really good kisser, and she wasn't ready to stop yet.

"Of course," she said in an even tone. She watched him getting the plates from the cabinet. "No problem at all for me," she added.

He turned, plates in hand. "I'm being a gentleman." At her silence, he added, "I'm being your lima bean."

She burst out laughing. "Lima beans are terrible."

~ ~ ~

A short while later, they ate at the kitchen island. Gabe was unusually quiet, and she found herself babbling to fill the silence, telling him all about her customers at Garner's.

When they finished their meal, she stood to help clear, but he put a hand on her arm. "That can wait. Let's play pool."

They headed to his finished basement, where a pool table took center stage. A fully stocked bar was on one side. The other half of the basement had been made into a small home theater with six reclining seats.

Gabe headed for the bar. "What can I get you? I've got beer, wine, whiskey, vodka, and the fixings for…piña colada. My little brother Angel's fault we've got piña colada. He's got a sweet tooth."

"Do you have any cranberry juice?"

He bent to look in a small refrigerator. "I do."

"I'll take vodka and cranberry."

Gabe produced a small can of cranberry juice,

fixed her drink, and poured himself a whiskey. She took a sip and sputtered. "That's strong." It tasted like mostly vodka, and there was no ice. "Are you trying to get me drunk?"

"I never said I was great at mixing drinks. You can doctor it how you like." He gestured to the bar, but he was already racking the balls up. "You break."

Zoe quickly decided to go with it and instead focused on the pool table. She'd spent years singing in bars and clubs and knew her way around a pool table. She grabbed a cue and slammed those balls. A solid thunked into the corner pocket.

"I guess you're solids," Gabe said, unbuttoning the top two buttons of his shirt.

She swallowed hard at the sight of golden skin and a smattering of chest hair. She took another sip of cranberry vodka that she was beginning to suspect was just vodka with a splash of cranberry. "Um, what are you doing?"

He unbuttoned the cuffs and rolled the sleeves up, revealing muscular forearms that she remembered oh-so-well from their surf lesson. "Gotta be loose to play pool."

"Oh." For a minute there, she thought he was going to strip. Not that there was anything wrong with that. In fact, the more she thought about it, the more watching him strip seemed like a very good idea. He had a beautiful chest. And shoulders. And back. And…everything.

They played in companionable silence for a while. Gabe got them both another drink. Zoe was feeling super good, a nice buzz, and kicking his ass in pool. She was going to have that dress in no time. Then she went for an impossible shot and sank the eight ball.

"Guess I have to strip," Gabe pronounced. He looked to her for agreement. That was ass backwards. She lost, so she should strip, but since she'd never agreed to it, maybe it was his turn to strip.

She ran her hands through her hair, feeling loose and free. "I thought we were betting for money?"

He pulled out his wallet, folded a twenty-dollar bill through his long fingers, and set it on the side of the pool table. She stared at the money. Somehow it didn't appeal to her as much as the idea of Gabe stripping. She took another sip of vodka. She looked down, surprised to see she'd finished the second glass.

"Hmm," she said. "Just a little stripping."

A ghost of a smile crossed his face before he took off his shirt. He was all golden skin and muscles, and the urge to lick and nibble that chest thrummed powerfully through her.

Zoe slapped a hand over her eyes and veered unsteadily to the side. "Put your shirt back on?"

"Is that a question?"

She peeked through her fingers. Still gorgeous. "No? You don't seem like a lima bean?"

He took her hand off her eyes. "Says who?"

Her breathing hitched, and she caved, placing her palms on that gorgeous chest. "Everyone?"

"You have a lot of questions," he said, letting her hands roam all over his pecs and that beautiful skin radiating heat. Beautiful. Sexy. Crazy.

She felt his voice rumble in his chest as he spoke. "I only want to hear one answer from you—yes."

"Hmm?" she asked absently as her hands roamed over defined abs. She glanced down to his happy trail leading to a bulge that promised so much more. She suddenly felt overheated, but she couldn't stop touching him.

His hand cupped her cheek. "Say yes, Zoe."

She tore her gaze from his bulge and met his burning eyes. She had no idea what they were talking about anymore, but it suddenly seemed important to do as he'd asked. "Yes."

His lips met hers in a gentle kiss that made her greedy for more. She pressed herself against him and let herself explore that wonderful mouth, pressing closer and tasting. He groaned and gripped her hair while he devoured her. His hands roamed up and down her back then slid to her ass, where he fit her against him. She was lost in sensation and her mind went blank, surrendering to it. Long moments later, he broke the kiss and gazed down at her.

"Another game of strip pool?" he asked, his hand still tucked firmly on her ass.

"Um…" She licked her lips and tried to think. Her mind was fuzzy. He nipped her bottom lip, released her, and racked up the balls again. She leaned against the table for support.

She was super-dee-duper vodka happy, which was probably why the only thing she could seem to focus on were his muscles flexing and bunching as he moved around the pool table. "Probably not—hmm."

Gabe broke and watched the balls scatter. He shot the seven toward the corner pocket and missed. "I'm not really your landlord, so you can get that out of your head."

"You're not?" She took her shot, missed, and frowned at the errant ball.

"You're not paying me rent," Gabe said.

She tilted her head to the side, got dizzy, and straightened up. "But I will pay you rent." She was super happy with that comeback. "So you are my landlord."

He took his shot, and her hands were itching to run up and down that muscled back. He sank two balls.

He turned to her with that slow, sexy shark smile

that said he ate women like her for a tasty snack. "I'm your lima bean, beautiful."

"Ga-abe," she sang. She couldn't resist wrapping her arms around him from behind because he'd called her beautiful, and he was beautiful too, and she'd never noticed men's backs were so lovely. She kissed his shoulder. "Thank you. I'm paying rent, though. I don't want to take advantage of you."

He turned and pulled her flush against his body. "Take advantage of me," he growled before claiming her mouth again. She was lost in heat and lust and the faint taste of whiskey. She could do nothing but cling to him, a hot puddle of need, until he released her long moments later. She wobbled back from him, a little off-balance when he wasn't holding her against him.

He turned and sank the eight ball. "Damn. I lost. Should I strip more, or should you?"

Her gaze immediately went to his bulging jeans. She swallowed. "Um…" She met his heated gaze; his breathing coming a little harder. "I think, maybe, you?"

He undid the jeans button and took a slow trip down on the zipper. She throbbed. The jeans dropped, and he stood there in black briefs tented over a massive erection. She didn't have to think twice. She leaped at him, and he caught her as she kissed him frantically.

She wrapped her arms and legs around him and kissed him like she'd never kissed anyone, hungrily, greedily, like she would die if she didn't get more.

She tore her mouth from his. "Upstairs?"

He groaned and set her down.

"What?" She shoved her hands in her hair and stumbled backward. "What's wrong?"

He gave her his back and pulled his jeans on. "I'd better walk you home."

No! The disappointment was like ice water dumped on her. "Why?"

"Because," he said tersely.

"But I want you," she pouted.

He groaned. "I'm trying to do the right thing here."

"You're a damn tease, Gabe Reynolds!" She turned and marched upstairs.

He caught up with her and helped her into the coat she was struggling mightily to get into. The damn sleeve wasn't cooperating. It was broken or something.

"I want to see you again," he said, slipping her arm into the sleeve. "Soon."

"Why? So you can tease me with your muscles and kisses and then kick me out again?"

"Shh, don't be mad." He wrapped his arms around her waist and kissed the side of her neck. She sighed and tilted her head. "I like you a lot." He kissed a hot trail down to her collarbone. "I just…got a little carried away. You're drunk, so we should wait."

She jabbed a finger in the air. "Then you shouldn't have played strip pool and made me drink cranber— vodka! And you're drunk too, so there!"

He chuckled and nuzzled her jaw up to her ear, which he licked. "I'm not. Unlike you, I can hold my liquor. You're the first person I've ever played strip pool with, and I got a little crazy. I'm usually very serious." He tilted her chin up and kissed the tip of her nose. "I've been called boring."

She gaped at him. "You are not boring! And P.S. whoever said that is an idiot!"

He kissed her softly. "Thank you."

"Come to my place for dinner tomorrow," she said for the sole purpose of luring him to her bed. "P.S. I make a mean takeout."

"I've got a family thing."

She felt like stomping her foot. All this lusty dizzy time only to get the heave-ho. "Whatever!" she sang and headed out the door.

He snagged her elbow and spun her back around. She tipped sideways a bit, and he pulled her against his solid chest. She rested her cheek against him, listening to his steady heartbeat. She closed her eyes, got dizzy, and opened them again.

"Tuesday?" he asked.

"I don't have the night off again until Friday."

"Friday, then."

She beamed and wrapped her arms around his neck. "Yes."

"Zoe," he growled, "you make me want so much."

"Then take—" Her reply was cut off by his kiss. His tongue invaded, and she welcomed it, swept away again as her knees went weak and his hands claimed her, holding her tight against him. She rubbed herself against him like a wanton hussy. She wanted to laugh she felt so giddy, but then he turned her whip fast, and her laughter died in her throat as he pressed her back against the wall, grinding into her. Yes. Like that. She moaned, grabbing his ass, urging him on. His strong hand held her jaw open for an all-consuming kiss that left her breathless, while his other hand grabbed her leg, lifting it, opening her to his powerful grind. Holy…her breath caught as he hit the right spot…omigod.

He lifted his head and spoke against her lips. "When the time is right." Another drugging kiss and a slow grind that had her eyes rolling back. "When you're thinking straight." A long kiss and grind that made her whimper desperately. He pulled back to look in her eyes, his own a glittering direct hit to her insides, which even now clenched as he pressed slowly, rhythmically, watching her.

"Yes," she said because she knew he liked her yes.

She felt his smile against her lips before he claimed her mouth again, grinding exactly where she needed until an explosion of sensation tore through her. She cried out, the sound swallowed by his kiss.

He pulled away, and when she stayed against the wall like a limp noodle, he pressed a tender kiss to her forehead. "I want a lot from you, sweetheart."

"Mmm…" was all she could manage.

He peeled her away from the wall, his hand on the small of her back, guiding her on wobbly legs out the door. She wasn't sure what he meant by what he wanted from her, but her heart warmed like it must be something really good. Something she brought out in him. That "sweetheart" made her feel all warm and gooey inside.

She smiled as she stepped onto the back deck because she loved a good orgasm and hadn't it been a long time since the last good one? Damn, she couldn't remember the last time a man had gotten her there that quickly and explosively.

She turned back. "Night!" she called cheerfully, but he was right beside her again, his hand on the small of her back, walking her to her place.

He kissed her on the tip of her nose when they reached her door. "Night, beautiful."

"Night, shark boy next door." She pulled the key

from her purse and held it up triumphantly.

He chuckled and shook his head. "Lima bean," he reminded her.

"I don't think so!" she exclaimed gleefully.

He took the key from her, opened the door, and guided her in. Fred barked twice.

"It's just me, Freddie!" she sang. He quickly settled down again, tired at the late hour. The door shut quietly behind her. Boy, Gabe was in a hurry to leave. She sighed, leaning back against the door for a moment. A brief flash of worry hit her that she'd started something she shouldn't, but the reasons why she wasn't supposed to seemed vague and unimportant. Landlord, shmandlord.

She made her way unsteadily to the bed. Who cared if she was leaving soon when she felt so good right now?

CHAPTER EIGHT

Gabe found himself whistling on Friday night while he did a quick check in the mirror, waiting for Zoe to stop by for their night of takeout and hopefully much more. He had to make sure she didn't drink too much this time. He would only offer wine, none of the hard stuff.

The doorbell rang, and he headed downstairs, reminding himself this was only their third date. He pulled open the door and went instantly hard. She wore a black leather jacket, open, with a purple turtleneck, gray skirt, and black knee-high leather boots. The outfit was both modest and form-fitting enough to get his imagination cranking. He wanted under that skirt, fast, hard, driving into her. The deep thrum of his pulse pounded through him, a damn primal thing, urging him to take.

She smiled cheerfully and took off her coat. "Hey!"

He had to force himself to smile back. His impulse

to claim her was shockingly strong and getting stronger every time he saw her. He was usually a laid-back take-his-time kind of guy. Zoe was lush with curves and owned it. He wanted to soak in that fresh openness, that spark she had, and then he wanted to do dirty things to her. He shifted uncomfortably as she turned from him because the rear view with her sweet round curves was killing him. He watched her hang her coat and purse on the nearby coat rack. Cool it. Dinner first.

"We have to eat out," he barked.

She startled. "Oh, okay."

Regular Prince Charming here. There was no way he could get through dinner with just the two of them and keep his hands to himself. He flashed to the other night when she came in his arms, and what if he just got a quick taste of her before they left. Just push up that skirt. He wouldn't even make her get naked. Just push her panties aside enough for his tongue—

"Is this okay?" She did a turn and looked at him over her shoulder. "I can put on a dress."

"Yes," he croaked. "It's casual."

She frowned and turned to face him. "I can change." She smoothed out the skirt. "I'll put on a dress."

"You don't have to." Unless she wanted to change in front of him. Or maybe he could help. "Let's see the dress."

"I knew it!" She turned to get her coat when the doorbell rang again.

He wasn't expecting anyone. Gabe reluctantly went to answer it. Great. His younger brother Vince. Just what he needed when he was trying to move things forward with Zoe. Two words had been used over and over to describe Vince—male model. He'd even been asked to model, but he'd turned them down. Gabe would describe him in one word—hothead.

"Hey, bozo," Vince said, barging in. His eyes lit up when he saw Zoe. "Hey, gorgeous."

Gabe made a noise in his throat that sounded surprisingly close to a growl. "Zoe, this is my brother Vince."

Vince took her hand and held it. "Stepbrother. Nice to meet you, Zoe." His voice was deep and melodic. Women loved it. From the look on Zoe's face, she was no exception. "I'm the stepbrother he warned you about."

Her eyes widened. "Oh, he never said—"

"What do you want, Vince?" Gabe snapped.

Vince turned to him and scowled. "Ma wants you at Sunday dinner. Not optional."

Gabe narrowed his eyes. "You could've called for that."

Vince put him in a headlock and rubbed his knuckles over Gabe's head. Gabe elbowed him in the kidneys and broke free. Dammit. His brother still hadn't outgrown stupid roughhousing. Vince had always been bigger than Gabe, even though Vince was a year younger. He glared at his brother.

Vince held up his palms. "I was working nearby." He turned to Zoe. "My construction company is building the new gym at the elementary school."

"He means his dad's construction company," Gabe said.

"It'll be mine eventually," Vince countered.

"You can go now," Gabe said. "Thank you, messenger boy."

"You're an ass," Vince said. He turned to Zoe. "Pardon my French. Does your boyfriend mind you hanging out with this loser?"

Gabe opened the front door and gestured for Vince to get out. Vince exhaled noisily and headed toward the door. He stopped and turned. "Zoe, would you like to come to Sunday dinner?"

Zoe looked alarmed as she looked from Vince to Gabe. He couldn't help the hard look he gave her. She would *not* be choosing his brother.

"Um, I don't want to intrude," she said.

"Just you and me, then, for dinner," Vince said smoothly.

Her cheeks turned pink. Gabe was about to stand between them and put his arm around her to stake his claim when she suddenly blurted, "I'm taking a break from bad boys."

Vince barked out a laugh. "Let me show you what you're missing, darling."

Gabe spoke up. "Tell Mom I'll be there."

Vince winked at her and left.

"Sorry about that," Gabe said.

She stared at the ground and took a few deep breaths, which irritated him. If she was going to get hot and bothered over anyone, he wanted it to be him.

"You like Vince the Italian model?" he asked in a deceptively calm voice.

She frowned. "He's a model?"

"He could've been." He wrapped his arms around her waist, pressing her against him. "Does he make you hot and bothered?"

She bit her lip.

"Zoe?" he prompted.

She lifted her chin. "He's too good looking. He knows it too."

"Would you have gone out with him if I wasn't in the picture?" He cupped her ass with both hands and squeezed. She sank against him.

"Maybe," she allowed.

"Maybe?" he growled.

"But he's a heartbreaker. All the good-looking ones are."

Now he was really starting to feel insulted. Not enough to stop fondling her ass, but still. "What am I, then?"

She flashed her beaming smile. "You're my lima bean."

He kissed her then, staking his claim, intent on making her remember who she was with. She smelled like strawberries again, and he couldn't get enough. He grabbed her hair and held her in place while he claimed her mouth, his tongue invading and thrusting as he longed to do deep inside her. She met him stroke for stroke, and he found himself backing her up, pushing into her against the wall, needing to press into her softness. He pushed up her skirt, and she moaned in the back of her throat. Fuck, he wanted her too much. Not here. Not like this. He jerked away, breathing hard, and shoved a hand through his hair.

"I told you you're my lima bean," she teased, straightening out her skirt. "You're being good."

"That won't last," he warned. "Come on. I want to see your dresses."

They went back to her apartment, where Fred was delighted to see them, barking and jumping like crazy. He made him sit before petting him, glad for the distraction.

Zoe emerged from the small closet with a black dress that looked like it would hug her curves yet barely show any skin. Knee-length, no big dip in the cleavage.

"Let me see the back," he said.

She turned it. No big dip in the back.

"What you've got on is fine," he said.

"Sure? It's no problem to change."

"Can I help?" The words were out before he could stop them.

She froze; then she smiled, shaking her finger at him. "That's why you wanted to see the dress. Bad shark boy." She laughed and put the dress back. Except he hadn't been joking.

She tucked Fred into his crate. "He still can't be trusted when I'm out. Last time I gave him free rein, he ate my pillow." Gabe grimaced. That was probably an expensive surgery. Zoe peered in at Fred and slipped him a dog biscuit. "Take a nap, lovie."

She grabbed her purse and stopped in front of him, looking all fresh and young. "Ready!"

He desperately wanted to kiss her again, wanted to find out if she tasted like strawberries everywhere, but he didn't think they'd ever get out the door if he did. His voice came out harsh. "Let's go."

Zoe gave him a strange look, but headed out.

He walked her to his Mercedes, his hand on the

small of her back. "You like seafood?" he asked automatically, but he could barely focus on her answer because all he could think about was getting her alone again, stripping her naked, losing himself in her softness. Taking, taking, taking—

"Gabe?"

He forced himself to focus on her eyes. "What?"

"I said yes."

He liked her "yes," but he had no idea what she was talking about. Were they on the same page?

He stopped. "Yes what?" he asked to be sure.

She turned to him with a bright smile that hit him in the gut because she was so full of life and he was the harbinger of death. "Yes, I like seafood."

He grunted and held open the passenger-side door for her, watched her curvy ass slide into the leather seat, felt that overpowering carnal urge, and convinced himself that if he really, really tried, she'd rub off on him, instead of the other way around. Her bright sunshine would keep the dark fingers of death away. Please let that be true. Because ever since that night when they talked all night, being with Zoe was not just…he couldn't…this would *not* just be a hookup.

"So what's Sunday family dinner like at your house?" she asked when he got in the car.

He pulled out of the driveway. "Noisy."

"Sounds fun," she said.

"Everyone's arguing and talking over each other," he added.

"Go on," she said with a smile.

He couldn't help but smile back. "My mom and stepdad have an open-door policy so home was always filled with too many people. Especially when we were teenagers."

"I think that's nice. They must be nice people."

"They are. It helped that we had a game room," he said.

"Did the game room have a pool table?"

He grinned, remembering strip pool the other night. Normally, he'd persuade the woman to strip in a game of poker, but with Zoe, he'd proceeded cautiously and let her look her fill at him instead over the less obvious game of pool. "Yup, we had a pool table. Same one we used the other night."

"You just wanted to show off your muscles, you shark! You faked sucking at pool."

He barked out a laugh. "It worked, didn't it?" He turned and headed toward Eastman. "I seem to remember you saying you were terrible and even drunk you weren't half bad." He glanced over to find her staring straight ahead.

"Is that how you pick up women?" she asked.

"Never played strip pool before." Strip poker, on the other hand…

"Hmm…why do I have a feeling that your pants are on fire?"

"You're calling me a liar?" he asked in mock indignation. "I'm hurt."

"Yeah, yeah. I think this is one of those lies of omission. How do you pick up women?"

"I'm supposed to spill all my secrets? How will I make any progress with you?"

She crossed her arms, looking cute in her indignation. "You've made plenty of progress."

"I take that as a compliment."

She grinned cheekily. "It is. Let me guess, you play a mean game of strip poker."

He bit back a smile. She was sharp. He liked that.

"So-o-oo," she said, "about strip poker…"

"You wanna play? I'm terrible. I'm sure you'd win." Which would work out very well for him. Again.

She pursed her lips. "I'm getting the picture here."

"What?" he asked, working hard on an innocent face.

"I know exactly how that game would end. You'd be naked as a jaybird, and I'd be the wanton hussy. Very smooth."

"Wanton hussy?" He grinned. "I'll take that."

"I bet you would."

He glanced over and noticed her skirt was riding high, revealing curvy thighs. He gripped the steering wheel tighter and hit the accelerator. Zoe was the first woman he'd wanted, really wanted, since Alyssa died. He'd been deeply in love and realized too late that she'd loved his money more than him. He'd been hurting and angry over the recent loss of his father and scrambling to make his own life mean something. He'd wanted to get back to basics—small-town life, marriage, kids, the whole deal. Wasn't that what you were supposed to do when you weren't chasing the almighty dollar? He'd thought she'd want to be a big part of that. She'd called him a selfish prick, berated him for quitting, and told him she'd find a new sugar daddy. She'd been so angry, but her eyes had been full of pain, which had confused him at the time. She was the one lashing out, dumping him, so why did she look so pained?

Their fight haunted him. He hadn't known the doctors had given her six months to live. Hadn't known him talking about their future was such a slap in the face. The last thing she'd ever remember him saying was *go to hell*. When all he'd really wanted to say was *please, Alyssa, I thought you loved me*. He wasn't at all sure her death had been an accident. He'd felt, deep down, she'd stepped in front of that truck on purpose. And he was at least partly to blame if she had.

Or maybe she couldn't face her future, slowly withering away. She was strong like that. Decisive.

He'd never know the truth. Either way, she would've died.

He'd been alone these past four years, not hurting anymore, but sort of numb, drifting through life. He hadn't asked out any woman, had felt zero interest in dating, so when he finally felt something for Zoe, something so powerful it hit him like a damn hammer, it was like awakening from a long sleep. Now all he wanted to do was give into his primal urges for Zoe and feel alive again.

"Have you had a lot of girlfriends?" Zoe asked, interrupting his rambling thoughts.

He had a feeling this was an important question to answer right. "Are you asking if I've slept around?"

"No?"

She was asking exactly that. He was beginning to learn her conversational ways.

"No, I haven't slept around. Yes, I've had girlfriends, but I'm a serial monogamist for sure. What about you?"

"I've been in love three times and none of them worked out. Obviously."

"Three times, huh? That's lucky. I've only been in love once, but it turned out I chose wrong."

"You wouldn't have chosen wrong if she was really the one for you."

It wasn't that easy. He'd fallen in love with no real

thought beyond how beautiful, how charming Alyssa was. What a great couple they made, moving in the same social circles of the elite. Their relationship had been shallow. She hadn't even told him something so important as that brain tumor. But it wasn't just her, his whole life had been shallow back then, gunning for partner. He wanted to be more than that now, which was why he spent his days in a type of community service, solving people's problems in cases that were more often than not out of the jurisdiction of the law. His take-home salary nowadays was mostly in hugs and grateful thank yous. He didn't need the money anyway. He had his own socked away as well as everything his dad had left him. Inheriting all of his father's assets was the only sign he'd ever had that he meant anything at all to him.

Gabe had given his two biological brothers, Luke and Jared, a share of their father's money, what they rightfully should've inherited, but he lived frugally in a house that was paid off and was doing just fine.

He turned to Zoe. "So your three guys weren't the one for you?"

"Guess not."

"How do you know if they're the one?"

She sighed. "I used to have a three-point system."

He bit back a laugh. "Really?"

"Don't laugh, it worked."

"What are the three points?"

"If their kisses made you swoon, if you always looked forward to seeing them, and if they were all you could think about, but I've had to rethink the whole thing because that's not how it worked out for my sister and her husband, and they're much more in love than I ever was."

A beat passed. "Do my kisses make you swoon?" he asked.

"Yes."

He grinned. "Good."

"But that might've been the vodka."

"The vodka, huh? What about when I kissed you before we left? Any swooning involved then?"

"Hmm…I can't remember."

He found himself smiling again. "I guess you need reminding."

"Guess so."

He pulled up to the restaurant and parked. "I don't think I've ever smiled as much as I do when I'm with you."

She beamed. "You're so sweet, Gabe."

"You keep saying that, but I'm really not." He felt it only fair to be honest. He had a not-so-sweet past. Being aggressive and calculating had worked well for him for years in both his professional and personal life. Not to mention the way death clung to him. Nothing sweet about that. More like cursed.

"You are," she insisted. He looked at her so sweet, so sincere, and worked really hard to push the fear away. Nothing would happen to her.

He broke out in a sweat, and his heart started pounding. He took a steadying breath. "I'll try, Zoe." He kissed her quickly and pulled away. "For you, I'll really try."

CHAPTER NINE

Zoe headed up the front walk of Gabe's parents' house, a ranch home in nearby Eastman, well used to Gabe's hand on the small of her back. It was a gentlemanly way to walk, she supposed, even if it did make her feel like he was inches away from feeling up her ass. But that was her own dirty mind and nothing he did. He'd surprised her after their dinner date on Friday night when he walked her to her door, invited her to his family's Sunday dinner, gave her a quick kiss goodnight, and left. She'd already told him she had a gig on Saturday. She'd thought he'd make a move or ask to come in or *something*. So-oo-oo disappointing.

But damn if it didn't make her feel desperate to have him instead of feeling like she was being hunted by a shark. What a smart lawyerly thing to do, turning that whole dynamic around.

He knocked on the front door of his parents' house, smiled tightly at her, and turned as the door swung open.

"Gabe, I'm so glad you made it," his mother said.

Gabe leaned down to kiss his mother's cheek. "Of course. Mom, this is Zoe."

"Please call me Allie," the petite woman said, shaking her hand warmly. "I'm just going to borrow Gabe for a moment."

She pulled Gabe to the kitchen with her. Zoe took a seat in the formal living room to her right.

An older Italian man with some white in his dark sideburns stopped in the doorway. "I thought I heard the door. And which one of my sons brought your loveliness to our home?" The man looked a lot like Vince, the male model she'd met at Gabe's place.

"I'm here with Gabe," she said. "I'm Zoe."

He stopped in front of her and shook her hand. "I'm Gabe's stepdad, Vinny Marino. I'm glad you're here. It'll keep things light." He winked. "Allie wanted to make tonight like some kind of serious family meeting, but I said leave the kids be, let them just enjoy their food."

"Oh. Is there something wrong?"

"Nah," Mr. Marino said. "Nothing to get worked up over. Can I get you a drink?"

"Sure."

"Right this way."

She followed him to a cozy kitchen, where Gabe

was speaking quietly with his mother. Gabe took one look at his stepdad and jumped up. "Dad, what's this I hear about tests?"

"I told your mother not to bring it up." Mr. Marino opened the refrigerator door. "What can I get you, Zoe? Lemonade? Soda? Wine?"

"I'll just take some water," she said.

"Is it serious?" Gabe asked.

Mr. Marino let out a long breath. "I'm fine, Gabe."

"Is what serious?" a deep masculine voice asked.

Zoe turned to see another tall, dark, sexy Italian model walk in. Omigod, it was Nico, all grown up. The boy the entire school had crushed on. She hadn't seen him in years. She felt herself flush. She'd written Mrs. Zoe Marino more times than she'd like to admit in her diary back then. Everyone had.

"Nothing," Mr. Marino said.

"Hey, Gabe," Nico said, clapping his brother on the back. He turned to her and smiled his perfect shiny white-toothed smile. "Hello, *bella*."

She smiled back. "Zoe Davis. I remember you from school. You were a grade ahead."

He cocked his head. "Yeah? Well, nice to see you again, Zoe." Clearly, he didn't remember her, but clearly she didn't care because she was hot from head to toe from coming face-to-face with her schoolgirl crush. Gabe's hand was on the small of her back again. She hadn't noticed him move.

"Back off, Nico," Gabe growled.

"Thanks for letting us borrow your Porsche," Zoe said, elbowing Gabe. "It's a beautiful car."

Nico smiled. "Yeah, it is. You're welcome. But, ah, no more borrowing my cars until you can drive a stick."

"You could tell?" Zoe asked.

"Gabe told me. You didn't mess it up that bad. Hey, I could teach you anytime. I own my own shop, Exotic and Classic Restorations." He pulled a card from his wallet. Gabe sliced his hand in a quick motion that had Nico winking at her and tucking the card away. He turned to Mr. Marino. "You better not be hiding shit from us, Dad."

"Language," Mrs. Marino said. "We'll discuss this at dinner when everyone gets here."

"There's nothing to discuss, love," Mr. Marino said.

Mrs. Marino blinked rapidly and rushed from the room. Mr. Marino muttered something under his breath and followed her out.

"What the hell was that?" Nico asked.

"Something's wrong with Dad," Gabe said with a quick glance at Zoe. She'd clearly come to dinner on the wrong Sunday.

Nico left, heading toward where his parents went.

"Do you think it's serious?" Zoe asked. "Maybe I shouldn't be here. It sounds more like a family thing."

"It's fine," Gabe said. "Don't worry about it."

She rubbed his back to comfort him, at a loss as to what to say.

"He's been more like a dad to me than my own father," he muttered, staring at the ground. "Anything that's good about me as a man comes from his example."

Her throat felt tight. "That's so sweet."

Gabe shrugged. "It's true." He wrapped his arms around her in a tight hug. "I apologize in advance for any drama. I warned you this family can get loud." He rested his chin briefly on the top of her head, and then he pulled back. "I think I picked the wrong Sunday to invite you over."

"I was thinking that too." She grimaced. "Should I go?"

"No. I want you here."

"Sure?"

He gazed down at her and stroked her cheek. "Yes. And my dad would throw a fit if you left."

"Okay."

A short while later, nearly the entire family sat around the dinner table with glasses of red wine, waiting for the last son, Jared, to arrive. To her right was Gabe. To her left, the male model with chiseled cheekbones, full lips, and deep brown eyes you could drown in—Vince. She was not at all surprised to learn he was still single. She was sure he had women throwing themselves at his feet.

Across from her was Angel, who really did have an angelic demeanor and dimpled smile to go along with it, and Luke, who she'd remembered as a clean-cut cutie and now looked like the slick Wall Street stockbroker he was, right down to his expensive haircut. He'd remembered her from school and greeted her warmly earlier. Nico was next to Luke. Mr. and Mrs. Marino were at the head and foot of the table.

"Can we eat?" Vince asked.

"Jared will be here," Mr. Marino said. "We wait."

"Who knows how long that will take," Vince complained. "He could have someone open on the table."

"Or in the break room," Nico said.

"There is a lady at the table," Mrs. Marino bit out. "Sorry, Zoe. I raised them better." She gave Nico and Vince a look. The two men fought back grins.

"It's okay," Zoe said. "I'm used to it. I've got three guys in my band."

Luke left the room, cell phone up to his ear.

Gabe whispered an explanation in Zoe's ear.

"Jared's an orthopedic surgeon."

A short while later, Jared strode in, his hair wet, fresh from a shower. "Emergency hand job."

The brothers chuckled.

"Manners!" Mrs. Marino said.

Jared shot his brothers a dark look. "Grow up. It was a crushed bone that needed to be set before permanent nerve damage was done." He kissed Mrs. Marino on the cheek before taking his seat next to Vince. He leaned down the table and peered at Zoe. "You look familiar."

Zoe smiled. "I was a grade ahead of you in Clover Park. Zoe Davis."

He smiled and laugh lines formed around his eyes. "Didn't you used to have"—he gestured around his head—"big, curly hair?"

She laughed. "Yes. I straightened it. Didn't you used to be covered in dirt?"

He smiled and shook his head. "I did love playing in the dirt. Now I'm up to my elbows in blood and innards. Surgeon."

"Jared, I'm begging you, not at the table," Angel said, looking green.

Jared put a cloth napkin in his lap. "I forgot we're eating with Mr. Sensitive." Then in a lower voice, he said, "Innards!" His tongue hanging out to razz him.

Angel looked to the ceiling.

Mrs. Marino called to the other room. "Luke, get off that phone and help me bring dinner to the table!"

Everyone passed around two trays of lasagna. Mrs. Marino ordered her sons to take a portion of salad from a giant bowl. Zoe helped pass one of several baskets of warm garlic bread.

After everyone had their food and began to eat, Mrs. Marino announced, "I've asked you all here because Dad has something to tell you."

"Aww, Allie, let them eat," Mr. Marino said.

"Is something wrong?" Angel asked.

Mr. Marino held up a hand. "It can wait."

"Not too long," Mrs. Marino said.

"After dessert," Mr. Marino said. "At least we can give them that."

"Who cares about the damn dessert!" Vince exclaimed. "Tell us what the hell's going on!"

"Apologize to your mother," Mr. Marino said sternly.

Vince immediately looked contrite. "Sorry for the language, Ma. I just need to know what's going on."

Several of the brothers chimed in their agreement. Zoe held Gabe's hand under the table. He squeezed it back.

"The doc ran some tests after my colonoscopy," Mr. Marino said with a frown.

"And?" Angel prompted.

Mr. Marino's lips formed a flat line. "And now they want to run more tests. See what stage I'm at."

"What stage?" Gabe asked. "You mean…cancer?"

"Something like that," Mr. Marino said. "Too soon to know what's going on. Now you all know as much as I do." He gestured to the food. "I'm sure you'll all love to eat after hearing about my colon."

"It's important," Mrs. Marino said.

"The tests will be fine," Vince said. "You're young. They test everything nowadays. Right, Jared?"

"Chances are good they caught it early," Jared said, his expression solemn.

"See?" Vince said, gesturing to Jared. "The doc says nothing to worry about."

Except the conversation stopped, and only Mr. Marino returned to eating. After a few moments of silence, he looked up. "Eat!"

Everyone resumed eating in awkward silence. Vince shot Nico a look. Angel stared at his plate. Gabe looked to her; he was pale and sweat had broken out on his forehead. She gave him a small smile, trying to reassure him. Finally, the brothers cleared the dishes while Mr. and Mrs. Marino took a walk after dinner. No one mentioned who should do what, so Zoe figured they always did things that way.

She brought in an empty lasagna pan and found Gabe by the sink, head down, Angel's hand on his shoulder. She stopped at the entrance to the kitchen, not wanting to interrupt their private conversation.

"What're we going to do if something happens to Dad?" Gabe asked.

"We'll pray," Angel said. "That's all we can do. And be there for him."

"He's not your dad," Vince said to Gabe. She hadn't realized he was leaning against the refrigerator until he moved. Nico and Luke stood closer to her, but Nico was busy watching his brothers and Luke was staring at his cell so they didn't notice her.

Vince got in Gabe's face. "What're you so worked up about?"

"He's as much my father as yours," Gabe snapped.

"You always did act like that," Vince boomed, "but that don't make it so. You're a Reynolds through and through."

"You're such an ass, Vince." This from Luke, who didn't bother to look up from his cell.

Vince turned, pointing a finger at Luke. "Fuck you. Fuck all of you." His arm swept the room. "You all act like something's happening to your dad. It didn't. He's mine, Nico's, and Angel's. The rest of you all are interlopers."

"Not this shit again," Gabe said. "Get over it. We've been family for twenty years now. No one's taking your daddy away from you."

"Love doesn't divide," Angel put in. Jared slipped into the room behind her and joined Gabe, Nico, Luke, and Angel in the next part. "It multiplies," they said in unison. They grinned at each other.

"You're all idiots," Vince said and stormed out the back door.

Gabe gestured for Zoe to join them, and she wondered how long he knew she was standing there. "Mom always said that to us so we'd stop fighting over who had the real mom and the real dad and which one of us they loved more."

"You always shared your mom," Angel said to Gabe. He turned to Zoe. "Our mom died when I was five. Cancer."

"Sorry to hear that," Zoe said.

"Cancer gets them all," Jared said darkly.

"Ah, fuck," Nico said, his expression stormy. He rushed out the back door.

Gabe took the tray from her hands and set it in the sink. He pressed his fingers against his temples and took a deep breath. "Sorry I brought you to the worst family dinner in history."

"No, no, it's fine," Zoe said. "How can I help?"

"You want to dry while I wash?" Gabe asked. He seemed tense, but maybe just doing mundane chores would help him keep his mind off things. There wasn't anything he could do for his stepfather right now. At least he wasn't pale anymore. For a minute at the table, she thought he was going to pass out or something.

Jared, Luke, and Angel looked to her, waiting for her response.

"Sure," Zoe said.

"We have a winner!" Jared said, raising her arm in the air. He kissed her cheek. "Thank you." He left.

Luke did the same. "Bless you."

Angel stopped in front of her. "Are you sure you don't want my help?"

"Go," she said with a laugh, pointing to her cheek.

Angel kissed her cheek. "Thank you." He left too.

She looked to Gabe. "I think I've been suckered into kitchen duty."

He pulled her close and kissed her tenderly. She melted against him, her body remembering exactly what his kisses could do. He ran his hands up and down her sides. "I just wanted you to myself."

"What about all these dishes?"

"Watch." He loaded them all quickly into the dishwasher. "Done."

"What about the pots and pans?" she asked.

"They need to soak. Come on." He took her hand and pulled her out the back door, snagging a large flannel shirt on his way out.

"Where are we going?"

"An old treehouse."

"Ooh! I always wanted a treehouse."

He led her to the backyard, where a treehouse was nestled up between two old oaks. It was up on stilts, but also had some wood nailing it to the larger tree.

"Are you sure it's safe?" she asked, looking at the ladder rungs nailed into the tree.

"Of course it's safe. My dad tested it out when they first bought the house." He boosted her up the rungs and followed closely behind.

She went inside. It was just a small platform with thin walls, a roof, and two windows on either side. She could imagine how much fun kids would've had up here. Gabe followed her up and laid the rolled flannel shirt down as a pillow for their heads. He lay down and reached for her. "C'mon. Look up."

She joined him to find a big rectangular hole in the roof. Stars twinkled beyond it. "Don't you think you should patch the roof?"

"It's a skylight." He took her hand. "Without the window cover. Me and my brothers would've loved a place like this. My parents only moved here four years ago, so this was some other lucky kids' hideout." He pointed. "There's the big dipper."

She looked up. The sky was black, and the stars shone brightly in the winter sky. She took in a deep breath, feeling more relaxed than she had all night. "This is nice."

"Yeah, gives you a little perspective," Gabe said. "And peace and quiet."

Just then they heard male voices arguing from somewhere in the backyard. "Who's that?" she whispered.

"Dad and Vince," he whispered back.

A few minutes later, a car door slammed and took off with a loud screech of tires. "Vince took off," Gabe said. "He's a hothead, if you couldn't tell."

"My sister's a bit of a hothead too," she confided.

He wrapped an arm around her. "Then we have that in common. We should get them together."

"She's married."

"Too bad. Vince needs someone to put him in his place. Otherwise he just runs amok."

"I really hope your stepdad's okay," she said.

"Yeah." He let out a shaky breath. "Me too." And just like that Zoe decided to stay a little longer. She had to give *Next American Voice* her answer tomorrow. She'd been waffling between the exposure and feeling like she was selling out, but now she knew for sure the answer was no. It would be okay for them, they had a huge waiting list of contestants. A weight lifted off her shoulders. She'd hang on a little longer for something to come through with her band. And she'd have a little more time with Gabe.

Angel called up to them. "I knew I'd find you here.

Ma wants you inside for dessert, and she says don't think you're getting away with just soaking the pots."

Gabe groaned.

"I'm just the messenger," Angel replied with a smile in his voice.

Gabe helped her up. He went down ahead of her. She started to walk with them when Angel pulled her aside and whispered, "I did the pots for him. Don't tell."

She grinned. "You really are an angel."

He shook his head with a smile. "Nah."

They returned to the table for homemade cannoli, which they all declared was the best they'd ever had while Mr. Marino beamed at the praise. He told her he was the main cook around here. Without Vince there, the group was subdued with only a little quiet conversation. Their dad's health was on everyone's minds, she could tell, and Vince leaving just seemed to emphasize that something wasn't right. The brothers took their leave with a few serious handshakes with their dad, who gamely smiled and tried to put on a cheerful face. Zoe had never felt so much sadness and love at the same time.

"I'm fine," Mr. Marino kept saying. "I'll be fine."

"Call me if you need anything," Luke said. "The best doctors are in the city."

"I've got connections," Jared said.

"Be strong," Nico said with a manly handshake, pat-on-the-back kind of hug.

"Call me if you want someone to go to the hospital with you," Angel said.

"You call me as soon as you know more," Gabe demanded.

"See what you started, Allie?" Mr. Marino complained.

"We all love you," Mrs. Marino said, wrapping both arms around his waist from behind. He turned and wrapped an arm around his petite wife, kissing her on top of the head.

"Thank you for having me," Zoe said.

"Sorry to bring you into such an embarrassing night," Mr. Marino said. "It wasn't my idea to talk about my colon."

"It was wonderful to see such a close-knit family," Zoe said. "Reminds me of my own."

Gabe moved by the door, in serious conversation with Jared.

Mr. Marino nodded. "We hope to see more of you around here."

"Thanks," Zoe said.

"Gabe hasn't brought any girlfriends around since he lost Alyssa," Mrs. Marino said.

A lump formed in her throat. Gabe had lost so much and now his stepdad was sick. She really wanted to be there for him.

"Don't speak of it," Mr. Marino said quietly to his wife. "It tore him up."

She stared at Gabe, who looked up and crossed to her side. "Why's everyone so serious over here?"

"We were just saying we'd like to see more of Zoe around here," Mrs. Marino said.

"I'll do my best," Gabe said. His gaze on her was heated and almost possessive, a heady combination that made her insides do a few delicious flips. He said his goodbyes, and then his hand was on the small of her back, guiding her out the door and into his car.

She waited for him to get in. He looked so sad. She hoped her staying would make him feel a little better. "I'm going to tell *Next American Voice* no tomorrow, so I'll be sticking around a little longer."

"You will?" he asked. She couldn't tell if he was happy or not.

She nodded and smiled. He looked down and then met her eyes. "That's the best news I've heard in a long time."

She let out a breath. "Good."

"You didn't do it because of me, did you?" he asked. "Because of my stepdad?"

"No," she said firmly, though if she was honest, it had played a part in her decision. But she knew he wouldn't want her to feel sorry for him. "That show just wasn't for me."

He nodded, started the car, and pulled into the street. "Tell me what you were talking about with my parents."

She hesitated.

"Tell me," he ordered in a voice that had her snapping to attention.

"Your mom said you haven't brought any girlfriends around since you lost Alyssa."

He blew out a breath. "Yeah."

"Oh, Gabe, I'm so sorry. You must miss her terribly."

"I'm sorry she died, but later I realized she was just using me." He paused. "Maybe we were just using each other. She wanted my money. I wanted someone beautiful on my arm to work the room at parties." He glanced at her. "I'm ashamed I lived that kind of life." He drummed his fingers on the steering wheel. "I'm trying to do better."

She didn't know what to say. She hadn't known him then.

"World's worst date, huh?" he asked.

"No, it was—"

"Excruciating?"

"Lovely."

He shook his head. "I don't deserve you, Zoe, but damn if I don't want you anyway."

"Um, thank you?"

He squeezed her hand. "Thank you for being you."

He was quiet the rest of the way home, and she knew his stepdad's news weighed heavily on his mind. He dropped her off at her front door with a chaste kiss to the forehead, then quickly left. A few moments later, she heard his car take off again. She let herself inside for a joyful reunion with Fred, hugging him close, wishing she could've done more to ease Gabe's worry.

~ ~ ~

Gabe was out of sorts all week. He kept calling home to find out his stepdad's test results, but there were numerous tests scheduled going into next week, so there was nothing definite yet. The uncertainty was killing him. He'd already lost his biological father, he'd lost Alyssa, he'd lost his twin, and now it looked like he was going to lose Vinny, the man who'd treated him like a son from day one, who'd been a real father to him in every way that counted. His own father had been cold, too manly to ever let his own sons know they were loved. It was why Gabe had tried for so many years to gain his approval. He'd managed it when he joined his father's law firm, but at what price? His brothers resented him. His father grudgingly gave him respect, groomed him to take over, but only as a good worker bee not as a son. He couldn't bear the thought of losing Vinny.

Which was why he found himself stopping by Garner's on Friday night to ask Zoe to run away with him.

"What're you doing this weekend?" he asked. Her hair was pinned up and despite his dark mood, he found himself fixated on her long neck and the dip in her collarbone. He wanted to taste her there and a lot of other places too.

"I'm supposed to be working here tomorrow, but only until four."

"Can you get someone to cover for you?" he asked urgently. He needed her light in his life, even if he felt selfish for wanting it with his dark history.

Her dark brown eyes were full of concern as she slid into the seat across from him. "Are you okay?"

He shook his head. "I just need to get away. You want to be spontaneous with me? Just show up at the airport and take the next flight out?"

"Are you sure you're okay?"

"I can't stop thinking about Vinny," he admitted. "I need to get away. Anywhere. Just not think about it for one minute."

She nodded. "You got it. I'll get someone to cover for me."

He let out a breath. "Thank you."

"You'll have to buy me dinner," she said, standing again with a broad sunny smile. "I want steak from you, mister."

He soaked in that smile. That infectious energy. Zoe was exactly what he needed. "You got it, and a whole lot more."

She cocked her hip, all saucy. "I like the sound of that." She headed off to the kitchen, and he snagged her wrist just as she passed by him.

"You'll like the feel of it even more," he said just for her ears.

"Grr-owr!" She swiped her claws at him like a tigress and went on her way, hips swaying in snug black pants.

He smiled to himself. This was the best idea he'd had in a long time.

~ ~ ~

"Ready to be spontaneous?" Gabe asked when he arrived at Zoe's door Saturday morning.

"Yup, I'm all packed."

He snagged her small suitcase. His was already in the car. He put it in the trunk, got in, and turned to her. "Nervous?"

"Not at all," she said. "I love an adventure!"

"Good," he replied. Why should she be nervous?

Just because he intended to share the hotel room, the bed, and her body as much as humanly possible. He glanced at her, looking so fresh and young and sweet. Had he ever been that open to life? So carefree? He felt it only fair to give her a heads-up that he had intentions. If she wanted to back out, now was the time to speak up. He'd put it to her gently. Ask permission like the good-for-you lima-bean boyfriend he was really trying to be.

"We're sharing a hotel room," he said.

"I figured," she said. "I brought cash for my plane ticket. Can't afford the hotel too."

He studied her, hoping they were on the same page here. She beamed back. "I'm so excited to make your dream come true! Spontaneous travel wherever fate takes you."

He was excited too. For a very different reason. She couldn't really be that innocent. She'd humped his leg like a champ when they'd kissed the other night. Remembering that, he smiled to himself and headed to the airport.

When they got to the airport ticket counter, Gabe asked for two tickets on their next flight out and waited in breathless anticipation for where spontaneity might take them. He glanced at Zoe, who smiled back while the counter attendant looked it up on the computer.

"That would be Pittsburgh, Pennsylvania," the man said. "Any luggage?"

Gabe and Zoe exchanged a look and burst out laughing. So much for exotic, last minute travel. "You still want to go?" Gabe asked her.

"Absolutely. I love Pittsburgh." He had a feeling she would've said that to any destination.

"Two tickets to Pittsburgh it is, then." Gabe pulled out his wallet.

Zoe handed a wad of bills to the counter attendant. Gabe snatched the money back and handed the guy his credit card.

"Gabe, I'm paying for my ticket."

"This trip was my idea."

"I know, but I went along with it." She tried to put the money in his hand, but he made a fist and turned back to the counter. The guy swiped his credit card. There.

Next thing he knew, her hands wrapped around him from behind, and both her hands slid into his front pockets. He went utterly still as one hand was very close to a very interested part, and realized just as she pulled away that her money was now sitting in his pocket.

She appeared at his side, bumped him with her hip, and grinned cheekily.

He leaned down and whispered in her ear. "I'd

accuse you of being sneaky, but I enjoyed it a little too much."

She laughed. They showed their IDs, got the tickets, and headed over to the long security line with their carry-on luggage. When they got to the front, they were both snagged and sent to a private area for a luggage inspection, thorough pat-down, and questioning. Apparently security didn't like it when you made a last minute ticket purchase.

"Where are you going?" the security guard asked in his no-nonsense voice after Gabe's luggage and body inspection yielded nothing more interesting than an obscene amount of condoms for a weekend trip.

"Pittsburgh," Gabe answered.

"Why the last minute?"

"We were being spontaneous."

"What business do you have in Pittsburgh?"

"Pleasure."

The security guard cracked an unexpected smile. "Yeah, heh-heh, we saw. You traveling with your girlfriend?"

"Yes."

"All right. You're free to go."

Gabe nodded, put his wallet, cell, and keys back in his pockets, slipped into his shoes, and grabbed his suitcase. Zoe still hadn't emerged from the private screening area where they took her. Dammit. Their flight left in half an hour. If she didn't come out soon, he was going to march in there as her lawyer. A few minutes later, she emerged smiling and chatting with the woman security guard about restaurants in Pittsburgh. He couldn't help but smile, watching her. Zoe took lemons and made lemon bars with whipped cream on top. He was getting goofy, but damn if he didn't want that sunshiny goodness for himself. She beamed at him and waved, and his heart stuttered.

He was falling for her.

"We've got just enough time to catch the flight," she said. "Let's go!"

"Not too fast," he joked. "They'll think we're fleeing something."

"This is ridiculous!"

He grabbed her and swung her around, feeling lighter than he could ever remember. "Let's go, sunshine."

CHAPTER TEN

The flight was short, only an hour and a half, so they got to Pittsburgh with plenty of time to sightsee. Zoe knew even a winter weekend in Pittsburgh could be fun. She'd been there before a few times for gigs in the Strip District, so she planned on being their tour guide.

"I'll book the hotel," Gabe said. "You rent the car." He handed her his credit card.

She handed back the card. "I got it."

He pushed it back in her hand. "I insist."

She slipped it into his pants pocket, and he went very still. "You can pay for my steak dinner." She headed for the rental counter.

"Zoe."

She turned. "What?"

Gabe spoke without looking up from his cell. "Two queens or one king-size bed?"

"Get two beds," she said automatically and got in

line. She traveled with her band all over the country and often shared a room with Jordan with two beds to save money. More for their pockets that way. Of course, Jordan had only actually slept in the room with her one time. He usually found some groupie to hook up with for the night and stayed with a stranger instead.

As she stood in line, she realized that was a dumb answer. This weekend made four weeks of dating Gabe, he'd been wonderful to her so far, and she couldn't deny the attraction. She turned to tell him one bed would be fine, but he'd stepped outside with his cell, and it was too late.

Twenty minutes later, they headed to the rental lot.

"You didn't get the sports car," he said when she led him to the economy section.

"This is less expensive."

"Yeah, but…" He gestured to the row of shiny red and black sports cars. "I should've been more specific."

She rolled her eyes. "Come on. I promise you'll still have fun."

She drove them to the Duquesne Incline, where they took a crowded ride up the hill in a nineteenth-century cable car for a view of the city nestled along the Allegheny, Monongahela, and Ohio rivers. When they got to the lookout point, Gabe put his arm around her as they took in the skyline, the three rivers glistening in the bright sunshine, the two stadiums, Heinz Field and PNC Park, where the Steelers and Pirates played respectively. It was starting to feel like spring now that it was mid-March. She breathed in the clean crisp air.

"It's nicer than I thought," Gabe said. "It's no Spain, but…"

"It's spontaneous and fun," she said with a grin.

He kissed the tip of her nose. "Yes. Too bad it's not baseball season yet. I'd love to see the Pirates play."

"Next time. You hungry?"

"Starving," he replied with a hot look that had her stomach fluttering.

"I've got the perfect place."

They took the ride down, and Gabe pulled her close, wrapping his arms around her from behind as they looked out at the view. That feeling washed over her again—electric and safe at the same time. When they got in the car, she blasted the radio and took off. "Next stop, Primanti Brothers!"

"What's that?"

"Only the best sandwich shop ever."

"Oh, really? I've had some pretty good sandwiches in my day."

"Not like this."

She found some parking and headed over to the

crowded shop. "Skip the wings and pizza," she said above the noise of the crowd while they waited to place their order. "You have to get the sandwich. What do you like?"

"You pick. I'm being spontaneous."

She smiled. "Excellent."

When it was their turn, she ordered two roast beef sandwiches with the works. They miraculously found two seats at the counter.

"Just take a bite," she said. "Don't look at it."

He took a big bite and chewed with his brows raised. "Are there French fries on this thing?"

She laughed. "Yeah. French fries and coleslaw."

"I never thought that would taste good right in the sandwich."

"I know, but it works, right? The hot and the cold together. And the Italian bread?"

He took another bite, closed his eyes and chewed. "Awesome."

They finished the afternoon with a tour of the Andy Warhol Museum. Gabe was a fan. "I had no idea Andy Warhol was from Pittsburgh. I always think of him in New York."

"Yup." She was having a blast surprising Gabe with all Pittsburgh had to offer. It really was a fun city.

Gabe checked the time on his cell. "It's almost six. Let's check in at the hotel."

"Sure."

Gabe checked them in at the Fairmont, a luxury hotel far nicer than she could ever afford.

"Wow!" Zoe exclaimed when they got to the room. "You got us a suite!"

He shrugged. "I wanted the view."

She crossed to the floor-to-ceiling windows. A telescope was set up with a view of Mount Washington with the Incline and the city. She turned. The living room had a large sectional sofa, a big flat-screen TV, a desk, and a dining table. She stopped. There were a dozen roses in a vase on the dining table. She walked over to the roses and breathed them in. "Are these from you, or did they come with the room?"

"Me."

"Thank you." She turned; his expression was fierce, hungry. The shark was back. She quickly continued the tour, heading for the bedroom with its king-size bed—he'd ignored her suggestion of two beds—and a bathroom with a shower and separate soaking tub big enough for two. She had to hand it to him. This was advanced seduction. The stage was set. But was she ready for the heartbreak? No guy had ever stayed with her more than eight weeks. She'd counted one time when she was starting to feel cursed.

She jumped as she saw his reflection in the bathroom mirror before she'd heard him come in.

"This is awesome, Gabe."

Gabe looked around. "Not bad for last minute. I made us reservations for dinner. Did you pack a dress or should we go shopping?"

Shopping, luxury suite, dinner. A far cry from her usual dates. "Just a skirt."

"We're getting you a dress. Let's go. We've got an hour until our reservation downstairs. It's the hotel restaurant, but it's supposed to be good. They have the steak you wanted."

"I was just joking about that. We could do something casual."

"A deal is a deal. Ready?"

"Give me a few minutes." She freshened up in the bathroom, took off her socks, and slipped into the black wedge heels that worked with pants or a dress. She tucked stockings into her purse and grabbed her coat. She found Gabe standing by the door in a button-down shirt and suit pants. "Ready."

He held the door open for her, and then his hand went to the small of her back, heating her as he guided her out of the room. Zoe told herself just to enjoy this weekend and not think too hard on it. Gabe wouldn't kick her out of her apartment if things didn't work out between them.

She hoped.

Of course not. He was sweet, even though he

claimed not to be.

She smiled tightly up at him as he guided her into the elevator. He didn't smile back. Instead his dark blue eyes burned into hers. When the doors shut, he pulled her close. "I want you in black." One long finger stroked upward, blazing a hot trail from her hip to the side of her breast. "Something that shows a lot of skin."

She swallowed as he placed a kiss on the side of her neck, where she was sure her pulse was beating way too high. "Are you going to pick my underwear too?" she asked, trying for a teasing tone and failing miserably.

"You won't wear any."

"Gabe—"

He hauled her against him, kissing the protest right out of her. She clung to him, overwhelmed with pure lusty pleasure, until the elevator dinged, and he set her away from him. She let out a shaky breath, hoping she didn't look as ravished as she felt.

The doors opened, and he guided her out, a hand on her back. She tried to reason with him again, facing him in the lobby. "Gabe, I'm not—" Her protest was cut off by a hard kiss.

He grabbed her hand. "Come on."

He pulled her to the concierge, where he quickly found out where he could get the kind of dress he wanted. It was within walking distance, and they were off.

"I thought this was supposed to be a fun shopping trip for me," she said, breathless at his pace.

He stopped. "It will be fun for you"—one corner of his mouth tilted up in a devious smile—"in the end."

She huffed out a breath. He grabbed her hand and pulled her along, seemingly eager to get her into a dress.

Fifteen minutes later, she waited in the dressing room as instructed in her bra and panties, and a saleswoman handed her a black dress in the requested size with double spaghetti straps, a V-neck bodice that would definitely show some cleavage, and a modest mid-thigh length. Oh. This wasn't that bad. She'd thought Gabe was acting out some X-rated fantasy.

She turned the dress. Come on! There was no back. Only the spaghetti straps that crisscrossed in back and a couple of tiny straps across the lower back that she imagined kept the whole thing from falling apart. The back ended in a near V, dipping obscenely low. This was not a dress you could wear a bra or underwear with. Maybe a thong if the waistband didn't come up too high. She set the dress back on the hook. This was definitely Gabe's X-rated fantasy, and she was a rated R kind of girl.

"Gabe!" she hollered.

"Yes?" He sounded close. Had he breached the ladies' changing room?

"Um, where's the saleslady?"

"I sent her away. Does it fit?"

She peeked her head around the curtain. "I can't wear this. It's very slutty."

"That's the point."

"I'm not slutty," she huffed.

"It's just a dress," he said. "Put it on."

"There's no back."

"Do you need some help?" He put his hand on the curtain to open it further, and she quickly shut it.

"Don't come in here!" She was standing in her bra and panties, for crying out loud.

"Zoe, you've made this such a great day for me. Just do this one thing, and I'll do my best to make it a great night for you."

She grabbed her shirt in defiance of his request when it was suddenly snatched from her hand. She yelped in surprise. He'd reached through the crack in the curtain.

"How did you know?" she asked.

"I can see you through the crack here. In the mirror."

She let out a stream of curses.

"The dress will cover you more than what you've got on." She could hear the smile in his voice.

"Though I like the pink satin."

"Turn around!"

She peeked her head out to make sure he did. Then she slipped into the dress. It fit perfectly, if indecently. She turned. At least her ass was covered. The back ended just above her butt crack, so her panties were showing a bit. She tucked them out of sight. One false move. She sighed and opened the curtain. "Okay, I'm wearing it."

He stared in open admiration, doing a slow perusal from her shoulders down to her bare feet, lingering on her cleavage, her waist, and hips. She let out an irritated sigh.

His eyes snapped to hers. "Take off the bra."

She took it off and slipped it out from under the dress. "Happy?"

He snagged the bra right out of her hand and stuffed it in his pocket. "Turn around. I want to see the back."

She slowly turned, heard the curtain close behind him, and waited. Suddenly his warm hands slid up the back of her bare thighs. She snapped her head around to find him kneeling behind her. "Gabe," she said in a shaky voice. "What are you doing? I'm not into—"

"Hush. Not yet." His hands stopped to rest on her hips, only those long fingers would've fit—

She gasped as he slid her panties down in one

quick pull. He stood, swept her off her feet, slid the panties all the way off, and set her down again. She stared at his index finger, where her panties now dangled.

He kissed her gently. "The dress is perfect."

"Gabe, I need those, you can't—"

"How is everything in there?" the saleslady called.

Gabe stuffed her panties in his pocket, grabbed her hand, and pulled her out. "We'll take it."

~ ~ ~

Zoe grumbled about the drafty breeze and feeling exposed on the walk to the restaurant, but that only made Gabe smile more. What an arrogant man. Telling her how to dress. Stealing her underthings.

"How would you like it if I stole your underwear?" she asked, making a grab for his pocket.

He snagged her hand and entwined his fingers with hers. "I'd love that."

Grrr.

They walked another block with Gabe distracting her with questions about her songwriting process when a flash of pink flew into a nearby trash can. Were those her panties?

"Gabe! Why did you throw them out?"

"Because I didn't want to argue over them," he said. "I'll buy you a replacement later."

She peered into the trashcan at her panties sitting next to a crumpled McDonald's wrapper, and then her bra flew in after it.

"How many original songs have you written?" he asked.

She clamped her mouth shut and glared at him. That was her nicest bra and panty set, and it hadn't been cheap. How dare he toss it!

He leaned down and nipped her neck, which made her jolt; then he took her hand and continued their walk. She fumed silently, not liking this domineering side of him one bit. He seemed unperturbed by her silence, striding with great purpose down the street, and then finally ushering her in the door of the restaurant.

Once inside, he helped her off with her coat and whistled softly under his breath. "Zoe, you are so beautiful."

"I feel naked," she hissed. "And that was expensive stuff you threw away!"

He just stood there, smiling his shark smile. He gave her another slow up and down that made her flush with excitement despite being pissed off at him. Next thing you knew, he'd ask her to strut the catwalk for him. *Here's Zoe in Gabe attire. Barely there fabric next to bare skin. Easier for your fucking entertainment.*

"Relax," Gabe whispered in her ear. His hand

rested on the small of her bare back, burning a hole through her with his touch.

"I can't relax when—"

"Right this way, sir, madam," the host said.

They were shown to a table in a quiet corner with a glowing votive candle and a single rose. She quickly glanced around and noticed two things right away—the rose was just for her, and she was way overdressed for this restaurant. The other women were in business casual outfits. Gabe's outfit could've fit in anywhere. She fumed. This whole dress thing was solely for his amusement.

Gabe pulled out her chair for her. How could one man be such a gentleman and such a shark at the same time?

She tucked the dress under her carefully as she sat. Then she leaned forward to quietly ream him out for toying with her, but was cut off when a bottle of champagne was delivered to the table. The waiter opened it and poured them each a glass with a flourish.

After the waiter left, she turned to Gabe suspiciously. "What's the occasion?"

Next thing you knew, he'd be demanding a lap dance. Once he got her drunk. He knew she couldn't hold her liquor.

He smiled tenderly at her. "I'm celebrating my first spontaneous thing. Thank you, Zoe, for coming along with me. It's been a really rough week. Today's been wonderful and that's all because of you."

Her irritation dissolved in an instant, knowing how upset he was about his stepdad. "I'm glad you took the plunge."

"That's what I like to hear," he said in a low, scraping voice that made her throb.

She took a sip of champagne. It was delicious. She sipped some more and began to relax. And the more she relaxed, the more fun she had with him. He was charming and great at conversation. He asked her where she'd traveled, and she told him about all the cities she'd played in America and Europe. He'd also been to Europe, and they talked of Paris. She was having a wonderful time, and the champagne just kept flowing. And this dress just slipped and caressed her as she moved even the slightest bit. Why hadn't she ever worn a dress with nothing underneath before?

She leaned forward and whispered, "This dress was a great idea!"

He grinned. "I thought so."

After dinner, they took a short walk to Point State Park and stopped by the huge fountain, all lit up at night, and admired the view where the Allegheny and Monongahela rivers met. She caught Gabe staring at her instead of the scenery.

"You're missing the view!" she exclaimed, gesturing

toward the water.

"I'm not missing anything," he said in a husky voice that made her shiver. "You're cold. Let's go."

He laced his fingers with hers and headed back.

"I wasn't cold, you know," she said, swinging her arm with his.

"You shivered."

"There are other kinds of shivers."

His grip on her hand tightened. "What kinds are those?"

"The delicious kind."

He sped up. "We really need to get to the hotel."

She giggled and kept up with him.

When they got back to the hotel, Gabe surprised her by heading straight to the bathroom and shutting the door. She'd expected him to kiss her or throw her on the bed. She slipped off her shoes, spread her arms wide, and spun around. She heard the water running. Was he taking a shower? Huh. She'd thought at least she'd get a hot kiss goodnight. She went to the window and admired the skyline, the twinkling lights, and the hills in the distance. She padded over to the telescope and bent to look out at the night sky. Wow. So many stars. This was cool.

"Zoe." His voice was harsh, and she immediately straightened and whirled around. Gabe stood there, fully dressed, not in a towel or robe like she'd expected. "I drew you a bath."

"You drew me a bath?" she echoed. Her very own butler.

"Come on before it gets cold."

She rushed to the bathroom. A bubble bath awaited, with a glass of wine and a plate of chocolate-covered strawberries on the nearby ledge. "Oh, Gabe. You spoil me." She turned to him and beamed. "This looks wonderful!"

"I'll leave you to it."

And then, shockingly, he left. Zoe didn't waste any time. She shimmied out of the dress, hanging it on a hook on the back of the door, secured her hair with a hair band into a bun on top of her head, and slipped into the tub up to her neck. *Ah-h-h.* She didn't have a bathtub in her apartment. She leaned her head back and closed her eyes. This was heavenly. She briefly wondered what Gabe was doing, she could hear him moving around out there, but she was too relaxed to care. She checked out the small bubble bath container on the side, some hypoallergenic luxury stuff. She blew some bubbles away, stretched out her legs languorously, and giggled to herself in pure pleasure. She stayed like that for a while, completely loose and relaxed, floating in the water.

She tried a strawberry. Omigod. So good. Juicy and chocolatey. She sipped the wine, which went with the strawberry perfectly. She could get used to this. She ate another decadent strawberry along with another sip of wine and had a pang of guilt that she was enjoying herself so much without the man responsible for all this wonderful stuff. "Gabe?"

He poked his head in the doorway. "You need something?"

"You want to try the strawberries?"

"Don't invite me in unless you're prepared to share that tub."

She smiled and nodded, and before she could give it another moment's thought, he stepped into the room and began to strip. She watched, not the first time she'd seen this show, but she hadn't seen the full monty.

"Next time I want you to strip for me," he said before hanging his shirt on the hook over her dress.

"But you're so good at it," she teased.

He didn't smile. Just set a condom on the wide ledge of the tub. Okay then. In the tub. That was new and—

The belt slowly came undone, the button, a slow trip on the zipper. She realized a moment later why that trip was necessarily slow. The pants hit the floor, the navy blue briefs followed, and a massive erection sprang free. She sucked in a breath. He might've been taking off his socks, but she wasn't sure because she couldn't stop staring at what she knew was in store for her. Oh, fu-uu-ck me.

"That's the idea," he replied.

Had she said that out loud? Her cheeks burned, and she started babbling to cover up. "The wine's so good and the strawberries too. They go really good together, I mean, well, I always get those two words mixed up. Anyway, you should totally try them. Did you like Pittsburgh?" Her voice came out embarrassingly squeaky at the end.

"Uh-huh." And then he slipped into the tub behind her, pushed her up onto his lap, his erection pushing against her bottom, and she was speechless.

CHAPTER ELEVEN

"You like the bath?" he asked as he nibbled her ear.

"Mmm…it was sweet of you."

"I don't want to be sweet." He nipped the side of her neck, making her gasp. "I want to make you scream my name."

"O-oh," she said shakily.

He placed hot, open-mouthed kisses down the side of her neck. "So what do you think?"

"You're very forward," she said primly.

He chuckled. "I'm in the tub with a beautiful naked woman who wore a slutty dress for me with no panties and *now* you think I'm forward?"

She turned to look at him over her shoulder. "I told you that dress was slutty, especially with no panties."

"You seemed to like it once the champagne started flowing."

She turned back around and played with the

bubbles. "I like anything once the champagne starts flowing."

"Maybe I should order us more champagne. This is one of those fancy bathrooms with a phone by the toilet."

She giggled.

His hand stroked her belly in lazy circles. "Zoe, you make life feel fresh and new. I love that about you."

Warmth speared through her at the words. Or maybe it was his hands, which had moved up to massage her breasts. "I do?" She leaned back, her head resting on his shoulder. His long fingers pinched her nipples. Heat shot through her, a deep throbbing that took all of her attention. "I-I don't know what to say."

"You don't have to say anything," he said, his voice lulling her. "Just let me have my way with you."

"Ha," she managed.

"I'm serious." His fingers stroked a hot soapy trail from her breasts to her hips, sliding toward her inner thigh. "Please."

"Please," she echoed.

He chuckled softly as he opened her legs wide, slowly stroking up and down, learning the feel of her, slipping one long finger inside before sliding back up to her favorite spot. She let out a blissful sigh. He was so gentle at first that she simply closed her eyes and floated through sensation as his magical fingers stroked her center while his other hand played with her breast. The sensation built slowly, in a way no man had ever taken their time with her, seeming to want only her pleasure. Her jaw went slack.

He moved the bubbles aside. "Watch."

She watched those fingers as she felt them, and the combination of both seeing and feeling what he did to her made the intensity skyrocket. Within minutes, she was moaning, unable to help it as he became more demanding, separating her folds, stroking quickly until she was writhing in his arms. He clamped an arm around her waist, holding her tight as he worked her, until she was trembling with the need for release, and then she broke in a climax that shook her to her core. But he wasn't done. He lifted her out of the water and pushed her forward, her hands resting on the wide ledge of the tub. She waited, still breathing hard, heard the rustle of the condom wrapper and then his hands clamped on her hips as he took her with one deep thrust that had her breath catching.

"Look at you," he said gruffly as he thrust deep again.

She saw them in the mirror. She looked thoroughly worked over, her hair half frizzy from the water, her cheeks flushed. He looked like he wanted to devour her.

He met her eyes in the mirror. "Yeah," he said as if he'd read her thoughts.

And then his wicked fingers were back as he thrust hard, and she didn't think she could take much more. His voice was harsh in her ear. "Scream my name when you come."

She couldn't speak, could only moan, and then he did God-knew-what move, some kind of spiral, pinch, and twist with his fingers that had her flying, her vision dimming as a slight ringing ran through her ears, and then she was back, tingling all over, his hands still gripping her hips, pulling her back as he thrust in, opening her onto him to take him as deep as he could go. She rocked helplessly as he pumped into her, felt his shuddering release, and just lay there, exhausted and limp.

He kissed her shoulder and loosened his grip on her hips. His voice rumbled in her ear. "I didn't hear my name."

"I think I passed out for a minute," she mumbled.

"Next time." She could hear the smile in his voice. He pulled out and stood in a noisy rush of water. She heard the water draining from the tub, but she couldn't move. She stayed draped over the side of the tub, resting her head on her arm, not trusting her legs just yet, her head a little woozy.

He slapped her ass. "Come on."

"Ow," she said weakly.

Then he was lifting her out of the tub, wrapping her in a towel, and carrying her to the bed. She snuggled into the pillow as he pulled off the towel and covered her with the blanket.

"Rest up," he whispered when he'd settled in next to her. "I want more from you in the morning."

"Mmm…"

He turned her, spooning her from behind, his still half-hard erection pressing into her bottom. She was asleep within minutes.

~ ~ ~

Zoe slipped into the shower the next morning while Gabe slept. Okay, she'd had too much champagne, too much wine, too many bubbles. But she didn't feel hungover. She felt euphoric. Damn, he was good. He overwhelmed her plain and simple. From the five-star hotel to the shopping, the bubble bath, the way he turned bossy and demanding once he'd set about seducing her. How easy it was to surrender. How shockingly rewarding. She throbbed, remembering.

"Zoe?"

"In the shower," she hollered.

"I'm getting us room service breakfast," he said through the door.

"Great!"

She luxuriated in the water pressure that was more like a massage than the trickle she got in her apartment. They'd talk over a nice breakfast. About this thing between them, and how she'd like to not end up homeless when it was over. So civilized that way.

"Quick question," Gabe said, much closer now. She startled as he peered at her through the glass block wall of the shower. The glass distorted the view, but she made out naked man well enough. Her throat went dry.

"Yes?" she croaked.

"You ever have shower sex?"

She opened her mouth to say we really need to talk, but couldn't get out the words because he'd joined her, and his thick rigid erection took all of her attention.

"Yes or no?" Gabe prompted, setting a condom on the small soap holder.

She blinked. "No."

His eyes gleamed. "I'm your first."

"Gabe, wait." She held up a hand. "Maybe we should talk."

He grabbed her hand, pulled her against him, and kissed her. Her knees went weak as he devoured her, no other word for the way he took control, she felt devoured as his hand gripped her hair, holding her in place for his kiss, his tongue thrusting in, his lips hard and unyielding as they slanted over hers, his whiskers scraping her skin. His kisses were dangerous, turning her into a puddle of need, making her cling to him. He pulled back and gave her a look that made her heart thud hard against her chest. That look said he wanted her for breakfast.

"Gabe," she said, breathless, "please...I think..." The words died in her throat as he dropped to his knees, grabbed her ass, pulled her into him, and sucked on her hard. Her breath hissed out.

He looked up at her. "You won't think, I promise you."

He kissed her intimately, softer now. Within minutes, she was rocking helplessly against his mouth as he gripped her ass, holding her in place. His tongue and lips quickly drove her over the edge with a white-hot intensity that had her screaming his name, which made him groan against her, the vibrations setting her off again, and he kept going and going until she was absolutely spent. She would've collapsed like a limp ragdoll without him holding her up. He stood, and she wobbled from the sudden lack of support. He rolled on the condom, and then he had her up against the wall, driving into her.

"Wrap your legs around me," he said.

She did, clinging to him tightly.

"Zoe," he murmured, his gaze at once searing and tender. "My Zoe."

Her mind shut down. There was just Gabe filling her, overwhelming her, pushing her to another explosive climax that left her trembling in his arms as he took what he needed from her with hard thrusts for his own release. He kept her like that, pinned against the wall, as he caught his breath. Finally, he pulled out, and she sank down the wall, her legs weak and shaky from clinging to him. Then he was pulling her back up, washing her gently, thoroughly, drying her, wrapping her in a towel, and carrying her to the bedroom.

She let out a sigh when she felt the soft pillow and bed under her once again.

"Rest, Zoe," he whispered, pulling her close, spooning her from behind.

"Mmm—oh!" He'd slipped inside her, still hard. "Gabe—"

"Shh. Just let me be inside you a little longer. When you wake, I'm going to do wicked things to you."

She let out a shaky sigh. He stroked her hair, relaxing her again.

They didn't make it out of the hotel room that day.

~ ~ ~

Gabe wasn't ready to have his weekend with Zoe end, so when they got back late Sunday night, he followed her right into her apartment. He had her naked in bed, flat on her back, within minutes. Her only words, a soft *yes*, drove him on. She gave him everything he demanded without hesitation, always with that soft *yes*. It was a major turn-on for him, having total control in bed. Not all women could let go the way she did— with complete, trusting surrender in a way that told him she loved it as much as he did. He was sensitive enough to adjust his lovemaking to a woman's responses, but Zoe had required zero adjustment to what he desired. That was the first time that had happened. Ever.

He wore her out. He wore himself out, and then he slept, spooning her from behind, his hand cupping her breast possessively.

He woke in the middle of the night, disoriented. Why was he awake? Zoe was still sound asleep, pressed up against him. He listened carefully—a noise like a scratching or scurrying from the ceiling. Damn, he didn't want to leave the bed, with her soft curves pressed against him. He'd had her so much already, but he wanted her again. He belatedly realized he should've asked her if she was sore instead of taking her the way he had.

He stroked from her breast down to her stomach,

spanning his fingers wide to touch as much of her as he could. She didn't stir. He heard the scurrying noise overhead again. If it was another bat, they might have a nest up there, or a hole in the roof. He eased himself away from Zoe and stood.

"Gabe?" Zoe mumbled.

"Go back to sleep."

"What's wrong?"

"I heard a noise in the attic," he said.

She sat up, the blanket clutched up to her neck. "You think there's more bats up there?"

He'd hoped not to disturb her, but now that she was up… "Maybe," he said. "You have a flashlight?" At least Fred was still at Daisy and Trav's house, so they didn't have his crazy barking.

She wrapped the blanket around her and fetched one from the kitchen drawer. He took it and headed for the attic. She followed closely behind him. He opened the access panel. Nothing. It was quiet up there. He moved the flashlight all around, peering into the rafters.

"Maybe it was just a squirrel on the roof," she said. "Something outside."

Gabe saw something on the rafter and reached.

"What are you doing?" Zoe screeched. "Don't touch it!"

He pulled down a bundle of envelopes tied with

pink ribbon. He shone the light on them. The envelope on top was addressed to Allie. "They're my mother's. This used to be her art studio."

"I remember. She did those picture books about the hedgehogs. What was it called again?"

He grimaced. "The Huddles. And later she added the Cuddles, a group of porcupines. Based on me and my brothers." The whole damn series was so embarrassing. The hedgehogs had been based on him, Luke, and Jared. They later did battle with the porcupines (Vinny, Nico, and Angel), until they resolved all their hedgehog-porcupine differences and learned to live together in harmony. So sappy. Angel, being the youngest and sappiest, was the only one who loved those books.

"Does she still do them?" Zoe asked.

"No. We grew up, and now she just does portraits."

"I'll have to reread those books again in the new Reynolds-Marino context." He could tell she was getting a big kick out of this.

"Please don't." He'd been the leader of the Huddles with a special scepter and cape with a giant H on it.

She took the flashlight from him and shone it on the bundle of letters. "It looks like they were hand delivered. No stamp. No return address."

He snagged the flashlight and made his way to the small kitchen, setting the letters on the counter. He'd give them to his mom next time he saw her. He turned, nearly bumping into Zoe.

"Aren't you going to read them?" she asked.

"She hid them in the attic. Obviously they're private."

She grabbed the flashlight and shone it on the bundle of letters. "Can I read one?"

He was kinda curious, but it was his mom, which made it weird. "Go ahead."

"I'll bet they're love letters," she said as she pulled the top one out. The blanket slipped off her shoulders and dropped to the floor. He slid a hand down her back, over her pretty ass, already thinking about taking her bent over the counter. Her voice came out soft, which made his cock pulse. "Gabe, please."

She was all softness—her curves, her voice, her soft brown eyes. It brought out something primal in him that made him want to both protect and dominate her.

"One minute." He grabbed the blanket off the floor and put it back on the bed, giving her a small amount of space.

She read out loud. "Dear Allie, you're all I ever think about..." She stopped and finished the letter reading to herself. A few moments later, she set the letter back on the counter.

"Why'd you stop?"

She turned. "It's from Vinny."

He didn't know what to make of that. It was strange those letters were hidden in the attic at his mom's studio.

"I guess I should've known," he said. "My dad always called her Allison, not Allie."

She crossed to him and put her hand on his arm. "Let's go back to sleep."

He slid his hands up and down her sides, reveling in her curves, inhaling her fresh strawberry scent. "You'll sleep when I'm done with you."

"Yes."

He groaned and pulled her back to bed. "I'm so damn lucky I found you."

She kissed him gently. "Me too."

He rolled on top of her, intending to take things slow, but the minute he was buried inside her, he lost control, driving hard and deep. She met him stroke for stroke, arching up into him in the closest thing to heaven he'd ever felt. Emotion welled unexpectedly inside him. "I love you," he said, surprising himself.

She didn't respond, merely panted because he couldn't stop thrusting hard and fast, even with the "I love you," so he lifted her hips to stroke her on the spot on the inside that always got a fast response.

"I-I-Gabe!"

That scream alone could bring him to orgasm, knowing he'd pushed her over the edge. He drove into her and his own release followed a moment later. He stilled, shaken by the depth of his own feelings. He raised his head. Her eyes were closed, a small smile on her lips.

He kissed those smiling lips, pleased he'd made that smile happen. "Tell me what you were going to say."

"Mmm…" She was drifting off to sleep.

He pulled out and turned her, spooning her from behind. He loved this position, her bottom cradling him. He pulled the blanket over both of them and then because he was still hard, he slid inside her and cupped his hand around her breast. She accepted the intrusion with a soft sigh. Even half asleep, she pleased him, accepting him without protest. Her breathing deepened into sleep a moment later.

She'd started to say it earlier. She'd said "I," he reassured himself.

"I love you," he said again in the dark. The words felt right and at the same time worried him.

Please don't die, he added silently. The familiar fear got a hold of him as it often did late at night. His mind replayed his father's death, Alyssa's funeral with his overwhelming guilt, the lifelong empty part of him from the loss of his twin, and now Vinny dying. He held Zoe a little tighter. Nothing could happen to her. If anyone had to die, it would be him.

Chapter Twelve

Gabe woke the next morning with a raging hard-on. He was turning into an animal consumed with his baser urges. Somehow in gaining control over Zoe's body, he'd lost control at the same time. She'd rolled onto her stomach at some point in the night. Let her sleep, he told himself. He forced himself to turn away from her. With a herculean effort, he slipped out of bed, pulled on his briefs, and started the coffeemaker. It was Monday. He had client appointments and had to go back to work. He stood in the kitchen, waiting for the coffee, and his eye caught on the bundle of letters. Zoe had left the letter she'd read out, open on the counter.

He took a quick look, not really wanting to read all the gory details, but still curious. It was a love letter from Vinny to his mom that ended with him pleading with her that three years was long enough to wait, that the kids could handle it. His heart pounded in his chest as he realized the awful truth. Vinny was the one that destroyed his parents' marriage. Not his father. He quickly shoved the letter back in the envelope. All of these years, him and his brothers, Luke and Jared, had been so hard on their biological dad, so good to Vinny, when it should've been the other way around.

He poured the coffee, drank it black, and fumed to himself. His father had died alone. His sons still turned against him. Even Gabe, who'd worked for the man, had always held himself at a distance.

Zoe slipped her arms around him. He startled, so lost in his dark thoughts he hadn't heard her get up. She wore a robe, and he immediately wanted to rip it off her. He wanted her naked always.

"Gabe, are you okay?"

He set the coffee down. "Are you sore?"

She blushed. "A little."

He wrapped his arms around her. "Tell me if I'm too much."

She looked down, clearly embarrassed. "It's okay. It's sore in a good way."

"I rode you hard, didn't I?"

"I liked it," she admitted.

He tipped her chin up. "God help me, I want to do it again."

"Yes."

He groaned and crushed her to him. "I promised

myself I'd give you a chance to recover." He released her. "Go get dressed." He backed up a step, his eyes still taking her in hungrily. "I have no control around you."

She gave him a small impish smile. "I don't want you to have control."

This woman was made for him. He didn't have to hold back with her at all. It was a liberation he'd never experienced before.

"I love you," he said. The words hung in the air. He stared at her, waiting.

She looked away.

"Forget it," he muttered.

She met his eyes. "Gabe, one weekend of sex doesn't mean—"

He was on her in a flash, kissing her hard, making her feel what she did to him. She opened for him, melted against him, allowed him to take what he wanted. He broke the kiss. "It's more than that."

"You've only known me four weeks," she said gently. "I was just your waitress for a month before that."

He couldn't argue with that. But he shouldn't have to argue about love. Shouldn't have to make his case. Dammit. He turned away from her and tried to rein himself in. He took a few deep breaths. She set something on the counter.

"Gabe," she said softly.

That soft voice brought out the animal in him, a primal urge that made him feel alive and uncontrollably ravenous for her. He took another deep breath before he slowly turned and saw the condom on the counter.

And then she dropped the robe.

The animal took over. He bent her over the counter, spread her legs wide, and took her exactly as he'd imagined taking her last night. He took what she offered, and then took some more. And when he was finally finished, spent, it was with the dark realization that while she gave her body freely, she held back her heart.

He got dressed and left without another word.

~ ~ ~

Zoe took a shower after Gabe left, her mind racing with all that had happened this weekend. She soaped up and began to wash. She had whisker burns on her breasts, her inner thigh, and the side of her neck. Those were just what she could see. As if she needed a reminder of all Gabe had done to her. Gabe's declaration of love was a showstopper. Pulled her right out of the sexy dreamworld she'd been living in and straight into reality with a bang. Because that was crazy. He couldn't possibly be in love with her so soon. That wasn't how love worked. It was a gradual thing. Several dates had to be involved, long phone calls, a gradual revealing of personal experiences. Not just one weekend. He was in lust, not love, and she wouldn't believe it unless he stuck around. She'd had more than a few *I love yous* from men, all revolving around sex, that never bothered with her again. And just look at how Gabe had left in complete silence as soon as he'd gotten what he'd wanted from her.

A stab of guilt hit her. Maybe he was hurt that she hadn't responded in kind.

She frowned. She hadn't meant to hurt him. But, at the same time, she couldn't say I love you back. Yes, she had strong feelings. He was a good man, had helped her out when she needed it most, had shown her a good time, but that wasn't love. It was too early for that and whatever it was he'd stirred up inside her needed time to learn what exactly it was.

Lust definitely. Strong like, absolutely. Not love.

~ ~ ~

Gabe went home to get ready for work, mad at himself for telling Zoe he loved her. He shouldn't have expected her to meet him where he was at. Hell, he was still shocked to find himself in love so fast, but he knew deep in his heart that was exactly what this was. He felt at peace with her—no small feat for him—after feeling so unsettled these last four years. And the sex. He wasn't letting go of that for anything. As long as she'd let him, he'd have her again and again.

Given time, she could learn to love him. Or was she like Alyssa, loving his money and what he could buy her more than just him? His chest ached. Every time he thought of Alyssa's death, he was swamped with guilt. He pushed the painful memory back to the dark corner of his mind where it lived, always popping up at the worst times, and headed to work. But he found it hard to focus on work. His mind was a muddle of all that had happened this weekend—Zoe screaming his name in ecstasy mostly, but also the letters that were proof that he'd once again wronged those he loved the most. His father had gotten a raw deal while Vinny got off scot-free. That was just wrong. By the time he wrapped up the day with a look at a despondent Ms. Walker's severance contract, he really needed a drink.

He called Shane to see if he wanted to meet at the bar. "Hey, buddy, you got time for a beer?"

"I wish," Shane said. "I'm on daddy duty tonight. Hold on." He called off in the distance. "Abby! No dancing on the coffee table!" Abby was his two-year-old daughter. Loud wails promptly ensued. "Ah, shit," Shane mumbled. "This one falls apart if I raise my voice." Shane tried to explain himself to Abby, but

Gabe knew it was hopeless once a female was upset. "I only raised my voice because last time you slipped and hit your head, remember?" The crying continued with heart-wrenching, gulping sobs. Then in a much gentler voice, Shane said, "C'mere, baby," and hung up.

Gabe couldn't imagine being outnumbered by females the way Shane was at home. You'd think he'd be dying for a guys' night at the bar. Of course, Rachel was probably working. She still did the bookkeeping for all three of their shops. He briefly considered going home, finding Zoe, and losing himself in her softness again, but dammit, he had to give her space after all the sappy love stuff he'd been stupid enough to blurt out. He called his brother Jared, who lived nearby in Eastman and was always good for a beer when he wasn't on call. He was finishing up his residency at Eastman Hospital.

"Dr. Reynolds," Jared answered cordially. He knew who was calling. He just loved to rub it in that he was the doctor in the family.

"Yeah, I got this rash—"

"No cure. Expect your dick to fall off in a week. Next patient!"

Gabe chuckled. "You up for a beer, Dr. Dipwad?"

"Fuck you and yeah."

"Meet you at Garner's."

"Give me twenty minutes."

Gabe was halfway through his beer when he felt a manly thump on his back.

"Hey, sweetcheeks," Jared said, taking the bar stool next to him. "Monday night beer. Just what I needed. I worked all weekend. Plight of the rookie surgeon." He signaled to the bartender, ordered something on tap, and turned back to Gabe. "So what'd you do this weekend?"

Gabe took a pull on his beer. "I went to Pittsburgh."

Jared barked out a laugh. "No, really."

Gabe raised a brow. "Really."

Jared's beer arrived, and he took a long swallow. "What'd you go to Pittsburgh for? Some kind of lawyer conference?"

"I decided to be spontaneous, show up at the airport, and go wherever the next flight took me."

"That's a boneheaded move." He paused and slowly smiled. "Who's the girl? Zoe?" Jared always was good at putting the missing pieces together.

"Yup."

"Ha! I knew it. Only time a guy does a boneheaded move like blow his money on plane tickets and, let me guess, five-star hotel?"

"Yeah," Gabe admitted.

"Is to impress a woman," Jared finished.

"Shut up."

"So what're you doing here with me instead of hanging out at her place? I'm figuring after a weekend at the five-star hotel, she's all over you."

"None of your damn business."

Jared chuckled and ordered nachos. His brother was always in good spirits. Lucky bastard.

They drank beer and watched the Knicks on the TV over the bar. Jared finished his nachos and glanced sideways at Gabe. "I saw Dad at the hospital."

Gabe's heart kicked up. "Did he get his test results back?"

"Not yet. Mom wants us at Sunday dinner. He'll know by then."

Gabe was suddenly furious at Vinny for being sick. The only reason he'd been able to handle losing his biological father was because he knew he still had Vinny. Now he was going to lose both of them. He couldn't lose any more people in his life. It made him want to rush home to Zoe and make her promise to never, ever leave him. And wasn't that just pathetic after the unrequited *I love you* hanging out there like an elephant between them?

He looked at Jared, who'd returned to the game.

"Aren't you upset?" Gabe asked tersely.

Jared turned, serious now. "He'll pull through."

Gabe stared at the bar. Fuck. And then he remembered the letters. How Vinny had betrayed them all, just like he was doing right now.

"I found letters in the studio attic from Vinny to Mom," Gabe said.

Jared set his beer down. "Oh yeah? Were they kinky?" He winked.

"They were having an affair for three years before they married."

Jared let out a whistle. "That's a long time."

"Vinny wrecked everything."

"I don't see it that way. Mom was unhappy before. She married him and got happy. No more sullen silences, no more fights. And we got three brothers out of it and a dad that actually gave a shit about us."

"Maybe if they hadn't had an affair, Mom and Dad would've worked things out."

Jared waved that away. "Ancient history."

"I don't know how I can ever look Vinny in the eye again."

"He's not a monster."

Gabe's hand gripped the beer bottle harder. "Vinny broke up our family."

Jared clapped a hand on his shoulder. "Nothing's changed. He was still Dad to all of us for years. And some of us weren't the easiest kids to live with either. Can you imagine being a stepdad to three boys that hated your guts? A teenager, a punk, and a daredevil?" Gabe had been the teenager, Luke the punk, Jared, still and always, the daredevil. He went skydiving whenever he got the chance.

"Our dad died alone," Gabe reminded him.

"He was happiest that way." Jared chugged his beer and finished it with a loud *ahhh*. "Not a people person, to put it nicely."

Gabe thought about that. It was true their father had never been an affectionate man, but he must've felt love at some point for their mother to marry him.

"I'm still pissed at Vinny," Gabe said.

Jared raised a brow. "So he's not on a pedestal for you anymore. Who can stand the height up there anyway? And don't forget Mom's no saint in all this. You gonna be mad at Vinny, might as well be mad at Mom too. She didn't have to shack up with him. Stick those letters back in the attic and forget you ever saw them."

"You don't think I should give the letters back to Mom in case something happens with Vinny?"

"Mom knows where they are. She put them there." Jared lowered his voice. "Seriously, don't open this can of worms now. What's done is done. We all survived."

Gabe took a long drink of beer, thinking hard. It still didn't sit right with him the way his own father died with no one on his side. He'd been cuckolded, humiliated, pushed out of his own home, and then his three sons had abandoned him for a new dad. They'd never wanted to visit him in his fancy city apartment, had given him major attitude, and often ran wild all over the city when they were forced to visit. Luke would steal cash from their dad's wallet, Jared would provide a distraction (often a small fire), and Gabe would go with his brothers to make sure they didn't end up kidnapped or in jail or dead. That whole situation had been fucked up.

Gabe scowled. A marriage was a legally binding contract. His mom had broken that contract and upended all of their lives.

"Hey, don't tell Luke," Jared said. "You know how long it took him to come around to Vinny." Luke had held out the longest, trying to stay loyal to his "real" dad, even as he pretended to his real dad that he hated his guts. Until Luke ran away from home at ten years old, riding his bike to the train station to move in with his real dad, and spun out on his bike, breaking his arm. It was their stepdad who took Luke to the hospital, who took him out for ice cream after. His "real" dad, when he saw him weeks later with the cast, had said only, "Guess you learned your lesson."

Gabe blew out a breath. "When did you get so smart?"

Jared chuckled. "Born that way."

CHAPTER THIRTEEN

Zoe spent every night that week at Gabe's place after her dinner shift at Garner's. Even Thursday night when she worked the late shift, he'd given her the key to his place and told her to stop by. He didn't even mind Fred staying with her, except, after that first night, Gabe moved Fred's crate downstairs because when she screamed Gabe's name as he always demanded, it set Fred off on a flurry of barking.

Gabe was more serious than he'd been on their fun weekend away. When he let her in the front door, he rarely smiled and when he did, the smile didn't quite reach his eyes. She read pain in those dark blue eyes.

"Is it Vinny?" she'd asked the first night she'd come over. She knew he'd been really worried about his stepdad before they went away for the weekend.

"Put Fred outside."

He waited for her to let the dog out; then he took her hand and led her up to his room. He started undressing right away, unbuttoning his shirt, watching her with a heated gaze. She didn't undress, knowing he liked to do that for her. She waited, hoping he'd let her in, his every movement radiating tension. He still didn't speak, and when she tried to, he distracted her with a kiss that quickly led to her stripped naked, panting, until he pushed her over the edge, making her scream his name again.

She still checked in with him each night, concerned about his lack of humor, his lack of warm smiles. Something was definitely not right with him.

"Are you sure everything's okay?" she'd ask.

"Fine." Then he'd grab her and all conversation ceased. He only seemed at peace after, spooning her from behind, holding her close. The only words he gave her were a murmur in her ear. "My Zoe."

He hadn't repeated the "I love you" again. She figured he realized it was just the heat of the moment and not the real thing. He still wanted her endlessly and that was enough for her. She was almost afraid to think of a future with him, afraid to jinx things with her history of breakups at eight weeks. It didn't make sense that he would fit into that pattern, but still, there it was, nagging at her. They were only at five weeks.

Friday night she had a gig in the city and invited Gabe to watch her perform with her band. They played a lot more of her original songs when they performed in clubs. Whenever Gabe heard her singing in the shower in the morning, he'd tell her she should put out an indie album, which thrilled her, and then he'd take over the shower, take over her, which overwhelmed her. In the best way possible.

She wanted him to get to know their music. The club, Harvey's, was a small basement venue, but with great acoustics. The front had a foosball table and a low-key bar, but all the action was in the dingy back room, where a small stage regularly featured bands and stand-up comedians. Gabe watched from a small round table as they warmed up. Jordan spent an unusual amount of time talking over the songs they'd perform and some improv stuff he wanted to show off her voice.

"What's up, Jordan?" she asked. "You seem nervous. We've got our set. Why're you trying to add in all this extra stuff?"

"Yeah, what's up?" Alex asked.

Wade stared, waiting for the answer.

Jordan looked around. Only Gabe and the guy that ran the place were here. He spoke in a low voice anyway. "Ronald Washington from Hep Six is coming to hear us play tonight."

Zoe whooped. "Hep Six? Omigod! This is so exciting!"

Gabe cocked his head to the side in question, but

she waved him away.

"Shh," Jordan said. "This is top secret, so don't tell anyone, even your stupid-ass boyfriend, Zoe."

She immediately went to defend Gabe. "He's not—"

"They might want us as an opener for their European tour." Jordan dropped that bombshell with a triumphant smile.

She opened her mouth, ready to squeal in excitement, when Jordan promptly covered her mouth with his hand. So much time had passed since Jordan had first mentioned Hep Six, she thought they'd been passed over.

"Haw de thaw happaw?" she said behind his hand.

Jordan dropped his hand and grinned. "Apparently, they picked another band—"

"Who?" Wade asked.

"Yellow."

"Ooh," they said in unison. Yellow was a really good jazz band, up and coming, playing larger venues all the time.

Jordan went on. "Yellow had to drop out after their lead singer had some vocal cord trouble."

Zoe put her hand to her own vocal cords protectively. Even when she screamed, she didn't go full throttle, always mindful of her voice. "So we're second choice."

"Yeah, but now they're desperate," Wade put in.

"I do best in desperate circumstances," Alex said.

"We have to be tip-top above the *zone*, guys," Jordan said. "We've been waiting for our big break. This is it."

They returned to warming up, all of them pumped. Gabe approached the stage area just before they began. "Break a leg, Zoe."

"Thanks! Now go back to your seat. This is a big night for us." She leaned forward and whispered, "A guy from Hep Six is here! They're awesome, and he wants to hear us!"

He kissed her then, a quick, hard kiss that pulled all of her scattered nervous energy and focused it back to the kiss, immediately calming her.

"Thanks," she breathed. "I needed that."

"I know." He turned and headed back to his seat, all swagger, making her smile.

~ ~ ~

Zoe sang, focused on Gabe, who frequently smiled and applauded enthusiastically. It was so good to see that smile back again. It was one of the best performances they'd ever done, and she was flying high. Ronald came up after to congratulate them.

"I liked your sound," Ronald said. "And you—" he looked right at her "—you're like a young Ella

Fitzgerald. That scat you got going on. Hoo-ee!"

Zoe beamed. Jordan put his arm around her proudly.

"Let me talk it over with the band and our manager Don," Ronald said. "You'll be hearing from Don on Monday one way or another."

"Thank you," Jordan said. "It was an honor to have you here."

Ronald smiled, winked at her, and headed toward the exit. As soon as he left, Jordan grabbed her and spun her around. "I think we're going to get it, Zoe-bean! You and that gorgeous voice."

She squealed and laughed. He put her down again. "Thank you," she said, "but P.S. you know it's a group effort."

Wade and Alex joined them. They huddled close, talking excitedly about the possibility of the European tour. It was for three months, but if ticket sales were good, Jordan said, they might add extra dates and expand it to America.

"What're you all excited about?" Gabe asked, appearing at her side with a smile.

She bounced on the balls of her feet. "We might go on tour with Hep Six!"

Gabe lost his smile. "Wow."

"This is really good news," she told him. "This is the break we've been waiting for."

Gabe shoved his hands in his pockets. "For how long? Where?"

"Europe!" she chirped. She hadn't been to Europe in ten years.

"How long?" Gabe pressed.

"For the summer. Three months," she said, suddenly realizing why he wasn't sharing in her excitement.

"That's great," Gabe said, only he didn't sound like he meant it.

Jordan slung an arm over her shoulders. "It is great."

Gabe narrowed his eyes at Jordan. Zoe shrugged Jordan off and pulled Gabe aside. "Of course I'll miss you, but we'll stay in touch. Anyway, it's not definite."

"A lot can happen in three months," Gabe said with a dark look at Jordan.

"Meaning?"

"You tell me."

"That we won't be together?"

He frowned. "I don't know."

She put her hand on his arm. "I want to be together. Maybe you could visit me for part of it. It's Europe!"

Gabe was quiet.

"It's no Pittsburgh," she teased.

A reluctant smile tugged at his lips. "It's no

Pittsburgh. That's for sure."

"It'll be okay," Zoe said.

He wrapped his arms around her. "I feel like I just found you, and I'm losing you."

"You're not. It's temporary. Anyway, it's still a maybe."

He pulled her away from the band to a quiet corner of the room. "Will it make you happy?" he asked, cupping her cheek.

She smiled. "Very."

"Then I'm all for it."

"You're so sweet and generous. I love that about you."

He gazed deep into her eyes. "I love everything about you, Zoe."

Her heart slammed into her throat. "Wow. That's just so—"

"Yeah." He dropped his hand and looked away.

"I'm falling for you too, Gabe."

His eyes snapped back to hers.

"I love you too," she said over the lump in her throat.

He stared at her for a long moment before crushing her to him. "People I love die on me," he said quietly in her ear. "Promise me you won't die. I'll die for you."

"Gabe, what are you talking about?" He was still

holding her tightly, and she couldn't see his eyes. "No one's dying on anyone."

He loosened his grip and dropped his hands. She caught his pained expression before he looked to the floor. "It could happen," he said quietly. "It *has* happened. My twin, my father, Alyssa, and—" His voice choked. "And now Vinny."

Her heart squeezed, and she hugged him again. He held her tightly. She hadn't known about the twin. She'd ask him about that later. Geez, that was a lot of death to handle. She pulled away enough to look in his dark blue eyes so full of pain. "It's okay. You had some bad luck. That's over now. From here on out, only good things. And P.S. Vinny's not dying."

He swallowed visibly.

"I hereby break your curse," she added.

One corner of his mouth quirked up in a small smile. He kissed her softly, and then he kissed her long and deep. "Let's go."

"I usually hang with the band for a few drinks after. You know, to talk about the set and what we want to do next time." She laced her fingers with his. "Join us."

"All right, but then we're going back to my place so I can remind you what you'll be missing in Europe."

She grinned. "I won't be missing it if you come

with us."

"Zoe, I can't miss three months of work. I'll have to start all over again building my practice."

"Didn't you say you wanted to do something different?"

"Bumming around Europe following my girlfriend around doesn't sound like a good career move."

"Then I want two weeks in Paris. The city of love."

"Isn't it the city of light?"

She narrowed her eyes.

"Or love," he quickly amended.

"Zoe," Jordan called, "we're going to Rodeo Clown. You coming?"

"We'll be there," Gabe answered for them.

When they got to the bar, Gabe waited in a crowd to get them drinks. Jordan pulled her down to the other end of the bar to sit with them. Jordan was doing his usual grilling, questioning the band members on what they could improve when all the while he had definite opinions on what they needed to work on. She listened patiently, mostly agreeing with Jordan's assessment of what they could improve. Gabe kept looking over, looking disgruntled and out of place at the bar that catered to a young grunge crowd. It was Wade's favorite bar.

Zoe turned away from Gabe's dark scowl.

Someone's hand settled on her shoulder. She turned. Jordan.

"This tour is going to happen," Jordan said urgently. "I can feel it. Zoe, you should let your landlord go. Freedom on the road is the only way to travel. You know the long-distance thing sucks."

"That never works out," Wade put in. "Long distance is what killed my marriage." He'd received divorce papers upon returning from a six-month gig he'd taken years ago with another band. Of course, he'd also slept with a different woman in each city, so that might've had something to do with it too.

Zoe glanced over at Gabe, who'd finally gotten their drinks and was heading straight for her. His stride was confident, his expression serious. Her heart kicked up as he got closer, as she saw the heat in those dark blue eyes. "I'm not giving him up that easily," she said under her breath.

"Big mistake," Jordan said.

"Well, it's my big mistake, isn't it?" She hopped off the bar stool and went to Gabe's side. She was tired of Jordan always acting like he knew what was best for her.

CHAPTER FOURTEEN

Zoe glanced over at Gabe as he drove them home that
night. At his short slightly disheveled hair, his strong
jaw that made him look like he could handle anything.
Even, she realized now, a deep pain he kept hidden
inside.

"Gabe, when did you lose your twin?"

His jaw clenched and unclenched. "Very early. My
mom said she lost him at three months. At least I
always felt it was a him." He paused. "I know it's
strange, but I've always felt like I was missing part of
me."

"That makes sense. I can't imagine anything closer
than sharing the womb. I mean, I feel close to you just
sleeping next to each other. I imagine twins are pressed
up against each other in there."

He glanced over. "You don't think it's strange?"

"Not at all."

"No one's ever understood that about me. People

say, you're surrounded by brothers, how could you miss the brother you never really knew? I can't explain. It's just different is all. I've always missed him."

"I'm sorry."

Gabe nodded, and they drove home in companionable silence. She closed her eyes and let her mind wander, thinking of Gabe growing up with five brothers, yet always missing the one. She'd always wished she was a twin. It seemed so cool to have a close sibling going through life at your side.

When they got home, she let Fred outside and tucked him back in his crate. Gabe waited for her, took her hand, and led her straight to his bedroom. She waited, knowing he liked to take charge, but something was different about him tonight. Instead of ripping her clothes off, he wrapped his arms around her and hugged her for a very long time.

Finally, he pulled back and cupped her face with both hands. "Being with you is the first time I felt complete. The first time I didn't feel like I was missing part of me."

Her heart squeezed and tears sprang to her eyes. "Oh, Gabe."

He kissed her. "Don't die on me," he whispered fiercely. "Promise."

"I promise. Not until I'm one hundred and ten."

He scooped her up and carried her to the bed.

"Not even then."

~ ~ ~

Gabe woke Saturday morning with a naked Zoe tucked in his arms, exactly where she belonged. He nuzzled Zoe's neck, inhaling her sweet scent as she slept peacefully. He'd never felt closer to another human being, and he wasn't going to lose Zoe to Jordan or Europe. He had to nail this thing down. What he really wanted to do was marry her, get a ring on that finger before she left, but even he knew that five weeks together, even with how strongly they felt about each other, was too soon. He stroked the curve of her hip. She'd probably say no if he proposed. The only time she'd not give him a yes. She was careful that way. He understood. She had some jerks in her past, had confided that to him a few nights ago. But at thirty-five, he knew what he wanted. It was her. Case closed.

Damn, he was going to miss her. He just knew they were going on that tour. He had to make her dreams come true, so she'd have great memories of their time together and come back to him. He remembered everything she'd said she dreamed of that night when they'd stayed up late talking. She wanted her own album, to drive a Porsche, make homemade ravioli, learn to surf, and be a princess in a castle. He'd already taken care of the surfing and driving the Porsche (sort of), so today he'd ask Vinny for help with the homemade ravioli. He planned on looking into a recording studio so she could make her own album. He knew a music producer from his city-lawyer days. And while he couldn't literally make her a princess in a castle, he planned on treating her like one.

She stirred in his arms, rolled over to face him, and gave him a sleepy smile.

"Morning, sunshine," he said, already reaching for the condom. He had to replenish his supply soon. They were going through them like candy. "I'm going to make all your dreams come true."

She blinked her eyes open and glanced down at him rolling the condom on. "All of my *big* dreams?"

He chuckled, climbing on top of her, settling between her legs. "All of your dreams. I'll start with loving you." He could say love now and know she was okay with it. It was an amazing thing.

"Oh, Gabe," she said softly, wrapping her arms and legs around him.

He lost himself in her softness. He always did. She welcomed him in, body and soul, made him complete.

~ ~ ~

Gabe arranged to stop by his parents' house that

afternoon for the ravioli making. But first he took Zoe to a jewelry store known for quality diamonds.

She wouldn't get out of the car.

"Come on, Zoe. What's the problem?"

Her eyes were wide. "What are we doing here?"

He tugged on a lock of her hair. "I want to get you something."

"What?"

"Whatever you want."

"Whatever I want!" she screeched.

"Yeah, come on."

"Gabe, I don't want you to spend a lot of money on me. Seriously."

"I want to." He cupped her cheek; her skin was so soft. "I love you."

Her eyes went soft. "I love you too."

He couldn't resist kissing her. She yielded immediately, her tongue darting out, touching his. A dark pulsing throb had him wanting to get her somewhere private, but he had to make do with a hot kiss. He pulled away and gazed at her pink lips, her breathing slightly quickened, her pupils dilated. How was he supposed to let her go?

He took her hand. "I want you to wear my ring."

"Why?" she asked suspiciously.

Not the response he'd been hoping for. And for the first time he realized that she might have some insight into the way his mind worked, playing the long game, trying to anticipate pitfalls and steer around them. Because the truth was he never would've brought up a ring if she wasn't going away. It was too soon for a marriage proposal, but he wanted that ring on her finger to stake his claim. To keep Jordan and any other interested men, of which he was sure there'd be plenty, away from her. Off limits. His.

"Because I want you to have something nice," he said.

"Then I'll take an inexpensive bracelet or earrings." Her expression was serene, not argumentative at all, which made him feel even worse for all of his ulterior motives.

"The ring means more."

She frowned. "Is this a proposal? Because I didn't hear a question in there."

He gritted his teeth. "Just let me buy you a damned diamond ring."

"No."

It was the first time she'd refused him anything. "Why not?" he barked.

"Because you want to give it to me for the wrong reasons. I might not understand all of those gears cranking in that big ol' brain, but I know well enough that you're jealous of Jordan and you hate the idea of me going on this European tour. You want to stake

your claim. Like some kind of manly one-upmanship."
She deepened her voice in an impersonation of some
caveman, probably him. "Zoe mine."

The fact that she was right on the money irked
him. "It's jewelry! Women love jewelry! Excuse me for
trying to buy you something nice."

"You can't buy my love. You can't buy my fidelity.
I give those things to you on my own. If you don't
trust me enough to handle a few months away for the
opportunity of a lifetime, for my biggest dream come
true, then maybe…" His heart clutched. "Maybe we're
not—"

He couldn't bear it. He pulled her close and kissed
her tenderly, needing to show her what was in his
heart because his words were screwing everything up.
She didn't pull away. She sank into him, allowing him
to lose himself in her softness once more. He pulled
away and, without another word, put the car into gear,
and pulled out of the lot.

"You can't always shut me up with a kiss, you
know," she said.

His hands gripped the steering wheel tighter. "It
works pretty well."

"Maybe in your world kissing the daylights out of
someone and throwing money at a problem works—"

"My world?" He snorted, and she got quiet. He
glanced over to see her glaring daggers at him. He'd

never seen Zoe mad before. She was his sunshine. His cheerful, bubbly, smiling ray of light.

"But that's not going to work in this case," she bit out. "I appreciate the idea of a gift, but I feel like you're going off the rails here because what you really mean to say is that you don't want me to go."

"Fine! I don't want you to go."

"I knew it!"

"Jordan loves you. And the truth is, three months away from me, you and him together, well, it's bound to happen."

"You just assume I'll sleep with him because we're on tour? Thanks a lot. I can see you think very highly of me. And P.S. he loves me like a sister."

Gabe shook his head. "Ask him. It's obvious to everyone but you."

"You're nuts. And jealous and possessive. That's not love, Gabe. That's just creepy."

"You think I'm creepy? Because I have perfectly normal feelings of jealousy when another man is moving in on my woman?"

She gestured wildly. "There are so many things wrong with that sentence I don't even know where to begin."

"How about you begin with the fact that you can't admit there might be something going on with Jordan? Why don't you admit you can't commit to me because of him?"

"I'm not admitting to things that aren't true."

His jaw clenched. "You're mine. In every way. Body and soul. Especially body."

"You're a freaking Neanderthal."

"Nice."

"This tour isn't even definite! All this fighting, all this Neanderthal posturing over nothing. At least now I know how you really are."

"And how is that?"

"Unsupportive and jealous. Maybe you don't want me to have success because you're not happy with your own life."

The accusation stung. Not the unsupportive jealous part because he admitted that he wanted nothing more than to keep her with him always and would do battle with any man that tried to come between them. But the fact that she thought he would hold her back because his own career sucked. Sure, his law practice was a joke. Half the time he didn't even get paid. He was more arbitrator than legal counsel, working through neighborly problems. Dammit, he didn't want to be that man. But he didn't want to go back to his old life either. What the hell was he doing with his life?

"You're right," he finally said. "I was jealous and unsupportive."

"Thank you."

"I'll stay out of your way."

"Good."

They drove to his parents' house in silence, the only sound the radio playing in the background. He pulled into the driveway and turned to her. "Let's go make ravioli."

She nodded, her expression grim, and got out of the car.

~ ~ ~

Vinny greeted Zoe at the door with a hug, making her feel a little better after that tense car ride with Gabe. She understood that Gabe didn't like the idea of her going away, but how could she turn down the big break she'd been waiting for her whole life?

Vinny rubbed his hands together. "Ready to cook?"

"Ready!" Zoe said.

"Zoe's going on a European tour," Gabe said.

"It's not definite," Zoe said, giving Gabe a look.

"European tour?" Vinny exclaimed. "Come in here, sweetheart." He gestured toward the kitchen. "I want to hear all about it."

Vinny led them to the kitchen and poured them each a glass of Chianti. "Salute," Vinny said. "To your health and big congrats."

"Salute," Gabe and Zoe said, clinking glasses. Zoe took a sip of wine and set it down because it tasted sour.

"Speaking of health…" Gabe started.

Vinny cut him off. "We're speaking of Zoe's European tour."

Zoe filled him in on Hep Six and her band while Gabe just stood there glowering, which made her babble on and on. When she finished, Gabe turned to Vinny. "I'm hoping she'll marry me when she returns."

Zoe stiffened. What was Gabe doing telling his stepdad something like that before they'd even had a chance to really talk about it? They still hadn't made it past eight weeks.

"A daughter who can sing." Vinny's eyes watered. "Now all I need is some grandchildren, and I can die a happy man."

"Don't talk about dying," Gabe said tightly.

"It's a figure of speech," Vinny said. "I told you I'm fine." He rubbed his hands together. "All right, let's get started. I made the dough ahead of time, so all we have to do is the fun part."

He sprinkled the counter with flour and had Zoe help him press it into a rectangle.

"It's nice to have someone to pass this knowledge onto," Vinny said. "Angel's the only one who's shown any interest."

"Now Gabe will learn too," Zoe said.

"I'll try my best," Gabe said, his voice rough and gravelly. Zoe knew he was thinking again of Vinny's illness.

Vinny expertly ran the dough through the pasta machine, making thin sheets. He had her try too. "Pull and stretch it a bit when it comes out. Not too much."

"This is fun," Zoe said, smiling at Gabe. He didn't smile back.

"We have to do it a few more times," Vinny said. "Until it's so thin you can see your hand through it. You want to take a crack at it, Gabe?"

"I'll just watch," Gabe said.

Vinny lay out the long sheet of pasta on the counter. "Next is the egg wash," he said as he quickly beat an egg with some water. He brushed the wash over the pasta. "It works like glue. Then the filling." He went to the refrigerator for the ingredients. "Very important that you get everything fresh."

He mixed up the filling quickly, not measuring anything.

"Wait," Gabe said. "How do we know how much to put in of each thing?"

"Just eyeball it," Vinny said. "Get the right proportions."

"Like two parts ricotta to one part basil?" Gabe

asked.

Vinny held up the bowl. "Like that."

"That's clear as mud," Gabe muttered.

Vinny showed them how much filling to put on half the sheet of dough, and Zoe helped him add it.

"Now we cover it," Vinny said. He folded the other half of the dough on top of the filling. "Press out the air pockets around the filling." Zoe joined him. "Good, Zoe, you're a natural."

When they'd finished, Vinny pulled out a couple of knives to cut the ravioli into squares and demonstrated how to cut. "You take over," he told Zoe.

Zoe quickly cut squares of ravioli. She was really looking forward to eating this. She hadn't had homemade ravioli in forever.

"How're you feeling?" Gabe asked Vinny.

"Fine, fine," Vinny said.

"Did you get the test results?" Gabe asked.

"Bah. It's nothing. Don't worry about it."

A long silence followed. Zoe looked up from her cutting. Gabe was scowling.

"You're good at hiding the truth, huh, Vinny?" Gabe asked.

Zoe froze at the tone in Gabe's voice.

Vinny narrowed his eyes. "What's that supposed to mean?"

"You're acting like you're fine when you're not. You're hiding a big secret. But you don't let on. Not at all."

"I don't like your tone," Vinny said. "I don't want you to worry. That's all there is to it."

A beat passed before Gabe finally said, "I found the letters. I know about your other secret."

"What are you talking about?" Vinny asked.

"The letters you wrote to Mom when she was still married to my father."

"That's private," Vinny snapped. "Did you read them?"

The two men glared at each other, and Zoe wished Gabe wouldn't have brought this up when she was caught in the middle.

"I read one," Gabe said. "That told me enough to know about the three-year affair."

Vinny's eyes were hard and direct. "It's none of your business."

"You made it my business when you destroyed my family," Gabe fired back.

"What are you doing?" Zoe asked Gabe.

Vinny scoffed. "Is that what you think I did? Baloney. Your mother was miserable. I made her happy. End of story."

"And you destroyed a marriage," Gabe said.

"That marriage was dead for years. Everything

worked out."

"For you. My father died alone."

Vinny took a deep breath. "Gabe, I'm sorry about that, but that has nothing to do with me and your mother."

"I think it has a hell of a lot to do with you two."

Vinny glanced at Zoe. "Maybe we should talk about this another time."

"Zoe already knows how things went down."

"Drop it," Vinny said.

Gabe put his hands up. "Forget I said anything. This family loves secrets."

"So this is a fun Saturday making ravioli, huh?" Vinny asked, planting his hands on his hips. "Well, not to me." He left.

Gabe stormed out of the house. Zoe stood there for a moment before she set down the knife and followed Gabe out the door.

~ ~ ~

"Let's go," Gabe said, already getting into his car. He had to get out of there and fast. He felt like his world was caving in on him. People he loved were slipping away from him no matter how much he tried to hang on. He knew Vinny was hiding the truth—he was dying. And Zoe was leaving. He'd finally found peace and now everything was going to hell again.

Zoe got in. "I know you're worried about your stepdad. Why're you getting so mad at him?"

Gabe clenched his jaw. He couldn't talk about it without breaking down.

She let out a long breath. "I'm sorry about Vinny. Maybe it won't be as bad as you're imagining it—"

"You have no idea what you're talking about. Obviously it's bad or he would've told us what the test results said. He's hiding it. Just like before."

"Gabe—"

"You're leaving, he's dying. I can't take anymore."

"I'm sure he's not dying—"

"You don't know that," he barked.

She got quiet.

When they pulled into the driveway, Gabe turned off the car and just sat there, staring at the steering wheel. Everything hurt, and he just wanted it to stop.

She touched his arm. "Gabe?"

He stared straight ahead. "If you go on tour, I think it would be easier just to say goodbye." But what he really wanted to say was *don't go.*

"Easier?" she asked in a shaky voice. He turned, and her expression went from incredulous to furious in a flash. "You're breaking up with me? From 'wear my ring' to dumping me?" She smacked his arm hard. "You suck," she said in a choked voice. "Don't talk to me ever again!"

She got out of the car, and he quickly followed. "Zoe, wait! I said *if* you go—"

"Don't talk to me!" She stalked off.

He stood there for a moment, trying to figure out what he was supposed to do. Had they really just broken up? He'd said *if*. The tour wasn't even definite. She'd find out on Monday. What if she didn't even get the gig, and they broke up for nothing? Should he fake support the possibility of the gig? Nah, she'd just get madder if it turned out she did get it.

Maybe he could still reason with her. He shouldn't have said that.

Bam! The door to her apartment slammed closed. There was no way he could reason with her now.

He scrubbed a hand over his face. How had he gone from making her dreams come true to broken up?

CHAPTER FIFTEEN

Gabe went home for another mandatory family dinner the next night in a foul mood. Zoe wasn't speaking to him. His stepdad was likely dying, and he was still mad about the affair that broke up his family. He'd tried to talk to Zoe again today, hoping she'd had a chance to calm down. She'd refused to have a reasonable conversation.

He'd stopped by her place earlier. "Tell me if you hear any news tomorrow."

She narrowed her eyes at him. "Why? So we can pick up where we left off if I didn't get the gig?"

That sounded excellent. "Yes."

She slammed the door in his face. Apparently that had been the wrong answer.

Now he walked in the front door of his parents' house, bracing himself for long faces and an even longer night. Lucky for him, Angel met him in the small foyer.

"Hey," Angel said with a smile. "How're you? Did you bring Zoe?"

"She's not speaking to me."

Angel winced. "Sorry. She seemed nice." He looked down and then met his eyes. "What'd you do?"

"Nothing!" Gabe barked.

Angel shifted uneasily. "Eh. It's probably for the best. Tonight could get emotional with Dad's big news. I'm praying it's good news."

Gabe lowered his voice. "You know it's cancer. The only question is how bad."

Angel crossed his arms. "We don't know that for sure."

"Why else would he be so secretive and wait until Sunday dinner? He's trying to break the bad news when we're all together to help each other through it. You know, have someone to lean on."

"Maybe he got good test results." Angel's chin jutted out. "Ever think of that?"

"No."

"It wouldn't hurt you to put a little positive energy out there."

Gabe thumped Angel on the back. "That's what we have you for."

"Hey, Beast, where's Beauty?" Nico called from where he was sitting on the sofa in the living room.

"I don't know," Gabe muttered.

"Giving him the silent treatment," Angel answered for Gabe.

"Wanna beer?" Nico asked.

"Hell yeah," Gabe replied.

The three of them headed to the kitchen. After they'd each popped the cap off one of Vinny's Sierra Nevada pale ales, Nico turned to Gabe. "Did you apologize?"

"Why do you automatically assume I'm the one who has to apologize?" Gabe asked.

Nico gave him a pitying look. "The man always has to apologize. Women one-oh-one."

"He's right," Angel put in.

Gabe shoved a hand in his hair. "She's going on a three-month European tour with a guy who's in love with her. All I asked was that she wear my ring."

"What ring?" Nico asked.

Gabe's lips formed a flat line. "The diamond ring I wanted to buy her."

Nico held up a hand. "Whoa, back it up. You proposed to her?"

Angel cocked his head. "After just meeting her?"

"I didn't just meet her, dope," Gabe said. He didn't mention it had only been five weeks. A man had to do what a man had to do.

"Lady troubles, Gabe?" Vince boomed as he went straight to the fridge for his own beer.

Great. Now he'd butt his nose in.

Vince snagged the bottle opener off the counter and popped off the top. "Let me guess. You want her to wear the ring to scare away other men."

"Fuck you all," Gabe muttered, taking a long swallow of beer.

"You know nothing about women," Vince said.

"Like you know so much," Gabe shot back. "You never have anyone sticking around."

"Maybe I don't want anyone sticking around." Vince smiled and took a pull on his beer. "Maybe I like being a play-uh."

Nico snickered.

"That's really not safe," Angel put in. He lowered his voice. "I hope you're using protection."

Vince snorted. "Yes, Father Marino. I'm using protection. When are you gonna get laid?"

"Who's getting laid?" Jared asked, arriving in the kitchen with Luke on his heels.

"Beer time, eh?" Luke said, snagging two beers and handing one to Jared.

"Who's not getting laid is the better question," Nico said, pointing his beer bottle toward Gabe and Angel.

"Angel's got to get his hands dirty," Jared said, elbowing Angel.

"Stop polishing that halo," Luke said.

"He's polishing something all right," Vince said. "And, Gabe, I can't believe you screwed things up with Zoe so fast. She is fine. Mm-mm-mm. Some sweet—"

Gabe grabbed him by the shirt and hauled him up close. "Don't say one more word about her."

Vince swiped his arm off him in one quick block. Gabe and Vince glared at each other.

"What's this?" their dad said, coming into the room. "You guys finished off my six-pack before I even got one?"

"Shoulda got two six-packs," Jared said.

"Here, you can have mine," Angel offered.

"Bah. I don't want yours," their dad said. "Backwash."

Angel wiped it off with the bottom of his shirt and offered it again.

Their dad looked around, nodding and smiling. "It's nice to see my boys getting along, sharing a brewski. Ah. Gimme a sip." He gestured for Angel's beer. "Don't tell your mother. She doesn't want me drinking now that I've got this health thing."

The men went silent. Guilt swamped Gabe. Why had he brought up that stupid letter with his stepdad? He was just mad at him for being sick, which wasn't his fault. He'd apologize as soon as he could get a moment alone with him.

"So what were we talking about?" their dad asked.

"Sports, politics, women?"

"Gabe screwed up with Zoe," Angel supplied helpfully.

"We were talking about the Knicks," Gabe said.

"Let me guess," Luke said. "She's too argumentative. You lawyer types don't want to argue once you get home."

"Not at all," Gabe said quietly. She was perfect, and he'd screwed up. But he could never tell his brothers that. They'd just razz him and give him a hard time and none of them knew shit about women beyond how to seduce them. Except Angel. He was devoted to one woman, a widow he would never touch out of respect for his dead best friend.

"All right," their dad said. "I'm gonna get dinner started. If you're not helping, get out. You can help out your mom. She's in our room going through all our clothes to make a donation to the St. Francis clothing drive. Make sure she doesn't throw out my lucky bowling shirt."

Everyone left the kitchen but Angel. An hour and a half later, they were all seated around the table. His stepdad had made homemade manicotti, which delicious, but Gabe couldn't help thinking of Zoe and how she'd helped make that ravioli. She didn't even get to eat it, thanks to him. Damn, everything made him think of her. He glared at his plate, wishing he could have a do-over with Zoe. Just have Saturday take two, where he kept it all about her and making her dreams come true.

And then his stepdad finally dropped the big news, and all Gabe could think about was how much he wanted Zoe at his side, holding his hand to help him get through the pain.

"It's stage two," his stepdad said. "That's not too bad, I guess. The doc gives me an eighty-seven percent chance of survival."

The family went absolutely silent. Gabe broke into a cold sweat. Even though he'd been expecting bad news, actually hearing it still shook him up.

Jared finally spoke up. "What's the doctor recommending for treatment?"

"Surgery," his stepdad said. "He wants to take out the section with the tumor, reconnect everything, test some of the nearby lymph nodes. Maybe chemo. We don't know yet."

"This is bullshit," Vince said, throwing his napkin down.

"Please, boys, er, men," his stepdad said, putting a hand up. "It'll be okay. And don't be like me. Get your colonoscopy at age fifty. I shouldn't have waited so long."

His mom stood. "You know what's bullshit?"

The room fell into shocked silence. His mom

never cursed and rarely got angry.

"That reaction," she said, pointing at Vince, who immediately looked contrite. "I expect better from the rest of you. When your dad shares news like…" Her voice got choked, and then her lip wobbled. His stepdad reached for her hand.

"Ma," Angel said.

She burst into tears and ran from the room.

"Excuse me," his stepdad said, following her.

The room went silent again. Gabe wiped the sweat off his face and took a long drink of water before he asked, "What's it mean, Jare? How bad is it?"

"Is he going to die?" Angel asked.

"We're all gonna die," Luke said.

"Shut up, moron," Vince snapped.

Jared told them what he knew. That chemo wasn't always needed for stage two. "I'm going to find another doctor for a second opinion before we go that route. I'll talk to Dad."

"I'll help any way I can," Gabe said. His throat was so tight he could barely breathe.

"Me too," Angel said.

Nico and Luke grumbled their agreement.

One by one, the brothers left the table, each to deal with the news in their own way. Gabe looked around for his stepdad and his mom to say goodbye and discovered they were in their bedroom with the door shut. He could hear his mom speaking in soft tones. He gave them their privacy. He'd call tomorrow.

Gabe drove straight home and pounded on Zoe's door until she opened it. He pushed his way in, afraid she'd slam the door in his face again.

"Vinny has stage two cancer," he choked out.

"I'm so sorry." She wrapped her arms around him, and he felt like he could breathe again.

~ ~ ~

Zoe let Gabe spend the night. Her anger with him dissolved the minute she saw the devastated look on his face. He was quiet, somber, already mourning his stepdad. He didn't want to talk about it, so she did her best just to be there for him. Fred was a nice distraction, and Gabe spent a good amount of time tossing Fred his squeaky bone toy. They watched some TV together, and Zoe finally got up the nerve to ask Gabe about his stepdad. "Did the doctor say anything about his prognosis?" she asked gently.

"He has an eighty-seven percent survival rate," Gabe said, staring at the TV.

"Gabe, that's great!"

He looked at her. "There's nothing great about cancer. Especially if he needs chemo too. That's very hard on the body. Jared's looking into a second opinion if it comes to that."

"I know. But honestly I think he's going to be okay. Those are really great odds."

He was quiet for a long moment. "Do you play the odds?"

"I don't know what you mean."

"Do you bet on the long shot, or go for the sure thing?"

Somehow she felt like her answer meant something significant to Gabe. She considered the question, her life spent in pursuit of a dream. "Definitely the long shot."

His eyes burned into hers. "I go for the sure thing."

She swallowed hard. "The reward is greater for the long shot."

"Sometimes." He pulled her into his lap. "Sometimes you have to balance risk and reward."

"What are you trying to say?"

"I want to go for the long shot." His arms wrapped around her. "With you."

"I'm a sure thing," she joked. "One kiss and I'm mush."

He cupped her cheek and kissed her tenderly. "Zoe, will you marry me?"

She leaped off his lap. "Why?"

"Because life's short, and I love you and want to

spend the rest of my life knowing I have you to come home to."

Her heart was racing. She tried to think it through. Earlier he'd been intent on getting her to wear his ring in a fit of jealousy.

"Does this have anything to do with me going on tour?" She paced in front of the sofa. "I mean if we get the gig."

"That plays a part," he said. "Maybe I would've waited a little longer to ask. But there's no question in my mind that I would one day ask."

She stopped pacing. "Why?"

"I just told you why. I've never felt like this with anyone before. I'm a sure thing for you. You go for the sure thing, I'll go for the long shot. Maybe we'll meet in the middle."

She wrung her hands together. "You're saying all the right things, but this just feels wrong. The timing with your stepdad and my tour."

He snagged her hand and pulled her into his lap again. "You need time to think about it."

"Yes."

"I'm not going anywhere." He kissed a hot trail along her cheek, her jawline. She tipped her head, relaxing into his embrace, her last thought that he might not be going anywhere, but she was. And then she stopped thinking as he pushed her back on the sofa, taking his time with her as he peeled off her clothes and worshipped her with his hands and mouth.

How could she tell him no when every cell in her body told him yes?

~ ~ ~

Gabe had Zoe right where he wanted her an hour later, naked in bed with him spooning her from behind. Being with Zoe made him feel alive, and he needed that reassurance right now with the way it felt death had caught up with him. He could push the old fear away, keep the panic down when he had her in his arms. It wasn't that late. Nine or so. He knew he should let her rest, but he already wanted to go for round two.

He pushed her hair back and kissed her temple. "Are you still mad about the ring?"

She looked at him over her shoulder. "Do you still want to say goodbye if I go on tour?"

"No."

She turned in his arms. "Then I'm not mad about the ring."

He rolled on top of her, entwining his fingers with hers and pulling them over her head. "Does that mean you'll wear my ring?"

"Please, Gabe, let's wait. I want to make sure we're doing this for the right reasons."

"We are."

"It's too soon."

He kissed her with all the love he was feeling, and she returned the kiss with equal passion. He couldn't stop kissing her. Her cell phone rang, and she made a small squeak. He lifted his head, still keeping her pinned underneath him. "Don't answer it."

"Jordan said he'd call either tonight or early tomorrow with the verdict!"

He knew it was silly to postpone the inevitable. He let her go.

She rolled out of bed and snagged her cell off the kitchen counter. "What's the news?"

She yelped and did a bouncing dance in place. Gabe put his arm over his eyes, working hard to move to supportive-boyfriend mode. She did a series of uh-huhs and hung up. "We got it!"

He sat up and smiled. "Congratulations."

She cocked her head to the side. "Be happy for me. This is what I've been working toward my whole life. Big audiences, name recognition, everything! Touring with Hep Six is going to open the door for so many opportunities."

"When do you leave?" His voice came out harsher than he'd intended. He swallowed past the lump in his throat.

"Three weeks," she said, her smile fading. "Jordan says they want us out there for two weeks of rehearsal before we start the tour. April twenty-fifth through the end of July are confirmed. They might add August dates back in the States if there's interest." She looked at him; her earlier happiness faded.

He hadn't meant to make that smile dim. He pushed down his own feelings. "C'mere." He opened his arms to her with a smile.

She ran back to him and leaped on top of him. He wrapped his arms around her. She propped herself up on his chest and stroked his hair, probably trying to soothe him. "Please be happy."

"If you're happy, I'm happy."

"I am." She beamed. "Gabe, I'm so, so happy." He wished his marriage proposal had made her this happy, but he could wait. He had to wait.

"Then I'm happy too." He rolled, pinning her beneath him, wanting to cement his hold on her. "We'll marry as soon as you get back from your tour."

"We'll talk about it."

He kissed her. "You always say yes when I've got you naked in bed."

"That's because I can barely speak."

He buried his face in her neck, inhaling her scent, trying to memorize all of her. He kissed her again because his body told her better than his words how he felt. He claimed her, thoroughly, desperately, with the unsettling feeling that no matter how much he hung onto her, she would still slip through his fingers.

CHAPTER SIXTEEN

"I'm ho-o-o-me!" Zoe called as she let herself into her parents' house for lunch on Monday.

"In the kitchen!" her mom said.

Zoe rushed into the kitchen, already smiling so hard her cheeks hurt. "We did it! We're going on tour with Hep Six!"

Her mom whooped and hugged her.

"I knew it!" her dad exclaimed, wrapping his arms around both of them. "Finally! Jordan really came through."

Zoe pulled away. "What do you mean Jordan came through?"

"He got you the gig, didn't he?" her dad asked.

"He got them to listen, but it was our sound that they liked."

"We're so happy for you," her mom said, smoothing things over for her dad as usual.

"I knew your break was just around the corner,"

her dad said. "You finally made the big time."

Zoe tensed. "So if I didn't get this tour, would you say I was small potatoes?"

"Now, Zoe—" her mom started.

Her dad frowned. "I don't know what's got you all worked up, girl. This is a happy occasion."

"I am happy," Zoe said. "I just…I don't know. I hope you didn't see me as a failure up to this point."

"Why would you think that?" her mom said.

Zoe felt tears threaten, and she forced them back. "Just because you were in the movies, Dad was on TV, Jaz was on Broadway, and I was playing clubs and waitressing."

"But you were working, following your dream," her dad said. "And it paid off."

"What if I had gone indie? Just put out my own album online."

Her dad's brows drew together. "Like anyone with a computer could do? You've worked much too hard to settle for the likes of that. After this tour, the record companies will be calling you, mark my words. You'll have a label behind you like that." He snapped his fingers.

Zoe deflated further. "And what if I don't?"

"C'mon, let's have lunch, and you can tell us all about the tour," her mom said.

Zoe followed her mom to the kitchen table, feeling

somehow like her good news was too little too late.

~ ~ ~

Gabe went in to see his stepdad at the hospital as soon as he was allowed visitors. He stopped short in the doorway. Vinny, who'd always seemed larger than life, looked almost fragile tucked into the hospital bed. His mom and his brother Vince were already there.

He crossed to his stepdad's side. "How'd the surgery go?"

"Hey, Gabe," his stepdad said in a tired, weak voice. "Went all right."

"Do you need chemo?" Gabe asked.

"Still waiting to hear on that," he replied.

"The doctor said the surgery went very well, and they think they got all of it," his mom put in. "That's the best news we could hope for."

"How's Zoe?" his stepdad asked.

"She's good, Dad."

"You deserve to be happy. I couldn't have asked for a better son." He closed his eyes.

Gabe's heart clutched. His stepdad had been saying a lot of things lately that sounded like heartfelt goodbyes. He glanced up to find his brother glaring at him.

"What about me, Dad?" Vince asked, but their dad didn't respond. "Your firstborn."

"I think he needs to rest," their mom whispered. "I'll call you when he wakes up."

Gabe took one last look at his stepdad and left. Vince went with him a moment later.

"How's it feel to be the golden child?" Vince asked.

"I'm sure he would say the same to all of us," Gabe replied calmly. "He's tired from the surgery. Give him a break."

They stopped in front of the elevator and waited in tense silence. Then they got on with a few other passengers and took the ride down.

Vince waited until they got to the parking lot before saying, "I came here to see my father and instead I get pushed aside for the golden child, the rich lawyer. Why can't you be more like Gabe? he asks. Why can't you study harder? Go to college like your brother."

Gabe turned, surprised. "He said that?"

"Yeah, thanks for that. Thanks for being the perfect son he never had."

"I'm not perfect, Vince."

"You know how badly I wanted to kick your ass growing up?"

"You did kick my ass."

"Nah. Not really. Not nearly as much as I wanted to."

"Well, we're at the hospital." He spread his arms wide. "Take your best shot. I'll just check into the E.R. when you're done."

Vince got up close. "You think I won't?"

"The point is," Gabe drawled. "I don't care. In fact, you'd be doing me a favor." He'd rather have his body hurt than the wrenching pain in his heart over his stepdad in the hospital and Zoe about to leave him. He raised his chin. "C'mon, hit me."

Vince pulled back his fist and feinted a punch to the jaw, ending with a soft nudge. "You didn't flinch."

"I told you I don't care."

"What the hell is wrong with you? You should care. I've got serious body mass on you. I could take you down in two seconds flat."

Gabe shoved him away, but Vince didn't budge. "You know, just because you can't love anybody but yourself doesn't mean Dad is the same way, you selfish bastard."

Vince shoved Gabe, but Gabe stood his ground. "I never once complained about you calling my mother Ma," Gabe said. "Yet you still can't deal with your father being Dad to the rest of us."

"I didn't have a mother," Vince spat. "You had a father. Why do you get to have both?"

"It's not a zero-sum game," Gabe said.

"What the hell is that supposed to mean?" Vince

hollered.

"It means me gaining a dad doesn't mean you lost a dad."

"That's bullshit. You got two dads, and I got a lot less of my one dad. Don't tell me that's not a zero sum. I lost, and you won."

Gabe gave up trying to get through Vince's thick skull. His brother was stubborn, and if he hadn't gotten over the stepbrother thing by now, he never would.

"Bye, Vince." Gabe headed to his car.

"Don't you walk away from me!" Vince hollered.

Gabe kept going. If Vince was going to lay into him, he would've done it by now.

"I still want to kick your ass, golden boy!" Vince called.

Gabe gave him the one-finger salute and got into his car.

~ ~ ~

Zoe woke up Saturday morning with a smile on her face for several reasons—all due to Gabe. First of all, he was doing his best to be supportive of her going on tour, even though she knew it was hard for him. And last night he'd gone to rehearsal with her and praised her up and down as the next big thing. Not to mention how he surprised her when they got back to his place.

He'd installed a pet door right off the kitchen. "So Fred can come and go whenever he needs to. I'll, uh, watch him when you're away. He already knows me, and he's used to it here—"

She threw her arms around him. "Fred would love that. Thank you!"

He shifted her and pointed out where he'd placed baby gates to keep Fred confined to the kitchen area at night or when they were out.

If she hadn't been falling for Gabe before, that sealed the deal.

Now she snuggled into Gabe's arms. He was, as usual, spooning her from behind. She was so used to that now it was going to be hard to sleep alone again. She turned in his arms. His eyes were still closed. "Gabe, you awake?"

He didn't respond.

"I love you so much," she whispered. "I have this stupid idea that we have to make it past eight weeks before it's real. Just because it seems like everything ends then, and wouldn't you know it, I'm leaving on our eight-week anniversary, but I'm not going to worry about that anymore. I'm just going to enjoy every single minute we have left." She took a deep breath. "And I'm going to look forward to the day I see you again after my tour. Though I'm still hoping you'll visit. Please visit." She wrapped her arms tight around him, and he mumbled something.

She pulled back a little. "What'd you say?"

"Mmm…today's going to be a good day." He stroked her cheek. "Especially since I'm not letting you leave this bed until we visit my stepdad."

"Gabe! I can't stay in bed all day."

"I want you," he growled, pulling her leg over his, making her feel how much he wanted her.

"Can I shower at least?" she asked in mock outrage.

"Of course you can shower." His hand slid over her bottom. "With me."

"You're hard to refuse," she breathed.

He yanked the covers off her. "I only want to hear yes."

"Yes."

He flashed a quick smile before dropping down to her ankles, where he began kissing his way hungrily up to her inner thigh, using his tongue and teeth, with occasional nips that had her jolting. Then he settled between her legs, pulled her legs over his shoulders, and pushed forward, spreading her wider with his shoulders. "Scream my name," he ordered.

"Yes," she hissed out as his mouth closed over her throbbing sex.

She gave him everything he wanted every time.

And loved every shuddering minute.

Much later, after they'd showered and she was a limp, clean noodle, she wrapped herself in a robe—Gabe liked to keep her in as little clothing as possible—and headed down to the kitchen, where Gabe had started breakfast. He had pancakes going.

"I smell bacon," she said in wonder. "I thought you didn't cook."

He turned, one corner of his mouth turning up. "Shane gave me a cooking lesson on Wednesday when you were working. Surprise."

"Are you serious?"

"I have to keep up your strength."

She shook her head with a smile and sat at the kitchen island. Gabe delivered a thick mug of divine coffee to her and returned to the stove. She wrapped her fingers around the mug, feeling all kinds of content. Usually she was so restless, always looking for the next big thing. With Gabe, she felt settled. A short while later, he motioned for her to follow to the dining room, placing a stack of pancakes, eggs, and bacon in front of her. There was a swirl of whipped cream on top. She could get used to this. She dug in. He went back to the kitchen to get something. Syrup, she figured. Then she startled when she heard a pop. Was that champagne?

"Champagne at breakfast?" she called to the other

room. "Is this heaven?"

He chuckled. "I hope so." He reappeared with two flutes of champagne and joined her at the table.

She lifted her glass to toast him and froze. "Gabe."

"Yes?"

"Something's in my drink."

He sipped his champagne, with a smile playing over his lips. "You don't say."

She stuck her fingers in the glass and pulled out a marquis diamond ring set in platinum. Her jaw dropped. A diamond of this size must've cost a fortune. She stared at it, speechless. Gabe took her hand and slipped the ring on her finger. "Zoe, marry me. Say yes one more time for me."

She burst into tears because she was leaving him for three whole months, and she was going to miss him so, so much. The next thing she knew she was in his lap, and his arms were wrapped around her. He kissed her tears. "Please don't cry. It's a happy time. Is that a yes?"

"I'm going to miss you so much," she choked out.

"We won't waste a single minute. We still have two weeks."

"It's passing by too quickly."

"Which is exactly why I'm keeping you in bed as much as possible. Eat. You're going to need your strength to keep up with me." He turned her in his lap to face the table and pulled her plate in front of her. She ate with Gabe's arm securely around her waist. Her ring flashed as she ate and every time she looked at it, her eyes welled up again.

She had to give it back. Because for the first time, she didn't want to go on that tour.

~ ~ ~

Several hours later, Gabe walked Zoe into his parents' house. His stepdad was home from the hospital, and Gabe wanted to tell him the happy news.

His mom met them at the door. "Shh, he's sleeping. Come on in. Have a seat."

They followed her into the living room. He helped Zoe off with her coat and his mom exclaimed, "What a ring! Gabe?"

Gabe smiled and nodded. "Yup."

"Oh, I'm so happy for you two! Congratulations!" She hugged him and then hugged Zoe. His mom took a seat in the nearby chair and gestured for them to sit on the sofa. "I can't wait to tell your dad. He really took a shine to you, Zoe. He'll be glad to know his ravioli recipe is safe with you."

"Sure is," Zoe replied in a soft voice.

Gabe studied Zoe, puzzling over that soft voice because he only ever heard it in bed or when he came on strong with her. With most people, she was bubbly, cheery sunshine. Oh, shit, had he pushed her into this? She hadn't said yes to his proposal, but he figured her tears meant she was overwhelmed with emotion. The good kind.

"Zoe?" he asked.

She turned. "Hmm?"

"You okay?"

She glanced at his mom. "I'm fine."

"This calls for a toast," his mom said. "I'll be right back."

His mom left.

Gabe grabbed Zoe's hand and kissed it. "Are you having second thoughts?"

"I'm having a lot of thoughts," she said.

He kissed her, and then because her lips were so soft and sweet, he kissed her again.

"Here we are!" His mom carried in a bottle of chardonnay and some glasses. "This is all we had. We'll get champagne for the next family dinner, where we'll tell everyone the good news together. I'm so excited to have my very first daughter."

Zoe smiled. "Thank you, Mrs. Marino."

"Call me Allie, I insist." She poured the drinks and lifted her glass for a toast. "To lifelong happiness and many grandchildren."

Gabe laughed and toasted his mom. He turned to Zoe to toast, but she looked a little pale. "What's wrong?"

She set her glass down. "I'm sorry. I'm not feeling well. Where's your bathroom?"

"Second door on the right," his mom said, pointing the way. Zoe rushed from the room.

"Is she pregnant?" his mom asked.

Gabe's head snapped back. "What? No, she's not pregnant. Why would you say that?" He used protection every time. There was no way she was pregnant.

His mom gave him a look. "I'm asking because you've only been dating a short time and when I pulled the wine out, she suddenly looked nauseous. I just don't want you to marry for the wrong reasons."

"I'm marrying her because I love her."

Zoe had sipped the champagne this morning and stopped, saying it tasted sour from the ring. It probably had. Why would his mom think he was marrying Zoe because she was pregnant? And that's when it hit him—the truth he should've seen much earlier.

"Like you," he said. "You were pregnant with me. That's why you married Dad."

His mom set her glass down and looked at her hands.

"I'm right, aren't I?" he pressed. "I always wondered why you married him."

His mom met his eyes. "Yes, that's why. We had a few good years, when you boys were little, but then he, well, let's just say he loved work a lot more than he loved me."

"Why did you wait so long to leave Dad? I mean, I saw that letter where Vinny said three years was long enough."

She shook her head. "I really wish you hadn't read my private letters, Gabriel."

"I'm sorry. It was just the one. I'll give them back to you."

She waved that away and sighed. "I tried to keep my marriage going long enough for you boys to be out of the house. I really, really tried. In the end, I couldn't do it. Three years was me waffling on leaving the marriage while Vinny waited patiently. Now that's love. He didn't know if I'd ever divorce your father. I knew it would disrupt your life. I so wanted everything to be perfect for you boys."

"But it wasn't," Gabe said.

"Your dad didn't know what to do with kids. He understood money and work. He certainly never understood me."

Zoe came back in. "Am I interrupting?"

"Not at all," his mom said. "Have a seat. How are you feeling?"

Zoe smiled. "Better. I think the bacon didn't settle

well."

"I cooked breakfast for the first time," Gabe said sheepishly. "Maybe it was undercooked."

His mom's eyes widened. "Well, good for you, cooking breakfast."

"Allie," his stepdad called.

His mom stood. "Coming!" She turned to them. "I'll come get you when he's ready." She hurried from the room.

Gabe turned to Zoe. "Are you pregnant?"

Her mouth formed a perfect O of surprise. "What? No!"

He grunted. "My mom thought maybe you were."

"I told you it was the bacon."

He lowered his voice. "When was your last period?"

She flushed. "Gabe! You're embarrassing me."

"It's just us. Tell me."

"I'm not telling you that. Change the subject!"

"I don't want any secrets between us."

She crossed her arms. "Well, too bad."

He studied her. "We've been having sex for two weeks straight."

"Would you be quiet?" she hissed.

"We've got two more weeks before you leave," he went on. "If you haven't gotten it by then, then I'll know for sure."

"There's nothing to know! I'm not always regular. I'm not even late! Can we please stop talking about this?"

"Okay, okay."

She settled down again.

"Are you sure?" he couldn't help but ask.

She wrapped her hands around his neck and pretended to strangle him. He kissed her quick. Then he kissed her slow because she was never more mellow and agreeable than when he kissed her. She melted against him, all softness again.

"Gabe, Zoe, you can come in now!" his mom called.

He took Zoe's hand and pulled her up off the sofa. When they got to his parents' bedroom, Vinny was sitting up in bed with pillows propped up behind him. A remote and glass of water sat nearby on the nightstand. He still looked a little pale, but he greeted them warmly. "So I hear it's official. Let me see that rock, Zoe."

Zoe crossed to his side and dutifully held out her hand.

"Nice work here, Gabe," Vinny said. "Congratulations. Can't say that I'm surprised. Gabe hinted as much last time you were here. Have you told your folks?"

Zoe shifted, glancing around the room, before

saying, "No. Just you two."

"Well, I'm sure they'll be very happy to have Gabe as a son-in-law."

"Actually, he hasn't met them yet," Zoe said.

"Well, I know them from around town," Gabe said. "I talked to your dad when you moved into the apartment."

"But you haven't met them as my boyfriend," she said. "That's okay. No big."

"We'll go there right after this," Gabe assured her.

Zoe didn't reply. Instead she sat on the side of the bed and told his stepdad all about the songs they were rehearsing for the tour. His mom shot him another look that he couldn't interpret, but his gut was doing a slow churn that said something wasn't right with his fiancée situation.

Chapter Seventeen

Zoe drove back to Clover Park with Gabe, wondering how in the world she was supposed to give back this ring now that he'd told his parents. She should've given it back before they left the house, but he'd been so happy, she hadn't had the heart to throw it back in his face.

"What's your parents' address?" Gabe asked.

"I don't want to tell my parents just yet," she said.

"Why not?"

"Because they haven't even gotten the chance to get to know you or us as a couple. I can't just spring it on them." And she couldn't get married just because she was going on tour either. Gabe should've waited until they were both sure that what they had was going to go the distance.

He reached over and squeezed her hand. "They can get to know me now."

"No."

"No?" he asked with an edge to his voice. "Was that proposal also a no? Because I'm getting a bad feeling here. You didn't exactly say yes."

She blew out a breath, working hard to remain calm and reasonable. "You shouldn't have told your parents yet."

"So that's a no."

"I told you I wanted to wait."

"Then why are you wearing it?" he demanded. "Why didn't you just throw it back in my face?"

She got quiet because that was exactly what she'd been trying not to do.

"Answer me!" he barked. "I think I deserve a straight answer."

"Fine! I was being nice!"

He stopped at a red light and gave her an incredulous look. "Nice? You think it's nice to pretend to be engaged? To let me make a fool of myself sharing the happy news with my family? That's as far from nice as you can get."

"Sue me."

His brows shot up. "Really? Sue you?"

"That's what you said when you did what you wanted."

He glanced at the light, saw it was green, and hit the accelerator. "When I did what exactly?"

"When you made a move because you felt like it.

Not because I asked you to."

"You wanted it too," he snapped. Then in a softer voice, he said, "Zoe, why won't you marry me?"

"Because."

"Because why?"

"Because when you put this ring on my finger—" she held up her hand "—I didn't want to go on tour, okay? I wanted to give up everything I worked for just to stay with you."

"Oh. Wow. I'm...that's pretty great actually, but I said you could go. I'll wait for you."

She started to pull the ring off her finger when his hand closed over hers. "Gabe, please, I have to give this back to you. I'm sorry."

"Just hang onto it. In three months it'll be official. I want you to have it in the meantime."

She didn't respond at first, but then she decided she'd better put it all out there. "The tour might go longer. Everything's up in the air. We'll see, okay?"

"Let's nail this thing down. Us—that's not up in the air. That's a definite."

She didn't say anything.

"Damn, I almost wish you were pregnant."

She stared at him, slack jawed. What guy wanted an accidental pregnancy? "Why?"

"So I could claim a father's legal right and make you stay."

She felt queasy. "Are you serious?"

He let out a breath. "No. That comes into play once the baby's born. I don't know why I said that. Do what you want. It doesn't matter what I say or do, does it?"

"Don't be like that. I want to enjoy these next two weeks."

"I'm not sure I can."

She closed her eyes, both upset and extremely nauseous. "Please let me out. I feel sick."

He pulled onto the shoulder. She ran out of the car and threw up again.

"We're getting you a pregnancy test," he said when she got back in the car.

"It's the bacon."

The next morning, at Gabe's insistence, she peed on a stupid plastic stick, and it said not pregnant. She held the stick up to him. "The minus sign means not pregnant. Happy now?"

He stared at it. "Not really."

She threw it in the garbage. "You're really stressing me out and that's the last thing I need before I go." She washed her hands, and he wrapped his arms around her from behind, looking at her in the mirror.

"I'm sorry," he said. "I don't want to lose you, that's all."

She turned in his arms and felt the stinging burn

of tears. "You won't. I promise."

He crushed her to him. "I'm holding you to that promise."

~ ~ ~

Zoe stood in a music studio on Thursday, mouth agape. She couldn't believe Gabe had rented her and her band a studio along with hiring a music producer. She'd told him she planned on renting some studio time with the money from her tour when she got back home. She had no idea he'd surprise her with it before she left. "Gabe, you shouldn't have. How much is this costing you?"

"Don't worry about it," he said.

She was still wearing his ring. She couldn't find an easy way to give it back without upsetting him. He was still worried about his stepdad, and she knew he hated the fact that she was leaving soon.

"No, seriously," she said. "How did you get Harry Birman?" He was a well-known music producer.

"He owed me a favor from back in my city lawyering days."

Gabe waved at Harry in the production booth, and he raised a hand back with a smile.

Jordan hadn't arrived yet, but Wade and Alex were already there warming up.

"You know we might not get a perfect cut on the

first try," Zoe said.

"I'll rent you the studio for as long as it takes," Gabe said.

"And then what?" Zoe asked.

"And then you can post it online and let the fans decide. This is your indie album."

"I swear you wrote down my bucket list and are checking it—holy shit. Did you write it down?"

"I have an excellent memory."

"It's too much. Really."

He caressed her cheek. "I want all of your dreams to come true." He kissed her. "Even when that means I have to let you go."

She blinked back tears. "We can still see each other. You can visit."

"Sure," he said, but he didn't sound at all sincere. She knew he didn't want to leave his stepdad, even though his test results came back clean. His doctor was optimistic about his prognosis, but Gabe didn't seem to quite believe it yet.

"Let's go, y'all," Jordan said, bursting through the door as if he wasn't the one making them wait. "One more week."

Everyone cheered. Zoe glanced at Gabe, who smiled back tightly. He tried so hard to be happy for her. She couldn't help but wish they'd met earlier so they would've had more time together before a separation.

They got right to work. Gabe moved to the production booth to watch. Zoe felt his eyes on her as she sang. She tried to convey all the emotion of the love songs straight to him.

After they'd finished for the day with four songs they were happy with, Harry came up and complimented her on the emotional resonance of her voice. She smiled. "It's because it's a very real emotion. Thanks to Gabe."

Gabe's gaze was heated. Harry glanced between them. "Then he's a very lucky man."

"I am," Gabe replied.

"Yo, Zoe, drinks at Chuck's," Jordan called.

She always went out with the band after a long rehearsal or gig. For the first time Zoe didn't want to go. "I'm going home with Gabe," she said.

Jordan crossed to her side, and she tucked her hands behind her, not wanting to get into a discussion over the ring. "We always go over the set, Zoe," Jordan said with a dark look at Gabe. "We can't afford to go soft now. We've only got one week."

"I know, I know," Zoe said. "We'll just talk now. I thought it was awesome. We'll come back tomorrow to finish out a few more songs and go with the best of them for the album." She turned to go, and Jordan grabbed her arm.

"Hands off," Gabe said in a low, threatening voice.

Jordan raised his palms.

Zoe left with Gabe's arm slung around her shoulders. That night Gabe was on her the minute they stepped in the door. It was hot, overwhelming, and she tried to lose herself in it, tried to push down the sense of time running out. Like they were on the clock and had to fill up on memories while they could to hold them over the separation to come.

"This isn't goodbye," she told him when he lifted her and carried her upstairs.

"Move in with me," he said.

"Yes."

He groaned. "I love your yes."

She smiled. "I love it too."

He set her down in his bedroom and stripped her down before she'd even gotten half of his buttons undone. "Give me more yes," he growled.

"Yes, yes, yes."

Then he tossed her on the bed and she gave him all that he demanded from her. No man had ever claimed her the way he did body and soul. She lost herself safe in his arms.

~ ~ ~

Zoe and Fred moved in and for one short week, Gabe felt utterly content. He should've asked Zoe to move in earlier, but at least now her stuff was here in the dresser drawers, in the closets, all over the bathroom counter. It reassured him. Made him feel like she really lived here and that meant she'd come back.

He reached for her Friday morning, their last day together, and felt empty space. He propped up on an elbow. "Zoe?"

She usually slept in. He headed over to the bathroom. Not there. His eye caught on the garbage can. The pregnancy test stick was in there. He thought he'd thrown that out last week. He leaned down to get a closer look at what appeared to be a plus sign. Didn't that mean pregnant? Did the minus turn into a plus after a while from sitting out? Then he remembered the box came with two tests, and he flew out of the bathroom. He hurriedly pulled on a T-shirt and jogging pants.

"Zoe!" he called. No answer. He ran downstairs still barefoot. Fred was outside and Zoe was with him, wearing pajamas and her jacket. He burst out onto the back deck. "Zoe!"

She startled and turned. "What're you doing up so early?"

He ran to her. "Does a minus turn into a plus later?"

She frowned. "We should talk."

His heart surged with love. He grabbed her and

spun her around. "I'm so happy. Tell me you're happy too. I can't believe it." He laughed. "How did this even happen?"

She shrugged. "Spillage?"

"You think?"

She shrugged again. "You know how you always want to be inside me just a little bit longer?"

He cleared his throat. It was because he couldn't get enough of her. He'd never acted like that before. Usually once he was done, he was done. "Yeah."

"I probably shouldn't have let you do that. I fell asleep. Maybe the condom got looser as you—"

"Yup. That could do it." He put his arm around her and led her back into the house. He couldn't stop smiling. "How come the first test was negative, though?"

"The directions said that sometimes there's not enough pregnancy hormone yet." Her voice caught. "But I was two weeks late, so I thought I should check. You know before I…leave."

"We'll talk."

She nodded glumly, which worried him. He worked hard to tamp down his excitement. A son or daughter with Zoe, his very own family. He couldn't think of a better future.

~ ~ ~

"This doesn't change anything," Zoe said once they'd settled on the sofa in the living room.

"Are you kidding? This changes everything!" He was so excited, which made her feel worse.

"I'm still leaving tomorrow."

"Are you sure you should be traveling?"

"It's not a big deal until you're further along."

He took both of her hands, fought back a smile, and lost. "We should get married right away."

"I told you nothing's changed."

"Yes, it has."

She got quiet.

"Don't go," he said urgently. "Stay here. Marry me. I'll turn the apartment into a studio for you. You can make all the music you want. I'll get the equipment you need, I'll hire a producer whenever you want. Just, please, stay here."

She couldn't help it. She broke down in tears because she couldn't pretend to be happy about it like Gabe. He pulled her into his lap, and she sobbed into his shirt.

"It'll be okay," Gabe kept saying.

She lifted her head. "And P.S. this is not the future I planned."

He held her face in both hands. "Well, P.S. this is the future I want."

She sniffled and took a shaky breath. Gabe's palm

slid across her stomach, where it stayed.

"I love you, Zoe, and I'll love this baby just as much. It'll be okay. I'll make sure of it."

That set her off again. Gabe did what he did best—scooped her up and carried her back to bed, where he proceeded to remind her exactly how she got this way.

~ ~ ~

Gabe spent the rest of the day trying to paint a picture of their future together that wasn't as bleak as Zoe seemed to think. But she kept ending up in tears and then he had to distract her, which ended up with him making love to her again. Not that he was complaining about that part, but that night, when she finally slept, he stayed up thinking about his own future.

He already knew the kind of dad he wanted to be. Like Vinny—involved, joking around with them, taking them places, playing ball or checkers or whatever else. Zoe seemed to think she was giving up so much, when Gabe felt like he was gaining so much. He hoped she'd come around to his way of thinking.

"I'll drive you to the airport," Gabe said the next morning as he spooned her in bed. He slid his palm across her stomach, splaying his fingers wide. He was obsessed with her stomach now, imagining what was growing inside there.

"Jordan arranged a car," she replied. "I told you that."

"Tell him we're getting married. Tell him you're having my baby."

"Gabe, please. I don't want to tell anyone yet." Her shoulders shook, and he realized she was crying again.

"Where's my sunshine?" he asked, turning her to face him.

"She got herself pregnant."

"No, she didn't. Her boyfriend did. What an idiot that guy is. He doesn't even know how a condom is supposed to work."

She smiled through her tears, and he kissed her, knowing she would relax in his arms, knowing he could make her forget her sadness. He had enough joy for both of them.

~ ~ ~

Gabe watched through his front window as Zoe got into the limo Jordan had rented for them to go off to the airport in style. Jordan smiled at Zoe. He couldn't see Zoe's expression, but he imagined she smiled back. He watched her pull away with the man he knew wanted to take his place and felt the gnawing ache he'd had in his gut turn into a churning mess. Now that Zoe was pregnant, he'd started to think maybe he should close up shop temporarily and go on the road with her. She'd need someone looking out for her, making sure she got the right nutrition, rest, and regular check-ups.

That night his stepdad called and asked him to meet him at Garner's for a drink. Gabe went without question, looking forward to telling Vinny the big news and his plans.

He found his stepdad at the bar, downing a glass of whiskey.

"Why here?" Gabe asked. "I thought you liked McGinty's." That was a bar in Eastman closer to where Vinny lived.

Vinny looked up. "I didn't want to see anyone I knew."

"Well, you know me."

He clapped his hand on Gabe's back. "I know, son."

"What's wrong?"

He tossed back the rest of his whiskey and signaled the bartender for two more.

"I never see you drink the hard stuff," Gabe said.

"I had some hard news."

Gabe froze. "Is it the cancer?"

Vinny smiled, more like a grimace. "You know what they don't tell you? Love cuts both ways."

"I don't understand."

"Falling in love with your mother, gaining three sons." His fist pounded the bar. "Best thing to ever happen to me."

"But that's good."

"And now I have to hurt your mother, break the bad news. You know how she cries. Just about kills me." The whiskey arrived. Vinny pushed one toward Gabe and downed his own, wiping his mouth with the back of his hand. He signaled for another one, and Gabe waved the bartender away.

"Dad, what bad news?"

"I lied, okay? The tests didn't come back clean. Doc says it's aggressive and spreading more than they'd first thought. Stage three. He gives me a fifty percent survival rate."

Gabe shook his head. "N-no, that can't be. You said stage two. Eighty-seven percent."

"Things changed."

Gabe's heart pounded furiously. He was finding it hard to catch his breath. *No, no, no!* he wanted to scream, but nothing came out. He glanced at his stepdad, his shoulders stooped, staring at the bar, and found his voice again. He had to be strong for Vinny.

"Dad." He got choked up and ran out of words. His hands were shaking, and he gripped the bar tightly. What did you say to someone facing this kind of prognosis? Death's grip tore at his heart. Not

Vinny. Not his dad.

Vinny clapped a hand on his shoulder. "Thanks." Then he took Gabe's whiskey and started drinking that. "You're the only one I told because I knew I could count on you to stay levelheaded."

Gabe forced himself to take a few deep breaths. Vinny had chosen him to share this news with. He had to stay calm, even if he felt like he was dying inside. "Do you have to get chemo?"

"Looks that way."

Gabe sat in devastated silence. How could he leave his stepdad when he was about to go through the fight of his life? Vinny had been there for him through thick and thin, even when Gabe hadn't always appreciated that.

"Drive me home after this?" Vinny asked. "I'm-m-m drunk."

"Yup."

Vinny was a cheerful drunk. He reminisced about when he'd first moved in with his boys to Gabe's mom's house. How Gabe and Vince had battled over sharing the attic bedroom, each used to being the oldest, each used to having their own room. How Luke and Nico had joined forces in high school to better win the hearts of the local girls. How Jared had looked out for shrimpy Angel with his tender heart.

Gabe had never been so depressed in his life, but

he tried to listen. It was the least he could do, let Vinny enjoy his memories with an enthusiastic audience. But one thought played on repeat through his head—death had caught up to him again.

He let Vinny finish his drink and then cut him off. "You've had enough. Let's go."

Vinny got off the bar stool and smiled goofily. "You got it, bub."

Gabe shook his head and led his stepdad out to the car. For the first time he was the one looking out for Vinny, instead of the other way around. He held it together for Vinny's sake, dropping him off with a hearty good night and an "everything will be okay."

It wasn't until he pulled into his driveway at home that he realized he'd never told Vinny about the baby. He walked on shaky legs into his house. Fred barked twice.

"It's just me," Gabe choked out. Fred got quiet. He made his way to the kitchen, stepped over the baby gate, and sank down next to the dog, running his hand over his thick fur. Then he finally caved, dropping his head in his hands as tears of grief and bitterness at the unfairness of it all rolled down his cheeks. Fred whined, licked his face, and settled close, pressed against Gabe's leg.

CHAPTER EIGHTEEN

Zoe arrived in London exhausted. She'd spent most of the flight motion sick and fighting back tears. Jordan sat next to her, which was the only reason she hadn't bawled her eyes out. She didn't want to tell him what was going on with her. Even though the baby was a surprise, she wanted it. She loved Gabe and knew he'd be a good dad. It was just hard to shift gears, to accept that life hadn't gone as planned. But, really, when had life ever gone as planned for her?

She figured she could get through the next three months without showing that much. She didn't want any special treatment, she just wanted to live her dream—big venues, enthusiastic audiences, playing with the best musicians in the world. It was all happening and all she had to do was show up, work hard, and pretend everything was normal.

When they got to the hotel, she was surprised when Jordan carried her luggage into the room and turned to go.

"Where are you going?" she asked. They always shared a room.

"It's all yours, Zoe-bean." He wouldn't look at her.

"Can we afford this?"

He glanced at her and looked away. "We have to."

"Why? I don't mind sharing."

"I can't pretend anymore." He set down his suitcase and crossed to her, looking deep into her eyes. "Zoe, I wasn't hooking up with another woman all those nights you had the hotel room to yourself. I was bunking on the sofa with Wade and Alex."

She blinked, confused. "Why? You could've had the other bed. I had two."

He stroked her cheek. "Because after sharing the room with you that one night I knew I couldn't do it again. Not as friends."

At her shocked silence, he went on. "I love you. I always have. I always will."

"Jor—" He kissed the words right out of her mouth, and she jerked away. "You said we were better off as friends after we hooked up."

"I wasn't ready to settle down at twenty-two. But, Zoe, I've loved you my whole life. The timing has been bad. But now the timing is just right. We can go so far together. Look at how far the band has come since I got on board."

"That wasn't just because of you." She backed away. "And the timing isn't better now. I'm with Gabe."

"Are you? You're not wearing his ring anymore."

Her eyes welled up.

"Thought I wouldn't notice, huh? I notice everything about you."

She blinked rapidly. The truth was she couldn't have left Gabe wearing it. That ring meant too much—marriage, a future settled down in the town she couldn't seem to break away from. She just knew she'd end up like her sister, "taking a break" from dance. Sure, Jasmine still owned the dance studio, but was she dancing? No. She'd hired an instructor to take her place. Who knew if Zoe would ever get back the momentum she'd finally got going in her own career? She had to grab that spotlight now that it was finally shining for her. That meant leaving Gabe behind. For now.

"I didn't want to bring it on tour," she said as a lame excuse. "It's too nice."

Jordan sat on the bed near where she was standing. "Nothing has been more right than you and me. I know you inside out. Since we were preschoolers banging away on the drums together." He drummed his hands in the air. "And now we're in the same place at the right time for more. We both love music. We could be the next big thing…together."

A horrifying thought hit her. "Did you plan this tour to pull me away from Gabe?"

"How could I plan it? Someone dropped out; we stepped in." He snagged her hand and pulled her to sit next to him. "I love you, Zoe. This is our time."

She burst into tears. She wanted it to be her time with Gabe. She'd only been away for one day, but she missed him so much.

Jordan pulled her into his arms. "Not exactly the reaction I'd been hoping for," he murmured, stroking her hair.

She cried some more because at one time Jordan loving her would've meant the world to her.

"What's wrong?" Jordan asked. "I haven't seen you cry this much since…I can't even remember when. Is it really so bad to hear that I love you?"

She pulled back and wiped her tears. "I'm sorry. I'm just tired from the trip."

He lay back on the bed and patted the mattress next to him. "Come here. We'll take a little nap. I just want to hold you."

She didn't believe that for one minute. She stood and crossed her arms. "You'll always be like a brother to me."

He tsked and rolled off the bed, standing with his jaw clenched.

"And a best friend," she added. "A lifelong friend. I want us to make great music together. To always share in each other's lives. But you have to find another woman, a very lucky woman, who loves you the way you deserve to be loved. I want that for you."

He grabbed his suitcase. "Got your message loud and clear. See you at rehearsal."

He left, the door slamming shut behind him.

Why did Jordan have to pick now to declare his love? Two years he had to make a move, yet he'd waited until now when they were on tour together, when she was missing Gabe so much. This was going to be a really uncomfortable, really long three months. She'd asked Gabe to visit her several times, but he never said he would. The bed called to her. She crawled in and slept straight through to the next morning.

~ ~ ~

Gabe had a horrible night. He'd tossed and turned, stuck in a nightmare of funerals and deaths and loss. The look on his dad's face just before he'd died. Beautiful Alyssa lying in a coffin, so young and perfect looking. Vinny's funeral. He woke at dawn, drenched in sweat, heart pounding. Vinny's funeral had felt so real—the casket, his mom sobbing, his brothers devastated, and Gabe frozen in place, knowing it was inevitable, knowing everyone close to him died. He grabbed his cell to call home, still finding it difficult to breathe normally. He had a text from Zoe: *I'm sharing a hotel room with Jordan, but don't worry, we always share a hotel room.*

He gripped the cell phone tighter, his mind trying to make it compute. What the hell? He felt like howling. What the hell! He stood and started pacing the room, seeing signs of Zoe here and there. Her framed picture of her family on his dresser. A bookmark she'd left on the nightstand. He went to the bathroom and stared at that big pink plus on the pregnancy stick in the trash can that he still hadn't thrown away.

No. There was no way she'd do that. He splashed cold water on his face. Think. Zoe knew him better than that. Knew he wouldn't put up with her sharing a room with Jordan. This couldn't possibly be true. He opened the vanity drawer, looking for more signs of Zoe. More signs that she was coming back. The bathroom was empty.

He returned to the bedroom and opened her nightstand drawer. The diamond ring he'd given her sat there, taunting him. He picked it up, sat on the end of the bed, and stared at the ring. It just didn't make sense. Not with her pregnant, not with the way they spent their last day together, making love, reassuring each other how much they loved each other.

She'd left the ring. Left him.

No, she was coming back. She promised. She was having his baby.

With shaking hands, he tucked the ring back in the drawer. Then he grabbed his cell, called her, and it went to voicemail. He couldn't speak over the lump in his throat and quickly hung up.

Fred barked, demanding to be fed, and Gabe went downstairs to take care of him, thankful for the distraction. One look at Fred's excited smiling face and wagging tail pushed the last of the panic back. Gabe breathed easier, and his mind started to clear.

"Who wants breakfast?" he asked.

Fred jumped around like a crazy pup who'd never eaten kibble before in his life. Gabe found himself smiling. He took care of Fred, got himself breakfast, and left Zoe a message to call him.

~ ~ ~

Zoe called Gabe back during a rehearsal break in the afternoon when it was still morning back home. "Hey, how are you? I miss you."

"Fine," he said. "How are you?"

"Just a minute." She stepped outside the studio for privacy. It had been a rough day so far, with Jordan fighting her at every turn. "Jordan is being difficult. I don't know how much longer the band will stay together."

"Zoe, I got your text about sharing a hotel room with Jordan," he said tersely. "Explain."

"What? I didn't send you a text."

There was a long pause.

"Gabe? You still there?"

He exhaled noisily into the phone. "It seems Jordan is causing trouble. I thought it was strange that you'd tell me you were sharing a hotel room but not to worry because you always shared a hotel room. You know I wouldn't put up with that. And you certainly wouldn't do a chicken-shit thing like put it in a text instead of telling me outright. He's really got it out for you. Watch your back."

Zoe sank to the steps of the small front porch. "You believed me."

"I trust you. I haven't trusted Jordan since I met him."

She leaned against the porch rail, her mind replaying the day. Her phone had been sitting out on a table so she could check it for a message from Gabe. Jordan must've snagged it when she was in the ladies' room. Her passcode was her birthday. Not hard for Jordan to figure out.

"Do you always share a hotel room with Jordan?" Gabe asked.

"I usually do," she said. "To save money on tour,

but he never slept in it. He always hooked up with some groupie and spent the night at her place." At least he said he did. "But on this tour we got separate rooms."

"What's different this time?"

She winced. "He said he loves me and can't share a room anymore. I told him I didn't feel the same way. I told him I was with you."

"I knew it! I knew he was in love with you. Didn't I tell you that?"

"I guess I just saw that he cared about me. Like a big brother." And now he was giving her the cold shoulder. All this time she'd thought he was such a good friend when he really just wanted to hook up. She knew Jordan. He never would've stayed. He'd been playing with her and keeping other men away from her.

"Does he know about the baby?" Gabe asked.

"No." She lowered her voice and glanced behind her. "I haven't told anyone here, and I don't plan to."

"How are you feeling?"

"Tired, overwhelmed, queasy."

"I wish I was holding you right now."

"Me too." She sighed. "When are you coming to visit? I need something to look forward to."

Silence.

"Gabe?"

"Vinny is worse than we thought. Stage three. He starts chemo soon. I don't know if I can leave him now."

"I'm so sorry," she murmured even as she selfishly still wanted him to be with her. She was pregnant and across an entire ocean on her own.

"I'll try to manage something. Even if it's just for the weekend. I just…can't leave him right now. He's counting on me."

She knew Gabe had this thing about death, that he felt like he was cursed, but Vinny was nowhere near death. "Gabe," she started.

"I know, I know. I just can't—"

Tears unexpectedly stung her eyes. "I gotta go. See you whenever."

"Don't—"

She hung up and wiped her eyes, feeling peevish and very much alone. Then she turned and marched inside to confront Jordan because she wasn't putting up with him acting like she'd wronged him when it was very much the other way around.

She found Jordan joking around with Alex and Wade like he didn't have a care in the world. The jerk! She stood next to them and waited. Alex and Wade got quiet, and Jordan slowly turned.

"Where you been?" Jordan asked. "You're holding us up."

"We need to talk," she said between her teeth.

"Ooh, trouble in paradise," Wade said. Alex elbowed him.

Jordan gave the guys an easy smile. "Love a bossy woman. Let's roll."

She stepped out into the hallway and Jordan followed.

"How dare you, Jordan!"

His eyes widened.

"How dare you!" Her hands were in fists and she fought the urge to slap him, because she couldn't ever remember being so furious. "Texting my boyfriend and implying I *slept* with you. Do you have any idea the trouble that could've caused? No, you don't! Because you don't think about anyone but yourself!"

He raised a brow. "So he was cool with it?"

"No!"

"But you said the trouble it could've caused."

"He listened to my side, and he believed me."

"Huh. He's different."

"That's it? No apology? No sorry I stole your phone and impersonated you? Sorry I tried to ruin your relationship?" Then it hit her. "Omigod." She sank back against the wall in horror. "It was you. You're the reason I never made it past eight weeks with any guy."

He lifted one shoulder up and down. "Two

months is around the time when most guys bail if they're not serious."

"You told them I shared a hotel room with you too."

He looked at the ground for a moment, and she waited for an apology or some sign of remorse or even denial. Instead he met her eyes, crossed to her, and whispered close to her ear, "I did it because I love you."

She shoved him away with both hands. "You ruined any chance I had at happiness and for what? To flirt with me after a show?"

He stood in front of her, his gaze burning into hers, completely unapologetic at the way he'd manipulated her life. "Those other assholes didn't deserve you. I did you a favor, so you should be thanking me."

"Thanking you!" Her hand came up of its own accord, but he caught her wrist before she could make contact. Then he snagged the other wrist and held them both at her sides.

"Yes, thanking me," he said. "If they really loved you, they would've asked you about the hotel deal instead of just dumping you."

Gabe was the only one that hadn't fallen for it. Why hadn't he? Probably because he was a lawyer and looked beyond the circumstantial evidence, but it was one hell of a bit of evidence, wasn't it? He'd been mad, she could tell, but he'd still talked to her about it.

"If I can't have you, they can't have you," Jordan said.

"You're crazy. Get your hands off me." She yanked her wrists away. "I'm still with Gabe. Nothing you can say or do will change that." And that was the minute she realized she should've kept that ring, should've married Gabe right away like he'd asked because her heart was made up and absolutely nothing would change that.

Jordan backed up a step and gave her a sideways look. "So you got him like that."

She lifted her chin. "Yeah, I do. And you know what? After this tour, you and me, we're finished. I'm not working with you again. In fact, why don't you just leave now?"

He glared at her. "Like hell. I'm not leaving on account of you. This is my big break too."

"I'm going solo as soon as we get back home."

"Ha! You'll fall flat on your face. You've got no head for business." He tapped her head, and she slapped his finger away. "You don't know how to line up good gigs—"

"I'll figure it out!"

He snorted. "Yeah, good luck with that." He turned and went back inside the studio.

She took a few deep calming breaths before taking her place behind the mike, telling herself not to listen to Jordan. She could make it on her own. And what she couldn't do, she'd hire out. It was time to believe in herself.

~ ~ ~

Gabe went to his parents' house later that day to check on his stepdad. He felt torn. On the one hand, his stepdad was going through hell, and Gabe couldn't shake the nightmare he'd had of Vinny's funeral. On the other hand, his last conversation with Zoe replayed over and over in his mind. She clearly wanted him there with her, and he wanted to be. He couldn't stand for Zoe to be so far away, pregnant, and dealing with a churlish Jordan. But he wasn't sure if he could leave Vinny for long. What if Vinny didn't make it? What if Gabe never got a chance to say goodbye?

Vinny was taking a nap when Gabe arrived, so he joined his mom at the kitchen table, where she was stirring sugar in her tea.

"Zoe's pregnant," he told her.

She stopped stirring her tea. "I see." She met his eyes. "And are we happy about it?"

He nodded. "I am. She's coming around."

"Are you still getting married?"

"I hope so. I need to see her again face to face and

nail this thing down." He hit the table lightly with his fist. "Just hammer out a deal that works for both of us."

"Gabe, this isn't a legal thing. Is she upset? Does she feel like it's not the future she planned?"

His eyes widened. "Yes. That's exactly what she said. How did you know?"

"Because I was the same way. It takes you by surprise, and you know your life will never be the same again. Being a mom isn't easy. It's a lot of work if you're doing it right. And I have a feeling Zoe would want to do her best. It's easier for the man. He just shows up at the end of the day, and he's fun daddy."

He stared at the table. He didn't see anything wrong with that. He wanted to be fun daddy. That's what Vinny had been.

"Is that Gabe I hear?" Vinny called.

"Yes," his mom answered. "I think he wants to say goodbye."

"Get your ass in here," Vinny hollered.

His mom inclined her head. "You heard the man."

Gabe appeared in the bedroom doorway, bracing himself for finding his stepdad looking frail, but he was sitting on the edge of the bed, looking a lot more like his old self.

"What's this about goodbye?" Vinny asked.

He sat next to him. "I didn't say that. I just

stopped by to see how you were."

"Ah, I'm fine. Your mom will take care of me. I know you want to go to Zoe. So go. Stay as long as you like. I promise not to die on you."

Gabe's throat felt so tight he could barely breathe. He worked hard to push the fear away for Vinny's sake. He leaned forward, resting his elbows on his knees, and took a few deep breaths. "Dad, when you say things like that it's hard to leave with a clear conscience."

Vinny clapped him on the shoulder. "I'll call if there's news, and you call me too. I want to hear all about this European tour. We'll do the face stuff. Whatever that is. Angel keeps popping up on my computer."

Gabe straightened. "Facetime."

"Yeah. We'll do the Facetime."

He studied Vinny's face. "Are you sure?"

Vinny smiled reassuringly. "Haven't I always been straight with you?"

Gabe nodded, his throat tight.

"Then you have to believe me. I'll be okay, son."

Gabe let out a breath, his eyes stinging. "She's pregnant."

Vinny broke out into a wide smile. "You don't say." He shook his head. "I'm going to be a granddad? That's just—" His voice caught, and he pounded Gabe on the back. "That's the best news I've heard in a long time. Go to her. And don't come back until you're ready. No rushing on my account."

Gabe relaxed a bit as the joy of his and Zoe's baby filled his heart again. It felt good to finally share the news with his stepdad.

"How's she feeling?" Vinny asked.

"She's a little queasy now and then. Tired."

"Give her a little extra TLC." Vinny raised his brows. "Tender loving care. You take care of the mother, you take care of the baby." He shook his head and beamed. "A grandchild! What a gift!"

A weight lifted from Gabe's heart. Vinny had a grandchild to look forward to. He'd hang on for that and hopefully a lot longer.

Vinny waved his hand in the air. "She might get a little emotional. She'll need a lot of hugs."

Gabe laughed. He could always count on Vinny for practical advice. "Yeah. I'll do that."

"Allie!" Vinny called. "Did you hear Gabe's big news?"

His mom stood in the doorway, smiling. "I sure did."

"We should meet her parents," Vinny said. "I'll make my homemade ravioli in her honor."

"She hasn't told them yet," Gabe said. "I'll let you know."

"You better get on that," Vinny said, pointing his finger at Gabe. "Don't wait too long."

"I will, I will." He stood. Then he had a thought. "Hey, would you guys like to watch our dog, Fred, when we're away?"

"I love dogs," Vinny said. "Allie?"

"We'd be happy to."

"It'll be a nice distraction for me," Vinny said. "Is he well behaved?"

"Sometimes. You need to let him know you're the alpha."

"Easy enough," Vinny said with a wink for his wife. "I already am."

~ ~ ~

Ten days later, Gabe was on a flight to London to see Zoe in her first concert. He'd shut down his business and given notice that it would be a three-month absence. He planned on staying with Zoe for the remainder of her tour though she didn't know it yet. He wanted to surprise her with what he hoped she'd see as good news. The decision to stay with her was not from a lack of faith, but an abundance of faith that she was worth putting his own life on hold so she could have her dream.

He took the early flight and made it to the hotel late that night, texting Zoe as soon as he arrived. Then he knocked on her hotel room door and waited, telling himself to take things slow. It was late, and she needed her rest for the baby.

She answered wearing the black dress he'd bought her that showed lots of cleavage and, as he well remembered, had no back. His mind flashed to that night, and he went instantly hard.

"Gabe!" she exclaimed with that beaming sunshine smile that made his heart stutter.

"Zoe," he choked out.

He dropped his suitcase, kicked the door closed, and wrapped his arms around her. Then she was kissing him, frantically chanting, "I love you, I love you, I love you." His hands slid under her dress, found only bare skin, and the small amount of control he'd had broke. He had her on the bed, dress pushed up to her waist in seconds. He freed himself and drove into her.

"Yes," she gasped. Her hands grabbed at him, urging him on, which worked for him because he couldn't stop for anything. He buried himself in her softness, forgetting everything but the woman he had to claim as his own.

~ ~ ~

Gabe woke the next day to the sound of the shower. He'd slept in. His time was all screwed up. It was afternoon here, morning to his East Coast body. He went to the bathroom and eyed the shower. It was much too small for both of them to fit.

"Hey," he said so he wouldn't startle her. Now that he'd had her last night, taken the edge off so to speak, he was really working on that TLC Vinny had told him pregnant women needed. He peeked his head around the shower curtain.

She smiled. "You won't fit in here." He glanced down at her stomach, which was still flat.

"Are you sure you're pregnant?" Because if it was a false alarm, he thought he could make the shower work if he held her legs close and—

"Yes, I'm sure."

His gaze trailed up to her eyes, which were sparkling with merriment. So much better than the tears she'd had just two weeks ago. "How big is the baby?"

She laughed. "Probably the size of a lima bean."

He grinned. "See? I was your lima-bean boyfriend. I put that lima bean right in there."

She splashed him in the face, and he closed the curtain, smiling as she did some vocal warm-ups in the shower. Her voice never ceased to amaze him.

He brushed his teeth and waited until she emerged from the shower. Then he wrapped her in a towel and guided her with his hand on the small of her back to where he wanted her—bed.

She giggled. "Gabe, I've got rehearsal soon."

"You know what I want to hear." He ripped the towel off her and pushed her back on the bed.

She smiled, opened her legs wide to him, and said the one word he loved most. "Yes."

He settled on the bed next to her, suckling her breast while his hand trailed south, finding her hot and wet. She tasted like strawberries. He moved to her other breast and suckled hard while his fingers stroked her sex, drawing a soft moan from her. He told himself to be slow and tender, but the way she was arching into his hand, asking silently for more, was more than his good intentions could take.

He kissed along her jawline and whispered in her ear. "Scream my name." Which was the only warning she'd get.

"Yes," she said softly. And then he was on her, thrusting deep, bringing them both to the edge. He slid his hands under her ass and lifted her, thrusting as her body clenched around him. He broke out in a sweat; he wasn't going to last much longer.

"Now," he demanded, knowing she'd give what he wanted. She always had.

He heard his name on her lips, felt that sweet release of hers milking him, and he just let go.

He rolled off her a few moments later and let out a

long breath. "Are you okay?" he asked belatedly.

"I'm great!" she said with a laugh.

"Do I need to be gentler because of the baby?" He pulled her close, pressing her head against his chest, pushing her leg over his hip. "I'll try. It's hard for me to control myself around you."

She squeezed him around the middle. "We're fine."

He kissed her hair. "Good, because I don't think I can be much gentler."

"I have to get ready soon."

He groaned. "I'm afraid I can't let you get dressed."

She pulled back and grinned at him. "Why is that?"

"Because I'll end up ripping your clothes off. You don't want to damage your clothes, do you?"

"Gabe!" She rolled away from him, but he grabbed her before she could get out of bed, pulled her back against him, and spooned her.

"Just a little bit longer," he said, quickly shifting her leg and slipping inside her again. She gasped, and he smiled. She really should be used to the way he couldn't get enough of her. He slid his hand around and cupped her breast.

"This is exactly how I got this way," she said.

He pinched her nipple, and she rocked back into

him, taking him deeper. Damn, it still felt good. "I know. I'm probably going to make you pregnant a lot."

"Gabe!"

"I love you." He stroked from her breast down to her stomach, where he rested his hand against their baby.

"I love you too." She let out a soft sigh, relaxing in his arms, and he felt like he'd come home.

She had a short rehearsal today before their evening concert. He planned on going with her to both. He had some things he'd like to discuss with Jordan man-to-man.

CHAPTER NINETEEN

Gabe watched rehearsal from the audience and was awestruck by Zoe. She was absolutely glowing on stage, even more than when he'd seen her playing back home. He didn't know if it was the pregnancy, or his visit, or just the fact that she was doing what she loved, maybe all three, but there it was, so he couldn't possibly see how he and his careless mistake had messed up anything for her. She was magnificent.

He also noticed Jordan really was giving her the cold shoulder. He didn't look at her, didn't speak to her except as part of the group, and he certainly didn't back her up on improv solos, merely left her on her own with only Wade and Alex to back her up. All the better to hear Zoe's voice, in Gabe's opinion, so Jordan's lack of a blaring trumpet wasn't hurting her there.

The band took a break. Zoe ran up to him, and he met her halfway in the aisle. She hugged him. "How'd we sound from out here?"

"You were amazing," he said, sneaking in a quick kiss.

"Thank you," she said with a laugh. "But I meant the acoustics. Is it good? Too much of one instrument? Can you hear me okay?"

"It's great. Maybe a little loud on the obnoxious trumpet player."

"Oh, you." Her dark brown eyes sparkled. And she really was glowing. Maybe pregnancy was good for her or the sex. Either way, he could help with both. "I didn't even sing full throttle, so you'll hear me more tonight. I have to save my voice."

"Even when you don't sing full throttle you're amazing."

"You're biased."

"It's not my opinion." He held her by the hips, unable to keep his hands off her. "It's simply a fact."

She wrapped her arms around his neck and spoke directly in his ear. "Can you get me some crackers? And a large bottled water. Sometimes when it gets hot under the lights, the queasiness comes back."

He stepped back immediately. "Absolutely. Where's the nearest store?"

"Just down the street. Turn right out of here, it's at the end of the block."

"I'm on it." He took off for the exit and heard her

laugh.

"Thank you," she called.

He turned. "Thank *you*." For having my baby, for making me happier than I ever thought I could be, for being you, he added silently. He headed out the door, where he found Jordan outside talking to Alex.

"Jordan," Gabe said, "just the man I wanted to see."

"Later," Alex said, stubbing out his cigarette and heading back inside.

Jordan narrowed his eyes. "What do you want?"

"What do I want? I want you to stop making things difficult for Zoe. She doesn't need any more stress on top of touring."

"Yes, Dad," Jordan sneered.

"You know what, I'm going to let that slide because I will be a dad. Zoe's pregnant, and we're getting married. So whatever crazy thoughts you had in that peanut-sized brain of yours about getting together with her you can get rid of right now. I'm going to be on the rest of this tour, and I'm going to make sure it's a good one for her. Are we clear?"

Jordan's eyes widened. "Zoe's pregnant?"

Gabe belatedly realized he wasn't supposed to share that news yet. Shit. Zoe was going to kill him.

Jordan turned for the door, and Gabe snagged him by the shoulder and turned him around. Jordan tsked and knocked Gabe's hand away. "Get your hands off me. Who do you think you're messing with?" He shoved Gabe backwards. "You knocked up my girl."

Gabe shoved him back. "She's not your girl. She never was."

Jordan got in his face. "I was her first everything. Did she tell you that? First kiss. First fuck. So, yeah, she is my girl and always will be. She'll come around. The men always leave and there's good ol' Jordan to pick up the pieces."

Gabe stood his ground. "So help me, Jordan, I will make your life a living hell if you upset her even once. I'm not going anywhere, so you're just going to have to get used to that. You might've been her first, but I'm her last."

Jordan's nostrils flared. Gabe stared right back at him, waiting for the larger man to swing a fist.

"Dammit!" Jordan exclaimed before stomping down the sidewalk, muttering to himself.

Gabe went back inside to quickly tell Zoe that Jordan knew before Jordan could. He found her sitting in the audience and slipped into the seat next to her.

"Hey, you got my crackers?" she asked.

"Not yet. I told Jordan you were pregnant, but it'll be okay, and he won't mess with you anymore." He gave her a quick kiss and took off.

"Gabe!"

He went to get those crackers because that was what TLC was all about.

~ ~ ~

Zoe waited backstage for their cue to open the concert. She had massive stage fright for the first time in forever and seriously felt like she was going to toss her cookies. She fought it as long as she could before she sprinted down the hallway to the ladies' room and threw up. Bah. She rinsed out her mouth and grabbed a paper towel. So unprofessional.

Jordan met her right outside the ladies' room. "Zoe, they're calling us. We got to go."

"You're talking to me again?"

"Your boyfriend said he would break every bone in my body if I messed with you."

She smacked his arm. "He did not. And P.S. Gabe's much too sweet for that."

"Yeah. Says you."

They got backstage and were hurried on stage. The lights came up. Jordan looked over at her and mouthed, "All you," as he always had. He meant her voice was the star, and they were just backup. Relief surged through her and when Jordan held up his hand in a silent count off—one, two, three—she grabbed the mike and let loose.

Zoe felt like she was sailing, in a strange free-flowing state, the music and movements pouring through her without any thought or effort. Just a free fall into the music and when she landed to enthusiastic applause, she was brought back to reality with a start.

"Yes!" Jordan was saying, whooping it up with the guys. "Take a bow, Zoe."

She took a small bow and gave a cheerful wave to the audience before heading backstage, looking for Gabe. A few minutes later he appeared, shaking his head. "Amazing," he said before grabbing her and spinning her around. She squealed, and he set her down. "Are you okay? Is the baby okay?"

"Yes, we're fine," she said with a laugh.

"Your CD is selling like hotcakes," he said. "I just saw them out in the hallway." She'd arranged for the CD from their recording studio session to be shipped to them for direct sales after concerts. She hadn't known if they'd sell, but she'd thought why not?

"That's great!"

"Zoe, this is big. I think you could make it solo. I watched that concert, and you outshine everything else out there. Your voice. That beautiful voice. And you write your own songs. I'm on board. One hundred percent behind your music career. All the way."

"I'm not that amazing. I got stage fright and threw up backstage."

"That was the baby's stage fright not yours."

"I can't believe you told Jordan."

"Is he treating you better?"

"Yes."

He gave her a smug smile. "Case closed."

"Now wait a minute, Mr. Shark Lawyer."

He took her hand, kissed it, and then pulled her along. "Come on, Mrs. Shark Lawyer. You owe me two weeks of yes. Did I mention I'm staying for the whole tour?"

She stopped short. "Are you serious?"

He smiled his dimpled smile. "Yes."

"Who's taking care of Fred?"

"Vinny."

"Oh!" Tears sprang to her eyes.

His hand went to the small of her back, guiding her outside. "I'm going to take those as happy tears."

She nodded and smiled as a tear escaped.

"C'mere." He wrapped her in a big hug and then grabbed her hand, entwined her fingers with his, and took her back to the hotel.

~ ~ ~

The next morning, Zoe found a note on the pillow where Gabe should've been.

Meet me at the castle and wear the dress.
Love, Gabe

She stared at it, crinkling her nose. What castle? Did he mean the black dress? Because he'd ripped the thin straps that held the back and front together, and there was no way she was wearing that thing out anywhere. It was Sunday, her day off, and she'd thought they'd do some sightseeing. Maybe Gabe thought the same and arranged for a castle tour.

She sat up. He'd left crackers and a bottled water on the nightstand for her. She got teary-eyed over the gesture. She ate a cracker, took a long drink of water, and headed for the bathroom. She stopped short at the tall armoire with a note taped to it: *Open me.*

She opened the door and gasped. Inside was a poufy pink dress. Like a princess would wear. It was her bucket list again from that night when they'd stayed up all night talking. The one thing he hadn't done yet. She fought back tears and lost. The hormones made her so emotional, and Gabe was so sweet. She pulled out the dress to admire it and saw a shoebox sitting under it. She put the dress back and peeked inside. Pink satin ballet slippers. How did he do all this? When? Her size even.

She didn't know how she'd gotten so lucky. So very, very lucky. What if she hadn't been his waitress? What if she hadn't needed a lawyer? Hadn't moved to that studio apartment? Hadn't gone with him to Pittsburgh? Oh, why wasn't she wearing his ring? It was a slap in the face. She wished she'd brought it with her.

She took a shower and got ready, taking extra care with her makeup. She pulled her hair up in a cute little updo with a twist. Now all she needed was the tiara, she thought with a giggle. She slipped on the dress and twirled around, feeling every bit the princess.

She looked around the room for more clues about the castle and found none. She texted Gabe. *Go downstairs*, he messaged back. *Your chariot awaits.*

She left the hotel room, hoping she'd find a car downstairs for her. Otherwise she was going to have a very expensive cab ride. And she didn't even know which castle he meant. Europe was full of castles. A driver held up a sign, For Princess Zoe. She laughed and got in.

They drove for about an hour and stopped at a huge castle along the river. The sign said it was open to the public. She wondered if she'd be walking in with a bunch of tourists gawking at her in her silly princess dress. She walked down the stone path alone, no tourists in sight.

"Gabe?" she called tentatively.

No reply.

The driver had told her to go all the way into the castle and wait.

She walked to a center foyer with suits of armor

and a huge hearth and found, finally, her prince. Gabe stood there in a tuxedo, looking every bit the part. He went to her, took her hand, and raised it to his lips. "Princess Zoe."

She giggled. "Prince Charming."

One corner of his mouth lifted, revealing the dimple in his clean-shaven cheek. "I rented the castle for the night. They have guest rooms upstairs."

She threw her arms around him. "I can't believe you made my whole bucket list come true!"

His arms wrapped tight around her. "Not a bucket list. This is the never-ending dream list."

She pulled away to find his eyes were shiny with tears, and she felt her own eyes well up. "I want to make yours come true too. Tell me them all, and then tell me some more."

"I only have one dream I care about. Marrying you." And then he pulled her ring out of his pocket and slid it onto her finger. And while she stared at it in shock, she hadn't known he'd found it, he went on. "I said I wanted to make all of your dreams come true, and I meant it." He tipped her chin up and looked into her eyes. "I'm going to be a full-time dad for two years at least, more if your music career is doing well. I'll help manage your career in any way you want—the business side, promotion, anything. I'll travel with you wherever opportunity takes you. Marriage and family won't hold you back. I want you to soar, and I'll be your safe landing place to come back to. Marry me, Zoe."

She couldn't seem to find her voice. She couldn't quite believe what she was hearing. Gabe was giving her more than she'd ever thought to ask for. "Gabe, I can't let you do that. What about your career? What about money?"

"You and the baby are my career, my honorable calling. And I have money. The first million I earned, the rest was from my dad's investments that I inherited. I can't think of a better way to spend that money than on you. You are my investment."

She burst into tears, and he wrapped his arms around her. He believed in her. She looked up at him. "I won't let you down."

"I know you won't." He wiped away the tears with his thumbs. "Please say yes."

"Yes!"

He grabbed her and spun her around. "I love your yes. Come upstairs. I want more yes out of you."

"Always, Gabe. Always yes to you."

He scooped her up in his arms and carried her up the grand stone staircase like a princess. He was the real deal. A prince among men.

A shark lawyer.

A boy next door.

A lima-bean boyfriend.

And P.S. a lima-bean husband too.

EPILOGUE

Gabe finally nailed things down when he married Zoe on August first exactly one week after they'd arrived home from her tour. Her parents had met them in Paris at the end of May and Zoe finally told them the news. It had been touch and go for a bit there as they sat at dinner in a nice restaurant, where Zoe first had to introduce Gabe as her fiancé, and then break the news about the baby.

Gabe had stepped in, assuring them how much he loved their daughter, and how he planned on being a full-time dad. After a bit of huffing and puffing on her dad's part, where he talked about "back in the day" and the "order things should be done," especially about them getting married after the baby instead of before, he got behind it. Her mom was just happy that Zoe was happy.

Then Zoe explained her plans to go indie and how indie was more common now and took out the middleman, letting musicians directly sell to their listeners with a greater profit.

"You're the future," her dad said to Zoe. "I'm just an old grumbling dinosaur. What do I know about the digital age of music? I'm old school."

Zoe hugged him. "You know a lot, Dad. And I want you to play with me too."

Her dad shook Gabe's hand. "You have my blessing…for all of it."

Classy guy. Then Zoe and her mom planned out the wedding in a small ceremony to be held in Gabe's backyard.

Zoe hadn't wanted to be showing in the wedding pictures, and Gabe wanted nothing more than to make it official, so the quick simple wedding worked perfectly. Fred acted as ring bearer, carrying the two gold bands on a small pillow strapped to his back.

And if that wasn't enough, his stepdad had done really well with chemo. Vinny told him Fred had been a great comfort to him. And the doctors were hopeful his stepdad would have a clean bill of health soon.

Gabe headed out back to check on the progress of Zoe's studio. He'd asked his brother Vince to get started on turning the apartment over the garage into a music studio as soon as he got a break in his schedule. And he was nearly finished now at the end of August.

"Hey, this is looking good," Gabe said, looking

around. Vince had done some research into soundproofing and redid the walls, floors, and switched out the windows' glass with acoustic glass. The equipment—computer, digital audio workstation, keyboard, microphone, and speakers—were all in place.

Zoe was already there, supervising. She grabbed the mike. "Hello, Mr. Shark Lawyer."

He smiled and put his hand across her baby bump. She was six months along now. "Hello, baby," he said into the mike. "Hello, Mrs. Shark Lawyer." He kissed her.

"You guys make me sick." Vince gathered his tools and put them in his toolbox. "Kissy kissy," he muttered under his breath.

Zoe giggled as she put the mike away, and then inclined her head meaningfully over to Vince.

"Vince, I wanted to ask you something," Gabe said.

"I'll be right back," Zoe said, heading for the bathroom. She had to go a lot now that the baby was getting bigger.

Vince finished putting his tools away and snapped the box closed. He stood and gave Gabe an annoyed look. "What? I told you no charge. It's a wedding present."

"And I told you I would pay you."

"Bite me."

Gabe hid a smile before saying, "Would you be godfather?"

Vince jammed his hands on his hips and glared. Gabe was onto his brother now. Zoe had pointed out that Vince blustered to cover up his emotions. Apparently her sister was the same way. She'd suggested him as godfather. After Gabe had thought about it, he'd agreed it would be good for the family and good for the baby. No one valued family more than Vince.

"Why me?" Vince asked. "Why not Angel, the freaking priest, or one of your real brothers, Luke or Jared?"

"We didn't choose each other as family, but I'm choosing you now as godfather."

Vince swallowed visibly and glowered. "Why?"

"Because no one I know holds family so close. I know you'll look out for him."

Vince dropped his hands. "Him? It's a boy?"

"Yeah, it's a boy." He grinned. "We haven't told anyone yet."

Vince let out a whoop and clapped Gabe on the back.

"So that's a yes?" Gabe asked.

"Yes!" Vince boomed.

"I'll teach him books, and you'll teach him tools and—"

"Sports—"

"And how not to get his ass kicked. I was a late bloomer."

"Very late," Vince said.

"So he'll need someone to teach him how to stand up for himself."

Vince shook his head, looking at the ground. When he looked up, he had to wipe his eyes. "Oh, man. You got me. Damn. Look what you turned me into. A damn blubbering baby."

"Sue me," Gabe said with a grin.

Vince shook his finger at him. "I'll sue you all right. Don't think I won't." He clapped him on the back and gave him a one-armed hug. "Bro, we'll raise him up right. This kid is going places."

"What about me?" Zoe asked with a smile from across the room. "Do I get to help raise him too?"

"You!" Vince boomed. "Of course! You're his ma. Get over here and give me some love."

"Not too much," Gabe put in.

Zoe walked over, and Vince gave her a careful hug, not pressing too close into her belly. Zoe smiled around Vince's shoulder at Gabe. He smiled back, his heart filled with love for the woman who'd given him everything he hadn't known he was looking for and now couldn't imagine living without.

Vince straightened. "All right, enough of this mushy stuff. Let me see the nursery. I want to check the crib. Did you secure the dresser to the wall?"

Gabe and Zoe exchanged a confused look.

"Of course you didn't," Vince said, scooping up his toolbox. "Let's go. Damn, this baby's lucky he's got me."

Vince took off for the house. Gabe took his time walking over with Zoe.

"That went well," she said. "I think I'll write a song about it." She deepened her voice. "The bros who raised that boy right."

Gabe chuckled. "I like the sound of that."

And that was just the beginning of a hugely creative period for Zoe, where she wrote song after song that all went onto her first solo album. Her breakout hit had a most peculiar name.

Lima Bean.

Some said it was slang for a new type of dance, some said it was referring to her baby, but Gabe knew the truth. He was her lima bean. And she was his heart.

~THE END~

Thanks for reading *Restless Harmony*. I hope you enjoyed it! Look for the other books in The Clover Park Series too!

Turn the page to read an excerpt from *Not My Romeo*, Vince and Sophia's story.

NOT MY ROMEO

KYLIE GILMORE

Vince Marino wants nothing more than to win the Clover Park library project and finally earn a promotion to partner in his father's construction company. But a last-minute bid for the project by Sophia Capello, daughter of their biggest competitor, throws Vince out of the running.

Sophia has to get Capello Construction back on track after her father left them near bankruptcy in a misguided attempt to win back his wife with an alpaca farm. Don't ask. It's up to Sophia to make up for her screw-up family once again and save the company.

Vince proposes a partnership with Sophia as the only sensible solution for both of them. But their fathers are life-long rivals and will never agree to it. And though Vince has never been tied down to any woman, there's something about the fiery Sophia that draws him in and keeps him pushing for more on both a professional and very personal level.

NOT MY ROMEO EXCERPT

"So tell me more about this fictional rake you get off on," Vince said as he drove Sophia home.

She straightened. "I don't get off on rakes."

"What gets you off?"

She got mad. He could tell by the way she took a few deep breaths, and her lips were practically a flat line. He suppressed a laugh that he knew would just piss her off.

"I am not having this conversation with you," she bit out.

It occurred to him that maybe she didn't get off at all, which was concerning. A beautiful healthy woman like Sophia never experiencing ecstasy.

"Did your last boyfriend get you off?" he asked.

"Simon?" she asked like he knew all about her ex-boyfriends.

"Yeah," he said just so she'd keep talking.

"Not really." She said it with such sadness that it

really started to bug him. Someone like Sophia never feeling passion. It couldn't be. She was full of fire. It wasn't healthy not to get that out.

"What about the guy before that?" he asked.

"Brian?" she asked. Even their names sounded pansy ass.

"Yeah."

She hesitated. "Almost."

"Almost?" He let out a huge breath of exasperation. What was wrong with these guys? What was wrong with Sophia that she'd settle for less? "Guy before that."

"Tim?" Another pansy-ass name. He was sensing a pattern here.

"Yeah, Tim."

"Not really."

"The rich donor guy?"

"Anonymous actor. He, uh, plays for the other team now." She waved a hand in the air. "So, you know, no."

He bit back a groan. "Sophia."

"I know, but he said he was confused for a while. It wasn't me."

He pulled over to the side of the road somewhere in Clover Park. "Has any guy ever made you feel passion? I'm talking fingers fisting in the sheets, raw, screaming top-of-your-lungs passion?"

She flushed, but she still answered. "No."

He stared at her. She stared back, a defiant gleam in her eyes, an unquestionable challenge.

"You want me to show you?" he asked.

She turned away. "Like you could," she mumbled under her breath.

He caught her chin and turned her back to him. "I promise you I can. One night."

"I don't do one-night stands."

"Two nights," he amended, feeling generous. It was the least he could do. It wouldn't be fair to show her the peak only to drop her back to the low boring side so quickly.

"If you could hear yourself right now, you wouldn't be smirking like that."

"I'm not smirking," he said. "I'm smiling."

"Just take me home, Vince. I'm exhausted."

He pulled back into the street. "Your loss."

She snorted. "Whatever." A beat passed. "You ever been in love? I mean really in love, heart thumping, head over heels, can't even think straight love."

"Nope. Not once."

"You don't sound torn up about it."

"I'm not. What about you?"

"No," she said, sounding very forlorn. "I've sort of given up."

"Well geez, don't give up if that's what you want.

What are you, twenty-five?"

"Twenty-six."

"You're young. I'm sure some pansy-ass guy is just waiting around the corner for you, dying to profess his love."

She brightened. "Yeah? You really think so?"

"Sure."

"One of the town council members has a son he wants to set me up with."

"Who?"

"You know, Randy? His son."

"Out of the question," Vince said.

"Why? He said he's in pharmaceutical sales. Stable, good job, looking to settle down."

"First of all, Randy is a lech."

"He is not."

"Trust me," Vince said. "I know. Second of all, a sales guy is not going to get you off. You can do better than that."

"Who should I date? Huh? A guy like you? No, thanks."

"What's wrong with me?"

"Two nights!" She gestured wildly. "That's a fucking proposition, not a date!"

His lips twitched. Something about the f-word coming out of her classy mouth gave him hope. Now that she was looking at yet another pansy-ass boyfriend, he wanted a chance to throw his own name in the ring. Nothing pansy ass about him. "You want to go on a date with me?"

"It would've been nice to be asked."

He double checked to see if she was serious. Her arms were crossed, and she was staring mulishly out the front window. "Fine. You want to go to dinner with me?"

"Where to?"

"I don't know. Wherever."

"No."

"Why not?"

"Because I don't think you really want to go. You're just saying that because I got mad."

He felt like pulling his hair out. This woman made no sense. He drove in silence, until he pulled up at her house. He glanced at the front door. "You think your dad's home?"

She clenched her teeth. "I don't know. He doesn't tell me when he's coming and going."

He pushed a lock of hair over her ear. It was silky smooth. He leaned closer. "I'm getting mixed signals here. You into me or what?"

"Or what," she replied. She got out of the car and slammed the door.

Guess he had his answer. Still, he couldn't help watching her hips sway as she marched up the front sidewalk. No way in hell she was going out with that lech Randy's son. For the first time in his life, he worried if he could ever be the kind of man someone might actually want to be with more than once. Even though he always told the women he dropped off at home immediately after a hook-up to call him if they wanted a second night of passion, they rarely did.

He had a feeling one night wouldn't be enough with Sophia.

Get *Not My Romeo* now!

Also by Kylie Gilmore

The Clover Park Series

THE OPPOSITE OF WILD (Book 1)
DAISY DOES IT ALL (Book 2)
BAD TASTE IN MEN (Book 3)
KISSING SANTA (Book 4)
RESTLESS HARMONY (Book 5)
NOT MY ROMEO (Book 6)

The Clover Park STUDS Series

STUD UNLEASHED: THE PREQUEL (Book 1)
STUD UNLEASHED: BARRY (Book 2)
STUD UNLEASHED: DAVE (Book 3)
STUD UNLEASHED: WILL (Book 4)

Acknowledgments

Big thanks to my most enthusiastic cheerleaders, my boys, and to my husband who encouraged me to follow my bliss in this writing career. Thanks, as always, to Tessa, Pauline, Mimi, Shannon, Kim, Maura, and Jenn for all you do. And thank you dear reader for making it all possible

About the Author

Kylie Gilmore is the *USA Today* bestselling author of the Clover Park series and the Clover Park STUDS series. She writes quirky, tender romance with a solid dose of humor.

Kylie lives in New York with her family, two cats, and a nutso dog. When she's not writing, wrangling kids, or dutifully taking notes at writing conferences, you can find her flexing her muscles all the way to the high cabinet for her secret chocolate stash.

Praise for Kylie Gilmore

THE OPPOSITE OF WILD

"This book is everything a reader hopes for. Funny. Hot. Sweet."

—New York Times Bestselling Author, Mimi Jean Pamfiloff

"Ms. Gilmore's writing style draws the reader in and does not let go until the very end of the story and leaves you wanting more."

—Romance Bookworm

"Every aspect of this novel touched me and left me unable to put it down. I pulled an all-nighter, staying up until after 3 am to get to the last page."

—Luv Books Galore

DAISY DOES IT ALL

"The characters in this book are downright hilarious sometimes. I mean, when you start a book off with a fake life and immediately follow it by a rejected proposal, you know that you are in for a fun ride."
—The Little Black Book Blog

"Daisy Does It All is a sweet book with a hint of sizzle. The characters are all very real and I found myself laughing along with them and also having my heart ripped in two for them."
—A is for Alpha, B is for Book

BAD TASTE IN MEN

"I gotta dig a friends to lovers story, and Ms. Gilmore's 3rd book in the Clover Park Series hits the spot. A great dash of humor, a few pinches of steam, and a whole lotta love...Gilmore has won me over with everything I've read and she's on my auto buy list...she's on my top list of new authors for 2014."
—Storm Goddess Book Reviews

"The chemistry between the two characters is so real and so intense, it will have you turning the pages into the midnight hour. Throw in a bit of comedy – a dancing cow, a sprained ankle, and a bit of jealousy and Gilmore has a recipe for great success."
—Underneath the Covers blog

KISSING SANTA

"I love that Samantha and Rico are set up by none other than their mothers. And the journey they go on is really hilarious!! I laughed out loud so many times, my kids asked me what was wrong with me."
—Amazeballs Book Addicts

"I absolutely adored this read. It was quick, funny, sexy and got me in the Christmas spirit. Samantha and Rico are a great couple that keep one another all riled up in more ways than one, and their sexual tension is super hot."
—Read, Tweet, Repeat

STUD UNLEASHED: BARRY

"Ms. Gilmore is an excellent storyteller, and her main characters are hard to forget, but her secondary characters are equally impressive. This is a character-driven tale inside of a sweet plot to get two nice people to fall in love and have their HEA."
—*USA Today*, Happy Ever After blog

"Forget alpha-male billionaires. Studs Unleashed will have you panting for that guy in nerdy glasses."
—New York Times Bestselling Author, Mimi Jean Pamfiloff

"I was pulled in quickly and between the fascinating characters, the witty banter, the flow of the story and the emotions I was feeling I was blown away! I loved every second."
—A Beautiful Book blog

Thanks!

Thanks for reading *Restless Harmony*. I hope you enjoyed it. Would you like to know about new releases? You can sign up for my new release email list at Eepurl.com/KLQSX. I promise not to clog your inbox! Only new release info and some fun giveaways. You can also sign up by scanning this QR code:

I love to hear from readers! You can find me at:
kyliegilmore.com
Facebook.com/KylieGilmoreToo
Twitter @KylieGilmoreToo

If you liked Gabe and Zoe's story, please leave a review on your favorite retailer's website or Goodreads. Thank you!

CPSIA information can be obtained
at www.ICGtesting.com
Printed in the USA
LVHW081707050419
613131LV00016B/614/P